THE SHADOW OF THE ALBATROSS

BY

MARTIN FRASER

16 Northolt Rd,
South Harrow, Harrow HA2 0ER,
United Kingdom

Copyright © 2025 Martin Fraser

Paperback ISBN:
Hardcover ISBN:

Cover Design by London Book Publisher

Dedication

In loving memory of my partner, Elaine Travers.

On Christmas Day 2022, I presented Elaine with a cardboard golden box containing the 6th draft of my manuscript for *The Shadow of the Albatross*. She was speechless and completely amazed as she opened the box. Started in February of that year, I had managed to complete the manuscript to this point in complete secrecy. She spent the Christmas period reading the novel and found it irresistible. She became my biggest cheerleader. Since then, the manuscript has received multiple revisions as part of the necessary editorial polishing process. She would regularly ask when I was going to start the follow-up. The answer came soon enough. When I began work on the *Cerberus File* in February 2023. She revelled in receiving each new chapter to proofread and seeing the story and character arcs develop.

Sadly, ill health dogged her in the second half of 2024. While we hoped and expected her to make a full recovery, fate cruelly intervened. She sadly passed away at the end of March 2025. *The Shadow of the Albatross* will be published worldwide on 29th September, on what would have been her 66th birthday and is dedicated to her.

Acknowledgements

No man is an island, and as Arnold Schwarzenegger pointed out in his book *Be Useful,* in reality, there is no such thing as a self-made man because everyone, regardless of their position in life, needs help somewhere along their journey. I spent my life sitting in the office of an International Bank, often wishing I was somewhere else. Now, I can sit in my study with music in the background and the sun streaming through the windows, as I fulfil my creative dreams, a world away from the often tedious and frustrating office life I left behind. The follow-up to *The Shadow of the Albatross, The Cerberus File,* is already "in the can", and work is underway on the third instalment.

There are many people to whom I owe a debt of gratitude. People who have kindly given their support, encouragement, or expertise during the process of writing this book. The late **Jennifer Miles**, my dog-walking pal and close confidante, for her support and encouragement from the very beginning, in good times and bad. Sadly, she passed away a few months before publication. My Brother, **Grenville Fraser**. A man who has probably read more thrillers than I've had hot dinners. For his constant support, benchmarking critiques, and advice throughout this momentous journey. **Eve Hall**. Former editor at Penguin Random House and Editorial Director at Hodder & Stoughton, for her invaluable assistance and for helping me realise what I was capable of. To my beloved and much-missed partner of over twenty years, **Elaine Travers**, for her love, enthusiasm, steadfast support, and meticulous proofreading of my manuscript. It is devastating that she didn't live to see this proud moment. To Screenwriter **Janet Lee Chapman**, who provided the outstanding Reader's Report for the Susan Mears Agency. Finally, the team at the **London Book Publishers** for making the dream a reality.

Table of Contents

Chapter 1

It was forecast to be a glorious summer's day, but as writer Ryan Jones left the train station in Poole for his early morning interview with the celebrated philanthropist, a ghostly thick pall of sea mist hung over the Dorset coastline. As he rounded the final corner, looming into view through the dense sea fret was his destination. Albatross House, designed in the brutalist style, was 150 feet of Portland stone and smoked glass, the embodiment of strength, power, and above all, money. It dominated the skyline like no other in the area. Three enormous interconnected towers overlooked the town and picturesque harbour. Jones approached the entrance, walking up the seven wide stone steps leading to the glass and stainless-steel frontage. He stopped at the entrance and looked up at the imposing eight-story structure before him. It's massive granite oblong blocks rising to the top of the structure, forming an octagonal ribcage for the thick glass panels which surrounded each of the office blocks. The top seven floors had windows stretching across the broad width of the building's entrance with balconies dressed with grey-green slate.

Gathering himself, Jones stepped through one of the two revolving doors and then through a second door before finally entering the foyer. To his left was a long wooden reception desk, and behind it was a security window. He walked across to the desk, and a young woman in a smart blue uniform asked if she could help him.

'Yes, thank you. I'm Ryan Jones and I have a 9 o'clock appointment to see Mrs Devereux.'

The receptionist checked her computer screen before replying, 'She is currently in a meeting, Mr Jones. I will let her know that you have arrived. Please take a seat over there, and I'm sure she will not be long.'

Jones thanked the woman and walked across to a leather sofa by the window, where he sat down. Olga Devereux, although not reclusive, was not in the habit of giving interviews. It was quite a coup for Jones, and he was excited but a little apprehensive at the prospect of meeting someone with such a global reputation for success and philanthropic generosity. He sat nervously waiting, trying to dry his clammy palms against his trousers.

Far above the foyer on the seventh floor, Olga Devereux sat behind a large leather and rosewood desk, on which was a picture of her late husband, a telephone, a laptop computer, and a beautiful white marble sculpture of an Albatross in flight. Sitting in front of her were four men, including her Chief of Staff Richard Rackman, and her eldest son and deputy, Hector Devereux, a tall, burly man whose speed of thought was matched by the quickness of his temper. There was unmistakable and palpable tension in the air. Security breaches were taken very seriously, particularly at the Albatross organisation. Olga stood up and walked slowly to one of the large windows and gazed out towards the sea.

The men shifted nervously in their seats, anxiously glancing at one another as they waited for the admonishment that was surely coming. Even Hector was not immune from the sharp edge of his mother's tongue on occasion. Olga Devereux was not someone who tolerated incompetence from anyone, especially from those she had trusted. In her youth, Olga had the face and body that in another age might have launched a thousand ships. Now approaching her sixties, she was still slim and strikingly attractive, yet behind the mask was a ruthless and fiercely determined woman.

Devereux sighed as she considered the situation that was now unfolding in front of her. Shaking her head in displeasure, she stared out across the misty water and into the bay. After a few minutes considering her options, she turned to face the waiting men.

'Well, gentlemen, it's not very impressive, is it? Richard, you are my chief of staff. This should never have happened! You know perfectly well that this organisation relies on absolute integrity; we cannot have people running around leaking critical information. This must be shut down now. Hector, call our friends in Rome and find out what they know about this. I want the accounts section locked down, get security to monitor all calls in and out, buffer all outgoing electronic messages until they are approved and cleared, and keep me advised. Now, I have another meeting, this one happens to be with a journalist, so sort this bloody mess out, and quickly. I don't want the press or anybody else getting wind of this. Richard, I want an update within the hour. That's all, gentlemen.'

With that, the four men stood up, looked at one another, and left the room without a word spoken.

Devereux picked up her phone and spoke to her secretary.

'Would you show Mr Jones up, please?'

In the foyer, the receptionist walked across the stone floor to the waiting area by the front windows, where Ryan Jones was pensively sitting.

'Mrs Devereux will see you now. Would you come with me, please, and I'll take you up to her office.'

They passed through the turnstile to the main lobby. The receptionist pressed the red recall button on the wall to summon a lift. As they waited, a lift on the far side of the lobby chimed. A moment later, the doors opened, and several people stepped out and walked towards the turnstiles on their way out of the building. As they approached, Jones caught sight of a particular man amongst a group of others walking towards the exit. He was very tall and immaculately dressed. There was something very familiar about him, a partial recognition; he couldn't quite place him, but he knew he had seen him somewhere before. Jones turned to watch the man as he passed through the turnstiles, hoping that the additional few seconds might somehow trigger the elusive memory. It didn't, the receptionist called out, and Jones, whose brain was still wrestling with the unknown man's identity, turned and followed her to the lift.

'I'm sorry, I thought I recognised someone there,' said Jones.

The receptionist leant across and pressed the button marked 7. A moment later, the doors closed, and the lift quickly ascended. A few seconds later, the lift stopped, and the doors opened again. They stepped onto the 7th-floor lobby and walked to the B block entrance, where Mrs Devereux's personal assistant met them. He introduced himself, a polite and courteous man, slim, probably in his 30s, and who clearly employed the services of a master tailor. He led Jones into his office and pressed a button on his intercom.

'Mr Jones is here to see you, Mrs Devereux.'

A few seconds later, a heavy wooden door opened, and a strikingly attractive middle-aged woman stood in the doorway.

'Good morning, Mr Jones,' said Devereux as she offered her hand to her visitor.

'Mrs Devereux?' she nodded slightly, holding his gaze with her own.

'It's a pleasure to meet you, it is very good of you to spare the time to see me,' said Jones, as he tried not to stare.

He had seen photographs of Olga Devereux and also television news footage, but seeing her in person, in the flesh, was quite something else. She reminded him a little of the late, great movie icon Elizabeth Taylor in her pomp. Olga's thick shoulder-length hair was dark, almost jet black with the odd fleck of grey creeping in, and her vivid blue eyes, sandwiched as they were between a double layer of eyelashes, had an almost hypnotic effect on him. He found it impossible not to stare at her graceful figure as she turned and led him into her office.

Her office was spacious, less of an office and more of a high-end hotel suite. It was modern and very much designed for open plan living with separate areas for work and relaxation. A variety of large potted plants were dotted around the floor. Huge, tinted windows surrounded the room, offering spectacular views across Poole Harbour.

They walked across a beautiful, plush carpet towards two large white leather sofas separated by an ornate oblong Italian coffee table.

'Mr Jones, I have read some of your work. I understand that you are writing an article about the Foundation.'

'Yes, that's right, I'm mostly freelance, but I have been asked to produce a series of special articles for Business International. They want to focus on the philanthropic achievements of some of our major international organisations. The media often puts emphasis on excessive company profits or the more controversial aspects at the expense of other, more altruistic but frankly, less newsworthy virtues. The Albatross Foundation, for instance, is one of those organisations that many people may not be familiar with. Yet it makes a significant contribution to people's lives through its background sponsorship and support of other, more well-known organisations and charitable works worldwide, and we hope to redress the balance.'

'I see,' said Devereux, 'well, we are happy to have a lower profile than many companies, I suppose, we prefer to work behind the scenes, to grease the wheels, so to speak, open doors, and use our organisation to facilitate the development of others.'

Jones sank back on one of the luxurious antique settees and waited for Mrs Devereux to join him on the opposite settee before continuing the conversation.

'You have held the reins of this huge multinational conglomerate for many years now and overseen its exponential growth and influence throughout the world, but despite this, and your appearances on the front of some of the more colourful periodicals, you have remained a very private person. Can you give me an insight into what drives and motivates you?'

The writer listened intently as Devereux recounted her early years with her husband. While he had given her a complete mastery of the business world, she had understood from a very early age the value of soft power. With her sultry beauty and a readiness to employ her feminine wiles, men had always found it impossible to resist her charms. As she grew older, she realised that it was not such a big step from influencer to manipulator, and the rewards were far greater. These, however, were not sentiments that she was prepared to share with a journalist, however apparently benevolent he appeared.

'What initially brought your family to the UK?' asked Jones, who was beginning to understand and experience for himself the magnetism that this remarkable woman exuded as he watched her at close quarters.

'My family is Russian; my grandfather was a member of the aristocracy. When the Russian Revolution broke out, the Bolsheviks butchered as many as they could find. My immediate family fled to Germany. When National Socialism took root in Germany, as Russian Jews, our very existence was threatened again. My great-uncle was able to use his contacts to enable some of the family to leave Germany, but many of my extended family, including my grandparents, were not so lucky; they were either shot or sent to the gas chambers. I was born here in England in 1960. My mother rarely spoke of the horrors of the war, but eventually, when she thought I was old enough to understand, she told me what happened. I vowed that my family would never be as powerless and vulnerable again, never.'

'And your husband? How did the two of you meet?'

'I met Robert at a Chess tournament. Amongst his many accomplishments, he was a Grand Master. I'd played since childhood and had been to many such events. We just started talking and had an instant rapport. He was already very successful and was focused on developing his business ventures, and chess was one of his many outlets, a way of relaxing, but even then, he was so single-minded and driven that he hated losing. We started spending a lot of time together. He was well-educated, articulate, and fun to be with. When we got married, it seemed natural to be involved in helping him develop his business interests.

'Who came up with the name Albatross?'

'That was Robert's idea, he wanted something that symbolised strength with a global reach, and he was a keen ornithologist, and an Eagle was just too obvious.'

'And the Foundation? Your husband started it, but it was you who turned it into a global power. How did that come about?' asked Jones.

'After my husband died, I felt I wanted to give something back, the corporate arm was so very successful, it seemed such a waste not to use the resources and contacts available to help the less fortunate across the world, so I set up the Foundation as a charitable organisation, we fund NGOs around the globe amongst other international projects.' said Devereux.

The conversation continued for some thirty minutes before Devereux's phone rang. She rose from her sofa and walked the short distance to her desk, and picked up the phone; other than several acknowledging comments from Olga, the conversation appeared to Jones to be very one-sided. After a few minutes, Devereux replaced the receiver and returned to the sofas.

'I am sorry, Mr Jones, but I am going to have to curtail our interview as something has come up that requires my immediate attention. I hope you will forgive me.'

Jones scrambled to his feet, clutching his recorder and notebook. The interview had been mesmerising, and he was disappointed that it had come to a premature end.

'Of course, I quite understand, I am grateful for your time, it's been very informative,' said Jones. Olga walked back to her desk and pressed her intercom. A moment later, there was a knock on the door. Her personal secretary walked in.

'Maxwell, would you show Mr Jones out, please?' She turned to Jones and shook his hand.

'It's been very nice to meet you, Mr Jones, I look forward to reading your article… goodbye.'

Olga closed the heavy door and walked towards a large wooden cabinet. Opening the doors revealed a well-stocked drinks cabinet. Pouring herself a large, neat vodka, she added an ice cube, then returned to her desk and sat momentarily looking at her phone before picking up the receiver and calling her Chief of Staff.

'Richard, can you come up to my office please?'

'Yes, Mrs Devereux, I shall be there directly,' said Rackman.

Devereux rose, walked to the window, and looked out across the harbour. The water was now bathed in sunshine as the sea mist retreated; it was an idyllic view, with the Purbeck hills glistening in the distance.

Olga's intercom buzzed, 'Mr Rackman is here to see you, Mrs Devereux'.

'Thank you, Maxwell, show him in please,' replied Olga.

Richard Rackman walked through the door brandishing a slim folder. His stern expression reflected his mood. Olga returned to her desk. Rackman, initially standing beside her, handed the folder to her before taking a seat in front of her desk.

'Well, Richard, just how bad is it?' Olga asked as she opened the folder and began glancing through the pages.

'You remember Safia the Afghan we got out of Kabul when the Taliban re-took control in 2021,' began Rackman.

'Yes, she was working with the Afghan National Security Forces, wasn't she? I've spoken to her several times, and she is highly competent.'

'She's been dealing with our Central and South Asian projects, and because of her previous experience, we also had her monitor our internal security and err.' Rackman paused mid-sentence.

'Well? Come on, Richard, out with it. Get to the point,' said Devereux, who was becoming impatient with her usually efficient executive as he appeared reluctant to broach what was, visibly, an awkward subject, as he searched for the right words.

'Well, as we discussed earlier, she was running an audit and noticed several suspicious emails from someone in Accounts to a woman named Olivia Hunter. She also references someone called Robert Sterling, who is apparently in Rome. Three weeks ago, one of our junior accountants approached our accounts manager and told him she thought she had uncovered a massive case of internal fraud and that it might seriously damage the Foundation's reputation. The Manager told her that he would escalate the matter immediately. However, it looks like she started investigating the inconsistencies herself.'

'What was in these emails, Richard?'

'I think you should see it for yourself.' He stood up, leaned over, and passed Olga the hard copies of the emails.

Olga read the contents of the first damming email, then quickly turned the page to read the subsequent messages. They shone an unwelcome light on some of the Foundation's overseas activities. She put the papers down and looked directly at her anxious Chief of Staff.

'Good God, Richard! I don't have to tell you how serious this is? Who is this person?'

'Her name is Monika Stein. She is German, single, aged 25, a good worker, diligent, has been with us for about 5 years, nothing out of the ordinary, keeps herself to herself, and has no family as far as I know.'

'This has got to be nipped in the bud. I want to know what else she has uncovered. Ask her to come up and see me at 4 o'clock, will you, Richard? I will decide what action to take after I've seen her.'

Threats to the foundation's activities or its global reputation were taken very seriously, and Olga Devereux would do whatever she deemed necessary to protect both, regardless of the consequences.

At 4 o'clock, the intercom on Olga's desk sounded, 'Mrs Devereux, I have Monika Stein to see you,' said her secretary.

'Thank you, Maxwell, send her in please, and will you let Mr Rackman and Hector know that I need to see them in 30 minutes.'

There was a knock on the door, the heavy door swung open, and a petite blonde young woman walked in wearing a smart grey two-piece skirt suit, high heels, and carrying a small envelope.

'Come in, Monika. Thank you for coming to see me. Please take a seat.'

Monika walked towards Olga Devereux's large desk and sat in one of the two chairs that were positioned in front of it.

'I understand that you have raised concerns about potentially fraudulent activity within the Foundation. Firstly, may I thank you for your dedication. I am sure you will appreciate that anything of this nature could have serious and far-reaching consequences, so it is something that I need to investigate personally and take the appropriate action.' said Devereux.

Monika sat apprehensively in her chair before opening her envelope and taking out several sheets of A4 paper.

Devereux listened intently as Monika began to unravel the tangled web of intrigue she had uncovered. She didn't have all the details, but she had enough to begin unpicking several strands of a finely woven subterfuge that underpinned something much darker.

'I can't believe it,' exclaimed the open-mouthed philanthropist, hanging on Moniker's every word as the whistle-blower detailed what she had discovered. 'However, did you manage to expose this? Have you shared this information with anyone?'

'No, Mrs Devereux, no one, I thought it best to speak to you first,' assured Monika.

'I think that is very sensible, Monika, we need to be discreet about this and those responsible dealt with. I am grateful, very grateful that you have brought this to my attention.'

The conversation continued until Devereux looked at her watch and then smiled at her companion.

'Monica, would you perhaps care for a drink, a glass of wine? I can't tell you how relieved I am that you have brought this to my attention. Now we can deal with this in-house. You have provided such an invaluable service, not just to the Foundation but to me personally. I deeply appreciate it. You know how important reputation is to this organisation.'

This was something that Monika had not anticipated; however, it was not uncommon for Devereux to reward outstanding service personally. Nevertheless, Olga radiated such charm that she decided that it could only help her future career by gratefully accepting her employer's hospitality. Devereux stood up and ushered Monika towards the two comfortable sofas before she excused herself and disappeared into an adjoining room. Monika sat on one of the beautiful, extremely comfortable white Italian leather sofas. The meeting had gone better than she had expected. Mrs Devereux had been very understanding, even appreciative, and there had been no anger, suspicion, or defensive reaction to what must have been a disturbing revelation for her. Monika sat back, now much more at ease and relaxed. She looked around at the artwork that adorned the room and waited for Mrs Devereux to return.

Devereux emerged from a small anteroom with a silver tray, which she brought to the coffee table between the two sofas, offering Monika one of the two Cobalt Blue crystal wine glasses.

'Here you are, thank you again, Monika, you may take it from me that I will deal with this matter swiftly,' said Devereux before returning to sit on the opposite sofa as Monika began sipping the wine from her glass as Devereux continued to talk to her.

Outside, in her secretary's office Richard Rackman, and Hector Devereux waited anxiously, it had been a long and busy day, Richard had had his hands full dealing with the fallout of Monika Stein's revelations and Hector had spent a good deal of the afternoon on the phone to his sister Oksana in Italy trying to trace how far the information contained in Monika's email had reached, and who the mysterious Robert Sterling was that had been mentioned.

Maxwell's intercom buzzed, 'Yes, Mrs Devereux.'

'Have Mr Rackman and Hector arrived?'

Maxwell confirmed that they had.

'Send them both in, please.'

The two men entered the room and walked towards Olga's desk, where she sat looking at the file Rackman had shown her earlier in the day.

'Well, gentleman, you have some explaining to do. I have just had a long and informative chat with Miss Stein. I am appalled at what she has discovered. Someone around here has been extremely lax. Richard, you are my Chief of Staff; it's your responsibility. I want the names of those involved. I'll deal with them myself. However, with Miss Stein's co-operation, the immediate problem has now been dealt with,' said Devereux, as she gestured towards the sofas

The men turned and looked at the ornate screen that shielded the sofas from view. Devereux continued.

'The two people mentioned in her email, Olivia Hunter and Robert Sterling, I want to know who they are and how they are involved, and quickly. Now, Richard, Miss Stein will be leaving us immediately. Make the necessary arrangements.'

Rackman stood up and walked across towards the white sofa where Monika Stein was sitting. Calling her name and getting no response, he tapped her on her left shoulder. She slumped forward across the coffee table. Startled, he lunged forward and grabbed her limp body before she hit the floor, then felt for a pulse on the carotid artery beneath her ear. She was still alive. Shocked, he turned and looked at Hector, who stood unmoved, then across to Olga Devereux, who stared back dispassionately without any flicker of emotion at all.

'Don't be so squeamish, Richard. ' She said, 'If this is not dealt with now, heads will certainly roll, starting with yours. Remember that. She's unconscious for now. House Services will be up shortly to take care of her, discreetly and permanently.

Chapter 2

Shafts of laser-like beams of sunlight pierced the darkened bedroom through the partially closed white vertical blinds. The golden morning rays moved imperceptibly through the room before edging their way across the large Super King-sized bed and onto the prostrate naked figure lying sprawled across its surface. As the bright sunlight reached his eyes, Greg Travers slowly stirred. Though still barely conscious, his eyes screwed up, he reached for a half-full glass on his bedside table but only succeeded in knocking it onto the floor, smashing the glass and sending what remained of the liquid flowing across the polished wooden floor.

He had no idea what day it was, never mind the hour. He sat on the edge of the bed for several minutes before attempting to stand up, running his fingers through his dark brown hair. Managing to avoid the freshly broken glass, Travers' first few tentative steps of the day were swiftly followed by a howl of pain as his unprotected toes collided with last night's large, empty bottle of Stolichnaya Vodka that was sent spinning across the floor like a gyroscope. Travers didn't know what hurt more, his throbbing head or his now throbbing toes. He wasn't usually given to swearing, but he made an exception in this instance and let out a string of expletives. From beneath the duvet, an arm suddenly appeared like the roving antennae of an emerging insect investigating its surroundings, and a blonde head followed it.

'What is it?' said the naked woman, emerging from beneath the bedding, clearly disturbed by the unexpected tirade of four-letter words.

Travers, startled, looked round.

'What the! Who are you? I mean, I'm sorry... er?' exclaimed Travers in a tongue-tied, incoherent mumble.

'Lisa, Lisa Scott, the casino last night, remember? At least then I made an impression on you. I didn't think you would have forgotten me quite so quickly, especially after what happened last night,' she responded with a mixture of anger and disappointment.

'Lisa? Oh yes, of course, now I remember, I'm sorry Lisa, I really am,' an apologetic Travers replied. 'It was quite a night, wasn't it? If it's any consolation to you, my head feels as though it has spent the last few hours in a tumble dryer. Remind me how it went last night? Did we come out ahead?'

'Ahead? You're kidding! You really don't remember? We won ten thousand,' she said.

'Wow, that's great!'

'No, it isn't! Because then you lost it, every fucking penny of it.'

'Oh,' said Travers, who was still struggling to recall bringing her back to his house after their drunken night at the casino.

'Why the fuck didn't you just walk away when I told you, when you had the chance, but oh no, you just had to play that one more game, all or nothing, and to prove what?'

As the fog began to slowly clear from Travers' brain, the events of last night's shenanigans began to come into sharper focus. Following his wife's recent tragic death a few months ago, Travers had lost all focus and discipline, and he knew it, but his scrambled mind was such that he no longer cared. He had begun indulging himself in more earthy pursuits. He had always enjoyed a drink, though hitherto not to excess, but now he was enjoying far more than just a social glass or two, and he was not particular about what it was, or how much of it he had. His frequent visits to the Casino allowed him to indulge himself and to forget the pain of his loss. Having been introduced to the high-rolling lifestyle by his wife, he was no stranger to the gaming tables. He had gambled before, playing Black Jack, Baccarat, and Roulette amongst others, with, to be fair, a high degree of proficiency. However, in those days, he was sober and in control. Now he was more likely to lose than win. Evidently, last night was the former, one of those occasions when too many cocktails, a beautiful girl on his arm to flatter him, and his skewed moral compass led him to the sorry state he found himself in this morning.

Travers walked across the wooden parquet floor of his bedroom to the kitchen; perhaps a strong cup of coffee and some toast would help revitalise him. He turned the radio on whilst he wandered around the kitchen trying to decide what to do first.

'Do you want some tea, coffee, or fresh orange juice?' enquired Travers, doing his best to sound a little more considerate towards his recently re-discovered bedtime companion.

'Juice please' came the reply from Lisa, as she emerged from the bedroom, her naked body only partially concealed by his long black silk Chinese dressing gown, which hung loosely over her shoulders and did little to conceal her exquisite figure. She joined him in the kitchen.

Having put the kettle on, Travers went to the bathroom before returning to the bedroom to dress. He splashed some cold water over his head and face, then stared at the alarming Dorian Gray-like reflection staring back at him in the mirror. His rugged good looks were looking a little more rugged than he remembered. His now pale skin contrasted alarmingly with the increasingly dark rings encircling his hazel eyes, no doubt the result of his current largely nocturnal lifestyle and lack of vitamin D. He reached for a towel and briefly dried his bedraggled mop of hair. After dressing, he joined Lisa in his conservatory, which was now bathed in sunshine. Sitting down opposite her, he savoured the first sip of hot black coffee, which he hoped would help speed up the sobering-up process and the pain of his hangover.

'Have you ever been to Poole?' asked Lisa.

'Poole? No, I haven't. It's supposed to have the second largest natural harbour in the world, after Sydney. Why do you ask?'

'I just caught the end of the news headlines on the radio, the Police have recovered the body of an unidentified young woman in Poole Harbour, just floating, fully dressed in the middle of the harbour,' replied Lisa.

'She must have done a Natalie Wood and fallen off a boat, I suppose,' commented Travers.

'Natalie who?

'Natalie Wood, the film star? She mysteriously drowned back in '81. Travers paused as he looked across at the vacant expression facing him. 'Never mind.'

'Anyway, how about lunch, hair of the dog and all that, some fresh air, it's a beautiful day, a bit of sunshine will do you good,' suggested Lisa.

It was a tempting offer, Travers thought; in fact, it was far too tempting to turn down even though he suspected that his liver was still probably 40% proof.

'You're on, let's walk across the common and pop into the Dog and Fox for a quickie, then get the tube to Covent Garden.'

30 minutes later, Travers and Lisa left his house overlooking Rushmere Pond in Wimbledon Village and walked across the common towards the high street. There were a large number of adults, children, and dogs on the common enjoying the sunshine and the warm weather,

some picnicking, others walking, or just playing. As they turned right into the high street, they were faced with the regular sight of the mounted horses from the Wimbledon Village Stables off for their daily exercise on nearby Wimbledon Common. Despite the daily regularity of the sight, the passing citizenry invariably stopped to watch the parade of horse flesh.

It took only a few minutes to reach the Dog and Fox, an iconic public house made famous by the Wimbledon Tennis Championships, which takes place a few hundred yards away along Church Road. During Wimbledon fortnight, the pub is packed with tennis aficionados, many of whom will have spent a long, hot day watching tennis. Then walked up the steep hill leading to the Wimbledon High Street roundabout, directly opposite which stood the Dog and Fox, an oasis for both the weary and the parched.

'Grab a seat in the sun, I'll pop in and get the drinks. Wine?'

'Yes, please, thanks,' responded Lisa.

A few minutes later, Travers returned with a small tray containing two glasses of wine and a small tumbler filled with ice cubes.

'How are you feeling now?' asked Lisa.

'Better than I did a few hours ago, at least my head has stopped spinning and I can feel all my fingers now, sadly, I can also feel my toes, there will probably be a bruise there tomorrow,' sighed Travers.

'Cheers,' said Lisa. After a few moments of deliberation, she turned and looked Travers in the eye.

'Do you want to tell me about it?'

'What?'

'I saw the certificates on the wall, a picture of you and presumably your wife, and a photo of you and the former Prime Minister. Last night I saw the same man pissed as a fart, win and then lose ten thousand pounds, have a one-night stand with a woman he had just met, and drink a whole bottle of Vodka before throwing up in the bathroom and collapsing onto the bed. I'm not stupid, and you don't have to be Sigmund Freud to see it … you have unresolved issues?'

'It's not important,' said Travers dismissively.

'Bollocks, of course it is, you want to try again?'

Travers was taken aback by the directness of Lisa's repost, but he admired her straight-talking honesty. She had not been put off by his less-than-gallant behaviour last night.

'All right, I worked, or I should say worked for the Government. My wife Cassandra was expecting twins about five months ago, but there were complications, and they all died. That's it. I went off the rails, straight to Skid Row. I needed to get away. The company offered me special leave and all the help and time I needed to sort my life out. I loved my job, but my heart wasn't in it anymore. Look, I am sorry about last night … and this morning,' said a contrite Travers.

'Sort yourself out? If last night is an example of sorting yourself out, it's going to take some time,' said Lisa. 'I enjoy a night out, but not all night, every night.'

'Come on, let's finish this drink and go and have some lunch,' said Travers. 'We can get the train from here to Waterloo and then the tube to Covent Garden.'

Travers and Scott finished their drinks, got up, and walked across the road just in time to get the 93 bus to Wimbledon train station, then on to Waterloo.

The London Grill in Henrietta Street, Covent Garden, was one of Travers' favourite haunts. He had been there a great many times over the years with his late wife. Since Cassandra's passing, he had returned there on numerous occasions, often enjoying a lazy breakfast that frequently stretched to an even lazier lunch before the pain of his loneliness reminded him that he still had a home to go to. Travers led Lisa to an area of outside tables in front of the restaurant, enclosed by a low, ornate metal fence surrounded by potted plants and boxes of floral displays. A large green canopy afforded a measure of shelter from the sun's extreme heat. Covent Garden was packed with locals, visitors, and tourists taking advantage of the wonderful weather. Travers and Lisa found a free table and, after glancing through the extensive menus, attracted the attention of one of the waiting staff.

'I'll have an Aperol Spritz, please,' requested Travers. 'How about you?'

'I'd like a Green Juice to start with,' she replied.

Acknowledging the order, the waiter disappeared inside the restaurant, returning a few minutes later with a small tray carrying the pair's drinks. He put them carefully down on the table before moving on to attend to another customer close by.

Travers stared aghast at the tall, full glass standing in front of Lisa. 'What the hell is that? It looks like something the dog brought up.'

'Avocado, Mint, Spinach, Apple, and Parsley. It's very good for you. Considering what you have been putting into your gut recently, you should try it.'

'God! It looks like embalming fluid. Why can't you have a proper drink? How am I supposed to keep my lunch down if I have to watch you drinking that? It makes me queasy just looking at it,' said Travers, making a mock expression of disgust, much to Lisa's amusement.

Travers leant forward and grasped his large Copa Balloon glass containing his Aperol Spritz, a measure of ice, and a large slice of Orange.

'Skal.'

'Cheers,' Lisa responded. 'What do you intend to do when your special leave finishes?'

'Oh, I don't know, judging by last night's demonstration, I am no nearer knowing the answer to that question than I was 4 months ago. I just went into an abyss when Cassandra died; everything just fell apart, nothing mattered anymore, my world stopped turning, and I just got off. Last night was a pretty good example of my new world. As for the future? I either go back to the office and carry on or move on to fresh pastures, have a clean break,' said Travers.

'And do what?'

'Well, I spent five years shuffling papers in the Home Office in Whitehall before moving to the MOD.'

'Where are you based?' asked Lisa.

'Thames House.'

'Wow, that's exciting, that's MI5, isn't it? Is that how you ended up being in a mug shot with the PM?'

Travers stared at his companion for a few seconds before deciding not to answer her question. The last thing he wanted to do was rake over old coals. He smiled, picked up his glass, and swirled around the remains of his cocktail before draining the glass.

'What do you fancy for lunch then?' asked Travers, swiftly changing the subject before he got drawn into a potentially awkward line of questioning. Lisa realised the conversation had been deliberately moved on and didn't pursue it.

Lunch with Lisa had been just the tonic that Travers needed. After several hours in the fresh air and warm sunshine, a very good Chicken Milanese washed down with a more than acceptable Perrier-Jouet,

Belle Epoque 2012. She had provided him with convivial and understanding conversation, which was more than he deserved after the spectacle he had made of himself the night before. Whilst Lisa excused herself for a few minutes, Travers looked out across the bustling market. He was now acutely embarrassed by his drunken fumbling last night before he passed out. After some ten minutes, she reappeared and joined him once more at the table. As Lisa retook her seat, a waiter arrived with a fresh tray of drinks that Travers had ordered in her absence. The conversation continued to flow with such ease and natural familiarity that they might have known each other for many years. After a further twenty minutes and two more drained glasses, Travers rose to his feet.

'I'll just go to the loo before we go, I'll only be a minute,'

He quickly disappeared through the doorway into the restaurant and made his way to the toilets. Five minutes later, he returned to find a noisy commotion outside. He moved through a throng of agitated people until he found his table. Lisa was kneeling on the floor, cradling a man's head in her lap. He was foaming at the mouth and appeared to be having some kind of seizure. The man struggled to lean up to reach her ear before slumping down again. A member of staff had already called for assistance, and it wasn't long before an ambulance arrived. Paramedics pushed their way through the crowd to render assistance to the fallen man. Lisa stood up and stepped back, looking around for the reassurance of a familiar face. Travers stepped forward, took her hand, and led her out of the crush.

'What the hell happened?' asked Travers.

'I don't know, the man had been sitting at the table behind us, I heard a glass go over and looked up. He was trying to get to his feet, then holding his throat, and gasping. He began walking and then stumbled. I thought he was going to collapse, so I jumped up and managed to grab him just as he went down. He was retching, foaming at the mouth as though it was some sort of epileptic fit, but it couldn't have been; he was trying to tell me something. I couldn't really make it out, something about Albe 'it was Albe', that was it. He was struggling for breath and couldn't get his words out. Then he just slumped down.'

A Police foot patrol had appeared on the scene during this time and took charge of the incident, as the paramedics loaded the unfortunate man into the ambulance, one of the policemen came across to where Travers and Lisa were standing and took notes as she recalled the events that had just taken place.

'Is he going to be alright, officer?' asked Lisa.

'Well, he's unconscious, miss, but the crew will get him to the hospital straight away. Thank you for doing what you did; it must have been very distressing. Can I have your name, address, and contact numbers, please, in case we need to get in touch with you?' asked the policeman. Travers and Lisa proceeded to give the officer their details as the ambulance pulled away, and some of the onlookers began to drift off.

It had been an abrupt and unwelcome conclusion to their agreeable lunch. He had not enjoyed such a civilised and genuinely pleasing time since his beloved wife had passed away.

'Would you like to come back with me tonight?' asked Travers. 'Or would you rather I hail a cab for you?'

'I had better go home, to be honest. It was a lovely lunch, Greg, thank you. I think a hot bath and an early night are what I need.'

'I'll call you in the morning to make sure you are all right.'

With that, Travers walked over towards the roadside and waved at an approaching black cab that pulled over. Lisa walked over, kissed and embraced Travers, and got into the taxi. Travers watched as the car pulled away down the westbound one-way street towards Bedford Street before turning out of sight.

With the day's activities prematurely curtailed, Travers decided to call it a day and return to Wimbledon Village. After the previous evening's debacle, today had gone well, apart from the unfortunate incident with the man taken ill at the London Grill. He had gone some way to retrieve his self-respect with Lisa, at least temporarily.

Chapter 3

Morning broke in a far less dramatic fashion than it did yesterday. Travers had slept remarkably well and, for the first time in some while, woke with a clear head and a sense of purpose. He rose from his bed, showered, dressed, and walked to the kitchen, where he poured a chilled orange fruit juice while the kettle came to the boil. He turned on the television in the living room and caught part of the local news. There was a brief reference to the incident at Covent Garden yesterday, but it did not provide any update on the unfortunate man's condition.

Travers had really enjoyed his time with Lisa and couldn't wait to see her again. He didn't want to ring too early and seem too keen, but on the other hand, if he left it too late, it might be perceived as uncaring given yesterday's events, especially if she thought that he might have repeated the previous night's alcoholic binge. He determined that it was better to ring than not; after all, it was now well after nine o'clock. He picked up his mobile and dialled her number, which rang without interruption until a voice message cut in.

'Hi Lisa, it's Greg. I hope you are ok today, I'm just checking in, can you give me a quick call back when you pick this up? Thanks.'

With that, he hung up. He had a full day ahead to fill. Something he had not been used to for several months. He still had official paperwork to attend to. Cassandra's family was financially very comfortable. Since his marriage, her family had been very generous. Once everything had been sorted out, he would be financially secure at least for the foreseeable future, but without the woman he loved and the children he had so longed for.

Travers tried Lisa's number again later in the morning, again with no response. He was beginning to think that he had somehow blotted his copybook with her. Two hours of replying to solicitors' letters punctuated by several phone calls was more than enough for him for one day. The thought of a couple of drinks at the Dog and Fox with maybe a burger and chips and some fresh air was enough of a temptation to warrant packing up the files at least for today.

Picking up his wallet and sunglasses, Travers walked to the front door. Opening it, he was confronted by two men standing on his porch.

'Detective Chief Inspector John Deery, this is a surprise. I've not seen you since your briefing on the Streatham stabbings at Thames House last year. I was just on my way out,' explained Travers.

'I'm sorry, Greg, it's important. Can we come in, please?' insisted DCI Deery. 'I assume you know Charles Stanley, Senior Intelligence officer at MI5.'

'Yes, of course, good morning, sir. You had better come in then,' said Travers, leading the way back into the house and inviting the two men to the living room.

'Before I go on, Greg, may I say how sorry I was to hear about your wife,' said the detective.

'Thank you, John, that is kind of you. I can't deny it's hit me pretty hard. I don't suppose a day goes by that I don't think about her. Anyway, how can I help you? I gather this is not a social call,' asked Travers.

'It's about the incident at Covent Garden yesterday,' said the Chief Inspector.

'Oh, that, well, I didn't see much of it, by the time I got there, the man was already convulsing, but it was very upsetting for Lisa; she was holding him when I got there,' explained Travers.

'Did she tell you what she saw?' asked Deery.

'Yes,' replied Travers. 'She told the Police officer everything at the time.'

'Yes, I know, I've read his report. Did she say anything else to you about what happened and what exactly the man said to her before he passed out,' asked Deery.

'She said it was incoherent, with lots of gasping and rambling, and he mentioned something about Albe,' said Travers.

'You're sure it was Albe?' pressed Stanley.

'Yes, she said he said it was Albe.' 'What's going on, Chief Inspector, what aren't you telling me?'

'With the help of our colleagues at MI5, we have identified the victim, his name was William Constable,' said Deery.

'Victim?!' said a surprised Travers.

'William Constable died late last night without regaining consciousness. The initial examination suggests that he may have been poisoned, but we won't know the full picture for several days yet until we have the toxicology report.'

'Poisoned? Why? Who was this guy?'

Stanley leaned forward 'Greg, I know you've had other things on your mind, but I need to remind you that although you are on extended compassionate leave of absence, you are still bound by the Official Secrets Act. What I am going to tell you is classified information.'

'I understand,' said Travers, who was becoming more intrigued by the moment.

'William Constable had been seconded to us by the Treasury; he was a senior financial auditor. We believe that a firm of accountants,

McKenzie and Hunt, here in London, which has extensive international connections, has been helping to launder large amounts of money belonging to criminal organisations. They also have the expertise to provide them with advice on cross-border asset movement,' Stanley continued. 'We pulled some strings and got him attached to official auditors Winston Adams, who were about to perform a regular audit on this company. Constable had to go and conduct an audit and see if he could secure evidence of criminal activity and report back. We needed proof.'

'Why didn't you get someone from our own Finance Department to do it, someone trained to deal with this sort of task?' asked Travers.

'Greg, these are not the kind of accountants that spend a couple of hours helping you fill out your annual tax return; these men are unprincipled, resourceful, and very successful criminals. We needed someone with the highest level of experience and expertise. Someone who is used to dealing with high-level corporate malpractice. He had been briefed and was aware that we had our suspicions.'

'Suspicions? I hope you told this poor man what he was getting into?' asked Travers disdainfully.

There was a momentary but perceptible pause that confirmed what Travers suspected. The only thing that mattered was results. Stanley glanced at his police colleague very briefly before turning back towards Travers.

'His job was to conduct a thorough audit and look out for any red flags, over and above the normal. We didn't want to overcomplicate matters by saying anything that might have made him unduly nervous or inadvertently give himself away,' concluded Stanley.

'I see, like he may end up on a mortuary table with his insides in a specimen jar, you mean,' added Travers sardonically. 'So what now?' asked Travers.

'He was only partway through his audit, but he had identified some entries that had aroused his interest, and he wanted to look into them further. His interim report is with our Finance team, they are going through it and trying to fill in the blanks, it's way over my head, so I am not even going to attempt to explain it, but we are talking about a turnover the equivalent of a small countries GDP,' he turned to Deery 'Detective Chief Inspector.'

'Greg, we believe someone found out about Constable and tipped off McKenzie and Hunt, and they arranged to have him killed, but at the moment we can't prove it. We don't know yet how the poison was administered. Whether it was given to him at Covent Garden via some kind of injection or slipped into his food or drink. When you were sitting there, did you see anyone sitting or standing nearby who looked anxious, nervous, or suspicious, or out of place in any way? Any incidents? Has anyone stop to talk to him? Anyone bump into him?'

'No, John, nothing, but as I said, I was not present when Constable collapsed, you need to speak to Lisa.'

'Ok, have you had any contact with Miss Scott today?' asked the Detective Chief Inspector.

'I've called a couple of times this morning, but she didn't pick up, I left a message,' confirmed Travers.

Deery and Stanley rose from their chairs. I don't think there is anything else at the moment. Our investigation is ongoing. If you think of anything else, give me a call, please. We'll try to get hold of Miss Scott; it's possible she may have seen something that may help us.'

The two men walked towards the front door, turned, and shook hands with Travers before opening it and walking down the driveway to their car.

Travers returned to his living room, poured himself a Hendricks Gin, added a dash of Bitter Lemon, and reflected on the extraordinary conversation that had just taken place. A man was potentially murdered right under their noses, involvement of an international money laundering ring, and the poor guy asked to walk into the lion's den with nothing but his notebook and pencil to protect himself with. He was glad that his job did not entail sending unsuspecting and ill-prepared people out on jobs like this with little or no backup. He picked up his phone, but again there was no reply from Lisa. Travers left another voice mail, followed by a text message, this time advising her that the Police were trying to get in touch with her regarding yesterday's incident but leaving out everything else.

It was another fine, dry, and warm day. The sky was predominately blue with the odd puffy white cloud. Travers had had a full morning with a couple of hours of paperwork followed by a visit by his friend DCI John Deery and his revelations concerning William Constable. A late lunch was beckoning, followed hopefully by a relaxing afternoon. Travers again collected his wallet and sunglasses and walked out of his front door, this time uninterrupted. He turned left, crossed the road onto the common, and continued walking until he crossed Cannizaro Road, continuing west until he came to the driveway and car park for Warren House. Built in the 18th Century, Warren House had been a grand party house with the likes of George III, Prime Minister William Pitt the younger, the Duke of Wellington, Lord Tennyson and Oscar Wilde amongst its notable visitors. Now, it was a popular upmarket hotel with extensive open grounds, and it was a place Travers was fond of visiting.

He walked through the entrance to the spectacular bar area where four large black and gold pillars supported the ceiling in front of an impressive, ornately sculptured marble fireplace. Travers stopped at the bar, ordered a Kir Royale Champagne cocktail, and made his way through the Orangery to the exit at the rear of the hotel, and selected an outside table in the sun. Several people were strolling in the landscaped gardens, which were open to the public.

Travers relished the first sips as the Briottet Crème de Cassis de Dijon Liqueur enveloped his taste buds and the warm sunshine bathed his face. He watched a Robin sway precariously, perched on a nearby bloom, as it stared back at him. It was almost a perfect moment. As he sat there, soaking up the relaxing atmosphere, his mind turned to his late wife. It had been a favourite hangout that they had enjoyed on so many occasions, if only he could share one more perfect moment with her again.

It had been almost five hours since he had first called Lisa this morning, and she didn't seem the type to ghost him even if he was too drunk to remember her name yesterday morning. He reached for his phone once more and dialled her mobile number. The phone rang, Travers let it ring for thirty seconds or so before hanging up. Ordinarily, he would not be concerned; he had hardly displayed any meaningful level of decorum and could scarcely blame her if she chose to look the other way. Perhaps it was the conversation with Deery this morning that gave him an uneasy feeling. Picking up his phone, he called the police. This time, he got an answer.

'Good afternoon, can you put me through to DCI Deery, please? It's urgent.'

The operator promptly transferred his call.

'DCI Deery.'

'John, it's Greg Travers, have you managed to get hold of Miss Scott since we spoke this morning?'

'Hello Greg, no, not so far. We are still trying,' said Deery.

'Ok, thanks, John, I have just tried her number again. I'm going round to see if she is all right. I'll get back to you later.'

With that, Travers hung up and swiftly finished his drink with one long gulp, most unbecoming of such an elegant libation.

He walked quickly back to his house, grabbed his car keys, and remotely opened the garage door, which was his grey BMW 645 coupe. Throwing his jacket onto the passenger seat, Travers started the car, and the magnificent four-and-a-half-litre V8 engine roared into life. Traffic permitting, he should be in Putney in around 10 minutes. Lisa lived on the Lower Richmond Road close to the river. As luck would have it, the fine weather seemed to have kept most of the drivers off the road, and Travers made good time. He managed to find the house number and parked outside. He didn't know what car Lisa drove and, in the absence of a garage, couldn't tell if any of the cars parked nearby belonged to her.

He approached the front of the house and rang the bell. While he waited for her to come to the door, Travers peered through the windows to see if he could see anything. Nothing seemed out of place; perhaps she had gone away. He rang the bell again just in case. Doing his best not to look overtly shifty, Travers walked around the side of the house to see if he could find a back door. There it was, slightly ajar. He knocked and called Lisa's name before opening the door wide enough for him to gain entry.

Travers stepped across the threshold into the elegant modern kitchen, and everything seemed to be where it should be. He walked through the room into a carpeted hallway that connected to several other rooms. Working his way along the hall, he paused to look into each room. Everything was neat and tidy; nothing had been disturbed. He reached the white-painted front door, which was bolted and chained, so if she had left, she did so by the back door and failed to close it properly. Travers turned away from the front door, now in front of him, and to the left was a staircase. He called Lisa's name again before venturing upstairs.

He began to climb, putting his right hand on the light wooden balustrade that led to the upper floor. At the top of the stairs was a small landing from which, through an open door, he could see a light grey tiled bathroom; there were also two other doors. Travers first walked into the bathroom, and it was empty. Next to the bathroom was a closed door. He reached for the doorknob, opened it, and allowed the door to swing open to reveal a small office. Some box files were stacked up on shelving, a laptop was still switched on, and a cold, half-drunk mug of tea sat on the table … along with her mobile phone!

Travers walked across the first-floor landing to the one remaining room, which must be her bedroom. The door was slightly open, and gingerly, he pushed the door with his fingers. In front of him, he could see a dressing table where several bottles of perfume and a makeup mirror had been knocked over. He pushed the door open. He had found Lisa. She was kneeling beside her bed with her head and exposed chest lying on the bed. A savage cut across her throat. Her dress and white duvet were soaked in her blood. Travers recoiled in revulsion at the sight. He stepped back through the bedroom doorway and tried to compose himself. What madman could have done this…and why? He stood transfixed, in shock at the appalling sight, before his shaking hands reached for his phone and called Detective Deery.

Still standing in the doorway, his eyes drawn to the nightmare vision of the butchered girl that he had only known for two days. It was a searing, life-changing image that would ingrain itself into his subconscious and haunt him forever.

'John, it's Greg, I'm at Lisa Scott's house in Putney. She's been murdered, you had better get over here and bring a forensics team with you.'

Chapter 4

Hector Devereux sat in front of his stylish white and gold oblong desk in his well-appointed office in C block on the 7th floor of the imposing Albatross House in Poole. Like his mother, Olga, Hector, her 37-year-old eldest son, also enjoyed spectacular panoramic views across Poole Harbour and the Purbeck Hills. His giant frame made even his large desk appear small. He inherited his great height from his father, but his ruthless nature was all his mother's. He was the de facto deputy head of both his Mother's charitable Foundation and the Albatross Corporation's business empire, created primarily by his Father. His responsibilities encompassed the UK operation of the corporate business and the coordination and oversight of all the Foundation's global activities. However, such was the breadth of the business that all the family was involved, with his younger siblings Christian, based in Miami, Alexander covering Asia and the Pacific basin, and sister Oksana in Europe sharing the responsibilities between them.

The Albatross Corporation itself was an umbrella organisation under which was a multi-national conglomeration of diverse businesses, developed or subsumed by the Albatross's ever-expanding corporate empire. They stretched across the globe, incorporating building and construction, oil production, mineral extraction, Communications, AI, munitions, brokerage, and a number of NGOs (Non-Governmental Organisations) throughout the developing world. While ostensibly independent businesses, their untaxed profits flowed back to the controlling and grasping fingers of the Albatross Corporation through dozens of crooked accountants. Olga and her husband had spared no expense regarding their children's education and futures. Post-graduation, each had worked overseas in several of the corporation's subsidiary companies, gaining valuable experience and a taste for power. With her husband's passing, Olga had assumed a far more autocratic and controlling interest in the business by installing her children as regional directors, as she tightened her grip and control still further.

With Olga attending a meeting in London, it was left to Hector to clear up after Monica Stein. It was not the first time such executive action had been deemed necessary. His mother was determined that the Albatross' philosophy of ever greater influence, wealth, control, and power should be the overriding principle that guides their actions and determines everything they do. Nothing should be allowed to threaten that mantra. As such, it was useful and sometimes necessary to have an 'off the books' capability in what was euphemistically referred to as the Special Operations team attached to their general House Services department that was able to remove or deal with the business's dirty laundry once in a while. Monica's body had been removed from the building via a secret central stairwell that had been installed when the building was erected and ran through the centre of B Block, emerging in the basement. The body was then spirited away unseen until it reappeared floating in Poole Harbour the following morning.

Hector's mobile phone rang. He put his cup of tea down and retrieved his phone from his jacket pocket, saying, 'Hi, Hector speaking!'

'Hector, this is Graham McKenzie from McKenzie and Hunt in London.'

'Yes, Graham, how are things?'

'I thought you ought to know we had an audit this week.'

'I hope they didn't find anything they shouldn't have?' enquired Hector.

'They were thorough, as you would expect them to be, but we take great pride in protecting our special client's privacy. You know we had a tip-off from your man in Whitehall, it caused us some concern?' said McKenzie.

'Oh? No, I didn't' said Hector.

'It seems that one of the auditors has been digging around rather more vigorously than he should have been. We understand from your contact that those dedicated public servants in MI5 have been taking an unhealthy interest in our business recently. Fortunately, we are very discreet. We are used to being under official scrutiny. They can huff and puff as much as they like, but they won't blow our house down. Nor will they find any smoking guns here.'

Hector growled under his breath. It was bad enough having to deal with a loose-tongued girl, but now the authorities were sniffing around one of their trusted accounting partners.

McKenzie continued, 'Having said that, if MI5 has planted him, we will need to be careful. I would recommend you review your internal security, just in case. Especially given the importance of your ongoing operations. We discussed the matter at length with our principals and took the view that the best thing to do was to arrange for the removal of our overly inquisitive Auditor. Given the understandable risk involved, we arranged for an outside agency to take care of him.'

'Shit! Graham, that's madness, you will have the whole of the bloody Fraud Squad and MI5 down on you like a ton of hot bricks,' said an angry Hector. 'What happens when they send someone else to finish what he started? They'll take you apart, brick by fucking brick?'

McKenzie continued, 'We did consider the potential repercussions. However, there is nothing linking us to the killing. One of our associates just happens to be an extremely well-connected and particularly vindictive Russian whose lucrative money laundering business was exposed and effectively closed down by this man, Constable. We just made sure that he found out that Constable was in town. After that, he simply needed reminding how much Constable had cost him and pointing in the right direction. He lost a fortune, and despite trying to keep his nose clean afterwards, he just couldn't resist the chance for revenge. He's been desperate to even the score. So when the authorities start nosing around, the finger of suspicion will lead straight to our Comrade Volkov; he's the perfect patsy.'

'And what happens when the police pick him up, question him, and he spills the beans and tries to cut a deal to save his skin?' asked Hector.

'I really don't think that will be a problem. Your man Petrov is arranging for him to be involved in a fatal car accident. So, with a little help from the soon-to-be-late Igor Volkov, things should tidy themselves up very nicely. The police will be presented with a dead man, a solid motive, and a high degree of probability.'

'Petrov?' questioned Hector. 'How is he involved?'

'Your Chief of Staff offered his services to us, a man used to tidying up loose ends, I understand,' replied McKenzie.

'I saw the news on TV yesterday about a man collapsing in Covent Garden, was that your auditor?' asked Hector.

'As far as I know, they haven't named him. According to the news reports, he was just carted off in an ambulance, but given how efficient the Russians are in these matters, if it was him, I wouldn't give much for his chances,' recalled McKenzie.

'All right, Graham. Thanks for the update. I will initiate a good housekeeping sweep here to make sure we are clean. Let me know if there are any developments.'

McKenzie and Hunt had been extremely useful partners over the years in concealing much of the vast ill-gotten gains made by some of the Corporation's less honest activities, not to mention greatly reducing their UK tax liability from their honest endeavours. However, if the slightest shadow of suspicion started to fall on their accounting partners, steps would need to be taken to minimise the risk to the Foundation and its assets.

Doing a full security sweep of all the Albatross personnel was time-consuming, but Hector knew the best place to start looking. He picked up the phone and rang Albatross's in-house security department on the ground floor.

'Hello, Safia speaking, how can I help you?'

'Safia, it's Hector Devereux. I need you to do a back trace on Monica Stein. Everything for the last month, phone calls, texts, emails, letters, social media, security footage, everything. If nothing comes up, go back another month. I want to know who she's been communicating with.'

The security department routinely ran background checks on all Albatross staff.

'Fast as you can, Safia, report back directly to me,' demanded Hector.

With the housekeeping sweep underway, Hector turned his attention to the other matter. He had asked Chief of Staff Richard Rackman to follow up on his enquiries into the Rome connection. Monica's email had referenced someone making a call to a Robert Sterling in Rome. Hector rose from his desk and walked across his grey carpeted floor, through the double doors into the foyer. Immediately opposite C block was A block, and the main building staircase was in front of its entrance. Hector descended the flights of stairs before reaching the 3rd-floor foyer. Turning left, he walked across the foyer towards the C block entrance and placed his thumb on the optical reader by the door. An almost instantaneous click confirmed that the magnetic doors had unlocked. He pushed through the double doors and walked around to the left until he reached Rackman's office.

It was a frosted glass-fronted room adorned with large potted plants. Hector knocked on the door before walking in. Rackman had just gotten off the phone and was updating a note on his computer.

'Good afternoon Richard,' said Hector.

'Hello Hector,' replied Rackman.

'I had a call from Graham McKenzie earlier. Do you know they had an audit this week, and MI5 sent in a Trojan horse? I don't know if this is related to the situation with Monica Stein; however, I have asked security to trace her comms and movements over the last month. Where do we stand with this Robert Sterling chap? Do we know who he is and what his connection with this is?' asked Hector.

Rackman replied, 'The short answer is no, not at the moment. The email mentioned that he was in Rome and that the information should be passed on to him ASAP, as to who he is or what capacity he's working in, at the moment, you're guess is as good as mine. I spoke to Oksana this morning. She has friends in the Guardia di Finanza. If this man were somehow connected with Monica or the authorities and is investigating us or someone linked to us, we should be able to find out.'

Chapter 5

At New Scotland Yard Headquarters on the Victoria Embankment, Superintendent Barclay walked into Briefing Room 2. Already sitting at the oblong table in front of him were Senior Investigating Officer Detective Chief Inspector Deery, his team, and pathologists Rachel Stewart and Charles Stanley from MI5. Each had a folder containing photographs and background material relating to the current investigation.

'All right, everyone, let's get on with it.' He turned to the Chief Inspector. 'John, bring me up to speed.'

'Thank you, sir, I have asked Charles Stanley, Senior Intelligence Officer from Thames House, to join us; their own inquiry is now overlapping with ours, and I think it would be appropriate and helpful to combine our investigations,' said the Chief Inspector.

'Agreed, good to have you with us, Mr Stanley,' said Superintendent Barclay.

Deery then reminded the Superintendent of the background detail before turning to the chief Pathologist, Rachel Stewart, for further updates. 'We believe Constable was murdered yesterday. I have asked Dr Rachel Stewart from Pathology to provide an update, Rachel?'

Doctor Stewart opened her black leather-bound folder, 'William Constable was killed by a large dose of TTX.'

'TT what, Doctor?' asked a puzzled Superintendent Barclay.

'TTX is better known as Tetrodotoxin, it's a deadly neurotoxin, derived from Tetraodontiformes, which includes the Pufferfish and Triggerfish, and some frogs, amongst others. TTX is seriously bad news if you get exposed to it. It is twelve hundred times more toxic than Cyanide, and there is no known antidote. It can enter the body through inhalation, ingestion, injection, or broken skin. Given the amount we found in his body, he was effectively dead the moment it entered his body; he never had a chance.'

'Where would someone get hold of this stuff?' asked Barclay.

'Not at your local pharmacy, sir, it has to be extracted from the host and then synthesised into a usable form,' answered Dr Stewart.

At this point, Deery broke in and continued with his briefing.

'When Constable collapsed at the Grill in Covent Garden, he was assisted by a young woman, Lisa Scott, who was having lunch with a male friend, Greg Travers, who happens to be an analyst at MI5. According to Miss Scott's statement, Constable reached up and attempted to tell her something. We are not sure exactly what was said, but reference was made to someone or something called Albe. Yesterday afternoon, Miss Scott was found dead in her house; her throat had been cut. Doctor?'

'The cut was made with a large serrated blade running from under the right ear across to the left, right to left, meaning the attacker was probably left-handed. The blade severed the Thyroid Cartilage, the Vocal Cord, the Cricoid Cartilage, the Carotid artery, and the Jugular vein. She would have died almost immediately,' said the Pathologist.

'There was no sign of a sexual assault or robbery, but there were definite indications of a struggle; she put up a fight before she was overpowered,' added Deery.

Superintendent Barclay, who had been making notes whilst the briefing had been taking place, looked across at the Doctor and thanked her before turning to Charles Stanley,

'Mr Stanley, do you wish to add anything at this stage?'

Charles Stanley closed the folder containing the documents in front of him and turned towards Barclay.

'We have suspected McKenzie and Hunt of large-scale money laundering for some time, but have been unable to produce any hard evidence to prove it. William Constable was a highly qualified and experienced auditor who had spent many years investigating companies and organisations, some of which were known to be operating illegally. I don't believe he would have given himself away. The fact that he was murdered suggests a connection, not a coincidence, and the fact that the woman who went to his aid and may have heard his last words has now also been murdered just confirms it. We are still going through Constable's preliminary report; if we turn up anything, we will pass it on.'

'Thank you, Mr Stanley,' added Barclay.

'All right, everyone, until further evidence suggests otherwise, for the present, we will work on the basis that these murders are connected and related directly to Constable's work. Review all of his recent audits, investigate anyone who might have a grievance, and check out McKenzie and Hunt thoroughly; if they are not squeaky clean, I want to know why. Find out where this TTX stuff came from; you obviously don't buy this at the pharmacy. You had better keep tabs on Miss Scott's friend Greg Travers, too; it's quite possible that whoever killed her might suspect that she passed something on to him and look to tie up any loose ends. John, keep me updated on any developments. Let me know if you need any additional resources, and keep Mr Stanley in the loop.'

Superintendent Barclay rose from his chair, walked across to Stanley, shook his hand warmly, and left the room. Deery, his six-man team, and Doctor Stewart gathered their papers and, after a few minutes' post-meeting conversation, drifted out of the briefing room and back to their respective offices.

Deery walked Charles Stanley to the entrance of the New Scotland Yard building.

'Right, Charles, you had better fill me in on William Constable. I need some background. Grey-suited bean counters don't volunteer for hazardous jobs that could get them killed. Being briefed by MI5 would send your average risk-averse pinstriped accountant into a tailspin,' enquired the Inspector.

The two men stood and looked out of the glass-enclosed entrance for a few moments before Stanley continued.

'Constable was a brilliant accountant and later auditor in the private sector; he decided to apply for a position in the Treasury. We are always keeping our eyes open for talented people who might be able to help us. We saw his application and arranged a meeting with him; he ticked a lot of our boxes. He was the right age, very ambitious, and eager to get on. We offered to help him get a foot in the door and support his application if he helped us out.'

'You didn't just help get his foot in the door, you got it into a body bag,' added Deery.

'I know John, I was the officer who gave him the briefing before he did the McKenzie and Hunt audit, so I don't need any lectures, please. I want the bastard that did it, and I will do whatever it takes to get him or her, dead or alive,' exclaimed a passionate Stanley.

'We'll need to get his work schedule and check up on everyone he audited in the last six months before joining the Treasury. Perhaps someone there might have a motive, but I want to focus on McKenzie and Hunt,' said the Chief Inspector.

'Right, well, if you need anything from me, Charles, you have my number. If we get any further leads from the Lisa Scott end, I'll pass them on. In the meantime, can I have a copy of your file on McKenzie and Hunt? We'll need to get hold of a list of their clients, past and present, and check them all out. There has got to be something there, there has to be. You just don't kill an auditor doing a routine check unless you are afraid, very afraid, they are going to expose something damaging. Killing a Constable and then an innocent girl, who just happened to be there? It doesn't add up, there is something big going on here, and we need to get to the bottom of it, fast.'

The pair shook hands, Stanley walked out of the entrance to his waiting car, whilst Deery returned to his office.

Chapter 6

The sight of Lisa Scott's body lying over her bed, with her throat cut, had left Greg Travers severely shaken. Despite working for MI5, his work was hardly glamorous, being largely computer-based, trawling the internet (including the dark web), gathering, collating, assessing, and presenting intelligence and analytics on people or organisations of interest, to be then passed on to other teams and allied organisations. The most visceral things he had encountered were photographic images or live operational streaming. The brutality of her murder had been stomach-churning. He had scarcely slept since the awful discovery, the sight of which defied all his attempts to banish it from his subconscious.

Almost everyone there had read the works of Ian Fleming and Len Deighton and was familiar with their famous literary creations and their creative links to the intelligence services. Some years ago, Travers had been talked somewhat reluctantly into attending a departmental team bonding day paintballing.

However, if he ever needed a reason to stay clear of fieldwork, this day provided it. On his first exercise, while crouching concealed amongst shrubbery and observing members of the opposing team, he tripped over a tree root. He accidentally shot one of his teammates, who had been kneeling directly in front of him, on the backside. On the second exercise, having entered the live zone a matter of seconds before, he was shot in the face. The force of the impact blew off his protective goggles. He hadn't seen or heard the shot coming. It was only a ball of paint. It stung a bit, but had it been a bullet, he would have had it! He had great admiration for the men and women of the intelligence community who risked their lives every day for King and country. Though, despite an appetite for some of life's finer things, it was, in his opinion, not an appetite worth recklessly risking his life for.

Since the tragic death of his beloved wife Cassandra and her unborn twins, Travers had sunk pretty low. From being a highly skilled and experienced officer in the Digital Intelligence Department, he had spent most of his recent weeks either drunk or in some cases, dead drunk. When he wasn't intoxicated, he was spending much of the night losing what money he had in the casino. For Travers, life had lost its allure and its meaning. The department had given him time off to sort his head out, but all it was doing was giving him an abundance of extra time to wallow in alcohol-fuelled self-pity. For a brief moment, he thought he saw a glimmer of light at the end of the tunnel.

Lisa Scott had appeared out of nowhere when their eyes met across the baccarat table at the casino. Elegantly dressed and articulate, she was fun to be with. The pain and futility of the previous few months that had plagued him seemed to fade. He was actually having fun again, even if he was still half-cut, at least that was what he kept telling himself. Twenty-four hours later, that faint hope was wrenched from his grasp, snuffed out like a flickering candle, until all that remained was the briefest of happy reminiscences, forever soured by the lasting recollection of the brutality of her savage murder. His melancholy state of mind was now matched by the bitterness of life's indiscriminate twists of fate.

Travers polished off his drink and glanced out of the window. The weather was still holding; it had been a fine, dry, warm spell, and the large high-pressure area responsible was still sitting resolutely across much of England. At least for the time being, it was showing no signs of moving on. Travers swiped through the list of contacts on his phone before deciding he would prefer his own company. Picking up his sunglasses, his jacket, and his mobile phone, he walked out into the sunshine, heading once more to the Warren House Hotel a few hundred yards away. A few hours in the sun, watching the world go by, with a jug of Pimms for company, and perhaps he would be able to shake off the miserable mood he was in, or at least distract himself for a while.

With Cannizaro Park stretching out in front of him, Travers made himself comfortable. Before too long, a well-dressed waiter arrived carrying a tray on which was a large empty glass containing some ice and a very full jug of Pimms stuffed with all manner of fruit and vegetables. He was reminded of Lisa's last drink, a ghastly green concoction, which made him feel quite nauseous. Still, she would be impressed with the fruit and veg on offer, if not with the quantity of Pimms.

The waiter poured the first glass, which included two slices of Cucumber, a couple of chopped Strawberries, a slice of orange, and a huge sprig of mint, which protruded from the top of the glass like a sapling stretching upwards from its pot towards the sun. Travers gazed at the glass, salivating at the prospect of the first thirst-quenching mouthful of the rich golden cocktail, just as a dog might over a freshly cooked roast beef joint. He looked around at the other people enjoying the fine summer day. A family group, a young woman, several couples, and a single man occupied a table furthest from him. As Travers picked up his glass, he caught the eye of the single man, who nodded in his direction and then looked away. Two hours passed by, and as the contents of Travers' jug of Pimms diminished, so too did his melancholy demeanour. Leaving his jacket over his chair, he stood up and walked back into the building to answer nature's call.

As he returned through the orangery, his mobile phone rang. He paused and retrieved it from his pocket. It was Deery again.

'Hello, Greg, it's John Deery. We've had the toxicology report. Constable was definitely poisoned and not with your run-of-the-mill poison either. It was TTX.'

'TTX? What's that? Sounds like an explosive!'

'It's nasty, very nasty, comes from tropical fish. Listen, we think that whoever killed Constable may have killed your friend, Miss Scott. We believe that Constable's killer silenced Miss Scott because they suspected he may have passed some information to her,' confided the Chief Inspector.

'Have you noticed anyone following you or loitering around the place?'

'I can't say I have,' said Travers, trying to think back over the last twenty-four hours.

'Well, keep your eyes open, just in case,' warned Deery.

'What do you mean, just in case? Just in case of what?'

'In case they think Miss Scott passed anything on to you. Oh, and if I were you, I would spend a bit more time drinking tea or coffee and a bit less time getting shitfaced. After all, Greg, you wouldn't want to be caught with your pants down, now would you,' joked Deery.

'Thanks, that makes me feel so much better. Ok, thanks for your call, John, I'll be in touch.'

Travers returned to his seat outside, which was still bathed in glorious sunshine. The number of people occupying the patio area had diminished somewhat since his enforced absence. He was now sharing the afternoon sunlight with just the single man and the lone woman. After his chat with Deery, he couldn't resist casting repeated glances at his two remaining companions. Much as he tried not to stare, he just couldn't help himself. Could he really be being followed?

The man was probably in his late thirties, with short dark hair, clean-shaven, and tall, judging by the length of his slender legs. He was still sitting at the same table as before with a glass in his left hand and a newspaper in his right. The woman who had been sitting close to the hotel's rear entrance had changed tables, moving from the shade to the sun. She was smartly dressed with a white jacket covering a bright red midi dress, a white wide-brimmed hat with a matching red ribbon, and sunglasses covering up much of her flowing dark hair. She seemed preoccupied with reading a book and appeared to be oblivious to his presence. Twenty minutes later, Travers drained his last glass and looked at the jug; it was empty. It was time to go.

Detective Chief Inspector Deery called his team to order. He had finally obtained a full list of McKenzie and Hunt's clients, all of which would have to be checked out thoroughly.

'Listen up, everyone, we know Constable was officially auditing McKenzie and Hunt. Unofficially, we know that he was also looking for evidence that might implicate them in serious organised criminal activity over and above simple tax evasion. We have a list of all their clients, all 150 of them. Every one of them will have to be checked out. We also have a list of all of Constable's own clients over the last six months. I want background checks on all of them and a microscope on McKenzie and Hunt, personnel, financials, everything, nothing's off limits. Unless he was incredibly unlucky and just in the wrong place at the wrong time, Constable was killed by someone on or connected to someone on one of these lists, and we are not going to rest until we find them. Get cracking.'

With that, Deery turned and walked back to his office, where he immediately picked up his phone. It was going to be a big task to do a detailed background check on so many people and organisations; he was going to have to get help.

At MI5, Charles Stanley sat at his desk, mulling over the current state of his investigation and the next steps. He deeply regretted William Constable's death and couldn't disguise a deep sense of personal responsibility. It had been his call to persuade Constable to conduct what he knew would be a potentially dangerous job at McKenzie and Hunt. Stanley had tried twice to get someone on the inside, but neither had panned out. This was the first time that he had managed to get such a highly qualified individual with such an unimpeachable CV to act on behalf of the service, and have a genuine chance to nose around. He wouldn't rest until his killer was brought to justice.

Quite apart from finding Constable's assassin, there was also the question of who tipped off McKenzie and Hunt. Stanley had made it clear to Constable that he shouldn't discuss this job with anyone else. On the assumption that he didn't, he was left with the unpalatable reality that the leak must have come from either MI5 or HM Treasury. It seemed inconceivable to Stanley that one of his close colleagues had betrayed him, and as a result, a man had lost his life, and in any case, the number of colleagues in the loop was so small.

All members of the intelligence service were routinely screened. Stanley concluded that the rat must be a Treasury man. It was a bit of a long shot, but checking the Treasury call logs was an obvious place to start, even though it was highly unlikely that anyone would make such a call using official channels. Then, there were the phone records of McKenzie and Hunt. It would be a long and laborious process unless they got a lucky break. However, it occurred to Stanley that as he now suspected that there was a mole at the Treasury he could potentially shorten the search by sending out another email to the Treasury, copying in the same individuals as he did when Constable's secondment to accountants Winston Adams was announced, advising that due to Constable's death, MI5 would send in one of their own auditors to finish Constables work.

Admittedly, it was a long shot. There was no guarantee that the traitor would either see the email or take the bait, or if he did, that he would warn the accountants using a traceable phone or some other electronic medium. However, they already had McKenzie and Hunt under surveillance, and the Home Secretary had now authorised their landlines and mobiles to be tapped using the Regulation of Investigatory Powers Act. So with a bit of luck, if someone did tip them off that they were still under investigation, the authorities should pick it up at that end and trace it to its source.

Chapter 7

Across the blue waters of Sandbanks, scores of kite surfers chanced their arms on the choppy Dorset waters, their kites populating the skies like so many butterflies with their multi-coloured wings fluttering as they looked to catch the prevailing breeze. To them, it didn't seem to matter whether the sun was out or not, but there could hardly be a better place to enjoy the recreation when the sun was out and the wind was up. It was a mecca for water sports enthusiasts. Sandbanks was both a spectacular and spectacularly expensive part of the south coast.

Sandbanks' Panorama Road contained what was referred to as Millionaires Row, a collection of thirteen mega mansions with a more expensive waterside real estate value than either Miami or Monte-Carlo, and Sandbanks itself was the most expensive stretch of real estate in the world. Home to the rich and famous, where multi-million-pound properties were often bought only to be immediately demolished and replaced with even more lavish homes. Sandbanks' three miles of golden sandy beaches were regularly voted amongst the best in the country and attracted visitors from all over the world. Apart from wind and kite surfers, Sandbanks and Poole Harbour were also a haven for boats, big and small, fast and slow, boats for every budget, including, of course, millionaires, and Poole's boatyards catered for them all.

Olga Devereux maintained a luxury suite on the seventh floor of Albatross House, which overlooked Poole Harbour. It was convenient and lacked nothing. It was the kind of opulent and extravagantly spacious accommodation that few hotels could hope to match at any price. She frequently stayed there overnight rather than going home, especially if she was working late. However, one of the benefits of great wealth was the opportunity to enjoy a lifestyle that few others could appreciate or scarcely imagine.

As Robert and Olga's business empire grew, so too did their desire for a bolt hole, a retreat away from the world's prying eyes. When the chance to acquire their own private island presented itself, it was an opportunity not to be missed. After Sydney Harbour, Poole was the second-largest natural harbour in the world. Within the harbour were several islands of varying sizes. At high tide, some of the islands almost disappeared completely under the rising waters. However, Parkson Island was ideal, hidden as it was from the mainland behind a larger island. It was approximately twenty acres at high tide with a good stand of pine trees. When the Devereux's purchased it, it was completely undeveloped, without running water or electricity, and it took some time before the provision of essential utilities was implemented. On the southwest corner of the island, a Helipad was constructed, and the building of their spectacular home could begin before long.

That was more than thirty years ago. Since then, the Albatross Corporation had become a formidable global business empire, and the family enjoyed lavish homes worldwide. Their four children had grown up and taken their place on the world stage, destined to play an ever-increasing role in managing the business and preparing for the eventual day when they and they alone would hold the reins of the vast organisation. The house on Parkson had changed too, updated with every conceivable technical innovation, including the installation of a communications centre which allowed Olga to effectively maintain control over every element of the Albatross's activities anywhere in the world.

A covered motorboat crossed the harbour towards Parkson Island, between the moored yachts that gently bobbed up and down with the moderately rolling swell. Two jetties stretched out from the island, an open wooden jetty on the northeast corner and a metal concourse enclosed on the southwest corner close to the Helipad. The boat passed around the other larger islands and held a south-westerly course. Swinging round to starboard, the boat turned and manoeuvred itself towards a covered metal jetty, which was effectively a large boat house, in which was a motor cruiser, tied up stern in. As the incoming boat reversed engines and stopped, one of the crew members jumped from the bow onto the jetty, carrying the bow line, which he quickly tied to the nearest cleat. As the crew completed the tying-up process, a tall, well-dressed middle-aged man stepped off the boat, greeted by one of Olga Devereux's assistants.

'Good morning, sir, if you will follow me, please. Your bags will be brought in for you,' said the stewardess.

'Thank you,' said the visitor as he followed the young woman along the jetty to an open door beyond which was a long illuminated corridor. At the far end of the corridor was a door with an electronic keypad on the right-hand side and a red LED light. When they arrived at the door, the stewardess keyed in a 6-digit code number into the keypad, at which point the red LED turned green, there was an audible click, and the woman opened the door. They passed through a large marble-floored atrium, the other side of which was an ornate wooden door. The woman knocked twice and then opened it.

'Mrs Devereux,' said the assistant respectfully.

'Ah, thank you,' responded Devereux. 'That will be all.'

She walked across the marble floor, stretching out her hand in greeting.

'General Ngoy, welcome to Poole. How was your flight?'

'Very good, Mrs Devereux, and thank you for sending a car to pick me up.'

'Well, it's much more convenient really, car rentals and helicopters involve digital paper trails, and we don't need any unnecessary complications,' added Devereux.

'Would you like a drink?'

'A whisky will do nicely, Mrs Devereux, thank you,' said Ngoy.

With their drinks in hand, the two walked out onto the veranda looking out across the harbour and sat at a table under the welcome shade of a large white umbrella.

'I find talking to people in person rather than via the internet is so much better, don't you? I appreciate how far you have had to travel, but I wanted to see you personally to tell you myself how much the foundation values our association and, of course, to reaffirm how mutually beneficial the arrangement is,' said Devereux.

'Thank you, Mrs Devereux, my principals are more than happy with the arrangement, the funds provided by your intermediaries have been of great assistance. We have been able to discredit and completely suppress the opposition parties, and the military government has now established complete control. Everybody wins, apart from our critics, but we deal with them as we deal with all dissenters.

Ngoy sipped his drink, with the wry smile of someone who enjoyed basking in the rewards that his criminality provided.

'Our diamonds, are they to your satisfaction?'

'Yes, General, perfectly satisfactory, the quality of the stones is quite excellent. It is an admirable arrangement; some of the stones we process ourselves, and the rest go to buyers, mostly in the Middle and Far East, who can arrange for their certification and distribution. I am also pleased to see the volume of Colbalt increasing, with renewable energy top of the world's political and economic agendas, demand is increasing. The more you can produce, the better for both of us, we can control the supply and, therefore, the price,' added Devereux.

'Now, you must be tired after your long trip. Amanda will show you to your room, after lunch, I'll show you around,' said Olga as she rose to her feet and pushed a button on the wall. A few moments later, the young woman who escorted Ngoy earlier entered and led him out and up the stairs to a guest bedroom.

Devereux refilled her drink, returned to the wooden veranda, and looked out across the harbour. As she did so, her mobile phone rang. She stepped back into her living room and picked up her phone, which was sitting on a glass table.

'Olga Devereux.'

'Good afternoon, Mrs Devereux, Giles Mulholland here. Is tomorrow's meeting still on?'

'Sir Giles, how nice. Yes, everything is proceeding as arranged. The first of our guests has already arrived. Let me know when you arrive in Poole and I will have you picked up.'

The following morning, preparations were well in hand. Five additional guests had arrived, one overnight and four others during the morning. Olga's eldest son, Hector, was also on hand. Succession planning was always on Olga's mind, and as her deputy, he routinely attended such meetings. Apart from his intimidating physical presence and unpredictable temper, Hector was organised and astute. He had also inherited his mother's trait of ruthless ambition with a total disregard for the law, but like her, it was a ruthless ambition based around family loyalty. He finished a video call with his younger sister, Oksana, and then walked to the living room, where he found his mother sitting on a chaise lounge, drinking a cup of coffee while watching the news on television.

'Mother, I have just spoken with Oksana. She doesn't have any news on Robert Sterling yet. She spoke to Alessandro at the Guardia di Finanza in Rome, all he can say at the moment is that Sterling has no criminal record and he's not on any of their watch lists, he may be with the authorities, but Alessandro is still making enquiries.'

'Alright, Hector, thank you. Sir Giles Mulholland should be arriving this afternoon. When he does, show him into the study upstairs and see that none of our other guests see him or know that he is here,' said Olga.

'Why keep them apart, given his involvement? Would it not be better if he were there to answer any questions,' enquired Hector.

'No, Hector, Giles Mulholland works for us, not them. The fewer people who know about his involvement, the better. Given the recent lapse in our security, the last thing we need now is a foreigner with a loose tongue or ambitions above their station,' said Devereux.

'Talking of loose tongues, this Mulholland character, do you trust him? What's to stop him ratting on us with the authorities if he gets cold feet?' asked Hector.

Devereux smiled. 'Oh, he has far too much to lose, quite apart from his fat Treasury pension, he has a well-connected and respected wife and four daughters. Besides, he knows I have a large file with photographs, dates, places, and times of his multiple indiscretions. More than enough evidence to ruin his reputation and his life forever.'

'You didn't tell me that. What evidence? What have you got on him?' asked an intrigued Hector.

'Some years ago, I decided we needed additional sources of inside information and influence. A list of suitable names was drawn up. Influential people who enjoyed a lifestyle that their salaries couldn't support, people whose personal predilections might be perceived as undesirable if they were to become public knowledge. We began cultivating. In Sir Giles's case, we threw a party in London, and I made sure he was on the guest list. He had a reputation for enjoying a good time, particularly when his wife was away, especially as gossipmongers said his marriage was a little shaky. So we made sure he had a very good time. It was a relatively easy process after that. He didn't need much persuading after showing him some very candid footage of him frolicking with two young ladies in one of the bedrooms, especially after I told him that they were underage. Still, they say that blondes have more fun, and those two earned their money.'

'Where was I while all this was going on?' asked Hector.

'You were working in Miami at the time, Christian helped me arrange everything,' added his mother. 'All I had to do was remind him how high he had risen in the Civil Service, and how far he might fall should his indiscretions come to light. Then show him the benefits available to someone with a more flexible attitude. All he had to do was look after our interests, do us a favour now and again, and in return, we topped up his pension with the odd bonus thrown in, and we would keep his guilty little secret a secret.'

'I see, just how many of these people do we have on the payroll, then, Mother?' asked Hector.

'Darling, real power is having access to critical information and the application of influence. The full list is in my safe,' said Olga. 'Now go and look after our guests, Hector. I'll be with you shortly.'

In Olga Devereux's media suite, her international visitors were joined by ten more via a video link and Hector.

'Good afternoon, ladies and gentlemen, thank you for joining us. I thought it was time we got together to review our current activities since our last meeting. As you know, the Albatross Foundation's interests are worldwide, and we have contacts and expertise around the globe. In some cases, we act directly or with our partners on joint projects, but act as facilitators in other areas. A number of Non-Governmental organisations operate under the foundation's umbrella in Africa, the Middle East, South America, and other regions, which means that we can legitimately channel a lot of charitable financial aid there. The Civil Society Partnership Review by the Department for International Development threatened to restrict our access to the Foreign Aid budget, but happily, we are still getting significant funds from there, too. This means that under the shield of our charitable operations, we can continue to use our expertise and resources to help you extract, process, and market the mineral deposits in your countries, tax-free and off the books. Whilst you enjoy the rich benefits and lifestyles that this arrangement offers.'

Devereux looked briefly down at her tablet, which contained a table providing a breakdown of the countries and regions represented at the meeting, along with a summation of their productivity and, more importantly, profitability.

'Shall we go alphabetically?' Olga proceeded to work through the report, country by country, with the representative of each area reviewing their productivity and any matters or issues impacting their profitability that required attention.

Towards the end of the two-hour meeting. Hector's Bluetooth earpiece bleeped. He caught his mother's eye, surreptitiously pointed to his ear, and tilted his head towards the door. She nodded slightly. Hector rose from his seat, excused himself from the meeting, and left the room. Outside in the atrium, Olga's assistant, Amanda, had Sir Giles Mulholland beside her, who had just arrived. Hector offered his hand to meet Mulholland's as they exchanged greetings. Mulholland was a tall man, well-groomed, broad in the beam, and every inch the city gent and one of the few people that Hector couldn't look down on.

'Good afternoon, Sir Giles, Hector Devereux. My mother is meeting some of our overseas associates at the moment. She's asked me to look after you. Would you follow me, please? Is this your first visit to the island?'

'Yes,' said Mulholland. 'Our previous meetings have either been in London or over the phone; it's beautiful here.'

'Yes, it is. It's ideal, really. May I offer you a drink, Sir Giles?' enquired Hector.

'Thank you, G&T, please, Hector,' replied Mulholland.

Hector walked across to a bar in the corner of the study, where he prepared a drink for himself and a Gin and Tonic for Sir Giles. The two men then walked across the thick shag pile carpet and stood in front of a huge double-glazed window that overlooked a well-manicured lawn below. Hector stretched out his hand to a chrome door handle and pushed the French door open, which led to a large wooden balcony. The men stepped onto the balcony and sat at a table surrounded by three wicker chairs. Hector was sorely tempted to discuss the nature of Mulholland's relationship with his mother, but he knew better than to risk her displeasure. Even so, as he watched the outwardly respectable Senior Treasury official sip his Gin and tonic, inwardly Hector smiled, picturing the devious honey trap his Mother had employed to ensnare the hapless man in her deceitful web. He would have loved to have been there, to watch it unfold for himself. He was therefore resigned to confining himself to small talk until his mother joined them.

About twenty minutes later, Olga entered the study and, seeing the two men outside, walked across the room to join them. They stood up as Olga approached the balcony doors.

'Mrs Devereux, good afternoon,' said Mulholland.

'Sir Giles, hello,' replied Olga. 'I hope Hector has been looking after you?'

'Indeed he has,' he said, pointing to his glass.

'How did the meeting go?' asked Hector.

'Very productively,' said Olga. 'All the NGOs are performing well, our profits are up, and the administrations and authorities are following our instructions, ensuring that the international media have plenty of access to the designated areas. The world must continue to see what we want it to see. Our altruism and a public-spirited philosophy.'

'And?' said Hector.

'Naturally, while the media see our new schools, our medical centres, water purification, and irrigation systems, our other activities go unnoticed. Diamond, Gold, Uranium, Platinum, and Cobalt production have all increased this quarter. Our international representatives are more than happy with the arrangement. The peasants benefit from the social improvements that the NGOs provide and so become less restive, our Marxist partners enjoy the benefits that unencumbered capitalism offers them, and our own wealth continues to grow tax-free,' added Olga.

Olga turned to Mulholland. 'Now, Sir Giles, to more serious matters. Hector had a call from Graham McKenzie regarding a recent audit of our accountants, McKenzie and Hunt. They said that they had it under control, have they?' asked Devereux.

There was a pause followed by a sharp intake of breath before Mulholland replied

'Well, MI5 has a list of UK companies they suspect may be involved in serious financial crime. They are always trying to infiltrate these organisations, either to break them up or to mine intelligence that may help them in other operations. McKenzie and Hunt are on that list, so far, all they have are suspicions, no proof, and of course, Graham McKenzie is nobody's fool. In my position, I see all the top-level communications that come into the Treasury. MI5 wanted to borrow one of our top accountants; the message came through my office. I asked them what they wanted him for, as it was an unusual request.'

Mulholland continued, 'They said he was to be attached to a firm of accountants which was about to conduct an audit on McKenzie and Hunt. It didn't take much to work out what they were up to. I thought it prudent to let McKenzie and Hunt know. However, given what happened to the man they sent in, I think it would be judicious to take precautions; they are bound to try again, or the Fraud Squad might just come in and shut them down. I've no doubt that McKenzie and Hunt will be working on countermeasures of their own, but if I were you, I would consider diversifying some of your more sensitive assets; there are other accounting options.'

'Good work, Sir Giles, your vigilance is greatly appreciated, and I have no doubt that your account manager in Switzerland will also be equally pleased when he sees the next deposit into your account there,' Devereux added with a wry smile. 'Keep us informed if there are any further developments, and if you need to contact us, use the agreed protocols. I want no traceable connection between us, is that understood?'

'Yes, Mrs Devereux, I understand completely.'

Chapter 8

Greg Travers stuck out a languid arm across the table, fumbling for his mobile phone, which was just out of comfortable reach. He had considered leaving it to ring, but the more it rang, the more he decided that the irritation of the noise was more annoying than the effort needed to pick it up. He had an appointment with his Solicitors in Wimbledon village this morning to finalise his late wife's financial affairs. It had been a long, drawn-out process, not helped by his near-constant malaise, but finally, the end was now in sight, and at least he could draw a line under that and perhaps take a small step forward. He stretched out and grasped the phone in his right hand.

'Travers.'

'Hello Greg, it's Nicky, how are things with you? I've not seen you in ages. What are you up to? I don't suppose you are free for lunch today?'

'Oh, hi Nicky. I'm ok, thanks, considering. Lunch? How long have you got?' asked Travers.

'I've got the day off, so as long as you like.'

'I have to see my solicitors this morning, how about One O'clock at the Bronze Dragon?' suggested Travers.

'Lovely, I could just do with a Chinese. I'll see you there,' said Nicky.

'Ok, I'll book a table and text you back to confirm it.'

After booking a table for two at the Chinese Restaurant, Travers gathered his paperwork, placed it inside his black leather briefcase, and made his way to the Solicitors on Wimbledon Hill Road. With the time-consuming donkey work already completed, today's visit should be no more than a formality. As it turned out, it was a very straightforward session. Cassandra's will had finally been executed according to her wishes, all the final documents had been signed, and assets transferred.

With his business concluded, Travers left the solicitors and walked the short distance to where he had parked his car. He had plenty of time to reach the Bronze Dragon. When he arrived in Kensington and Chelsea, he parked his car and, with some time to kill, popped into the Chelsea Pig for an aperitif before walking down towards the Chelsea Embankment. As was common in fine weather, there was a throng of people milling around, some looking across the river Thames, others just meandering and taking the air. The restaurant entrance was guarded by two large bronze Chinese ornamental dragons. Travers was greeted at the entrance by a smartly dressed oriental waiter who confirmed the booking and led Travers to his table across a beautiful red and gold embroidered Chinese carpet. Travers estimated that the restaurant was probably no more than half full. The waiter pulled the chair a little to allow Travers to take his seat.

'Would you like to order a drink, sir?' asked the waiter.

'Thank you, I'll have a 175 Soave Classico, please. My friend should be here shortly,' replied Travers as he looked round towards the entrance. The waiter had barely turned his back when Travers heard a familiar voice in the distance.

'Hi Greg,' came a distant call.

Travers turned to see his former colleague waving as she approached his table. He stood and embraced her warmly as they met.

'Hello Nicky, it's great to see you. What would you like to drink?'

'What are you having?' asked Nicky.

'I've just ordered a glass of Soave Classico.'

Nicky glanced down at the drinks menu as the waiter walked towards their table carrying a small silver-coloured tray with Travers' glass of wine.

'I think I'll have a glass of Chablis,' replied Nicky.

As the waiter placed the glass of wine on the table in front of him, Travers thanked him, then requested Nicky's glass of Chablis and asked for a few minutes' grace before ordering.

'How have you been?' enquired Nicky. 'We've really missed you on the team.'

'I'm surprised you've not heard the jungle drums. After Cassandra died, everything just went tits up. I needed to get away. I felt the world closing in on me, and I needed space. I wasn't interested in work or people. I wasn't interested in anything. As you know, the department was very understanding and gave me a leave of absence. Since then, I've just been living in my own little vacuum, nothing mattered, least of all myself. I've spent most of my time pulverising my liver,' said Travers.

'What about your personal friends, couldn't they help?'

'I talked to Cassandra's parents and our solicitors, but then I had to go. As far as anyone else was concerned, no, I'm ashamed to say that I pretty much cut everyone off, I just didn't want to know, I was so self-absorbed with my own misery that I just couldn't be bothered.'

Before she could add any further comments, the waiter returned with his notepad in one hand and Nicky's Chablis in the other. He turned to Nicky first.

'I'll have the Thai Prawn Tom Yum Soup to start, followed by Fillet Steak Chinese Style with egg fried rice, please.'

They waited and quickly scribbled down the order in hanzi before turning to Greg.

'I'll have the Aromatic Duck followed by Kung Po Chicken with Egg Fried Rice, please.'

With that, the waiter turned away and headed off toward the kitchen.

Travers picked up his glass of wine, raised it to Nicky, and proposed a toast.

'Good health, Nicky, it's lovely to see you.'

'You too, Greg, it's been too long, and despite your attempt at self-destruction, I must say that you are looking well, considering.'

Nicky continued 'What is the situation now? What are your immediate plans? Or don't you have any?'

'Up to a few days ago, my only plans revolved around getting absolutely hammered at least four times a week and the rest of the time sleeping it off until my head stopped spinning. Did you hear about the incident at Covent Garden?'

'Yes, I did. Some guy had a medical episode at a restaurant,' replied Nicky.

'Well, I was having lunch with a friend there when it happened. He collapsed into her arms, mumbled a few words to her before being carted off by Paramedics. The Police were there, taking witness statements, etc.'

'Oh god, how awful,' said Nicky.

'The next day … she was murdered, her throat was cut. The police think the two incidents may be connected.'

'Shit!' she exclaimed embarrassingly loudly.

'Yes, quite,' added Travers, anxiously looking round at some of the other people seated at nearby tables who may have overheard Nicky's sudden and unrestrained comment. As his gaze crossed the room and returned towards his own table, he saw an attractive woman several tables away, who seemed to be tucking into a bowl of noodles with great relish.

'I am so sorry, was she a close friend of yours? It's such a dreadful thing to happen, poor girl.'

Travers did not reply; his mind was elsewhere. Receiving no reply, Nicky glanced up to see Greg looking beyond her, over her shoulder, into the distance.

'Greg? … Greg!' called out Nicky, trying not to draw attention to herself.

'I'm sorry, Nicky, what did you say?' said Travers as he turned his head slightly and looked once again at his companion.

'I was saying how sorry I was about the girl who was killed.'

'Yes, it was a terrible shock, we'd only met a couple of days before. I had been round to see if she was ok the day after the incident and found her body, which was appalling. There was blood everywhere.'

'Why do the Police think the two incidents are related?' asked Nicky.

Travers' attention was once more elsewhere, drawn again to the woman eating noodles.

'Greg, what is it?' asked Nicky curiously.

'It's that woman, over there. The one wearing the jeans and the white T-shirt, with her hair up.'

'What about her?'

'I don't know, her clothes are different, her hair is different, but there is something about her, she looks familiar, I just have the feeling that I have seen her before, recently, I just can't place her,' added Travers. 'I don't know Nicky, I got a little spooked when the Police asked if I had noticed anyone following me. Up to that point, I hadn't noticed anything, but now, I see people hiding in shadows everywhere, and I assume they are all watching me. I suppose I am just feeling a bit paranoid. To be honest, what happened to her has been a bit of a reality check. I suppose I just don't want to become another statistic.'

At that point, the waiter arrived carrying a large tray containing their first courses. They paused their conversation while their food was served, and the waiter left them.

'Why would someone be following you anyway? I don't understand,' asked Nicky.

'I don't know, the guy who collapsed whispered, or at least tried to whisper something to Lisa before he passed out. The police have said he was deliberately poisoned, and whoever did it may suspect that vital incriminating information was passed onto Lisa and by extension to me,' said Travers.

'What was it that was so important that it cost her life?' asked Nicky.

'I don't know. It was nothing really, a few mumbled words that didn't seem to mean anything. She gave all the information to the police. Anyway, bon appétit,' said Travers as he speared the nearest piece of his Aromatic Duck. It was like the first cup of tea in the morning or the first taste of chilled lager on a hot summer day; it was a moment to savour.

'How's your soup?' asked Travers.

'Lovely, thanks,' replied Nicky. 'Given what's going on, what are you going to do? You can't just hang around and wait to see if anything happens to you. If you want my advice, you will go back to work. You seem to have forgotten that you have almost unlimited resources at MI5 and beyond. More importantly, you have spent years tracking down people and groups like this.'

'When a Detective came to see me about the Covent Garden matter, Charles Stanley came with him. Have you met him?'

'Yes, I don't know him very well, but I've met him a few times and I've seen him around the office. If he's involved with this investigation, why not talk to him about returning to work? There is no one better than you to find the right rocks to look under for some of these people. Who would you rather have constantly looking over their shoulder, you or them?'

As Travers considered the wisdom and the logic of Nicky's comments, the waiter reappeared with the main courses. The conversation stopped abruptly, Nicky and Travers sat back in their white upholstered chairs whilst the waiter distributed the array of dishes across the table.

Detective Deery spent some time reviewing the details of William Constable's career, although, in his late thirties, Constable had had an illustrious rise. Highly qualified and by all accounts very personable, he had started and developed his own accountancy firm, and as his reputation grew, he attracted several high-profile clients. He then began to specialise in auditing and financial crime and had made quite a name for himself in financial circles. His burgeoning success in exposing financial crime had naturally brought with it a degree of unpopularity in certain quarters.

Deery looked down the list of audited companies and individuals. It was quite possible that someone on this list had taken a fall and had been looking for payback. His team was methodically working its way through every name on the list. Each owner and each company director would be vetted, cleared, or, if necessary, interviewed until they could all be eliminated as a potential suspect. However, the fly in the ointment was the cold-blooded murder of Lisa Scott! Was it a random act of brutal murder, or was there a connection? He could understand up to a point, a vindictive criminal wanting to get even with someone they felt had ruined their illegal operation, but Miss Scott was an innocent passer-by, so why kill her? What possible threat could she have posed? Unless Constable had given her something or said something to her that could implicate the murderer.

There was a knock on his door. The detective looked up for an instant and put his report down.

'Come!' he barked. One of his team members opened the door and hurriedly walked in, grasping a sheet of paper.

'What is it?' called out the Chief Inspector.

'Boss, something interesting, we've got a match from someone on our audit list and a man involved in a fatal road traffic accident a couple of days ago. When the name flashed up, I called up the linked accident report. The local police think that the fuel line ruptured, and an eyewitness said the car went up like a Roman candle.'

'And does this Guy Fawkes have a name?' asked Deery.

'Well, there wasn't much left of him, but the car is registered to Igor Volkov.'

'Volkov? Sounds Russian, shit, that's the last thing we need. Please tell me he was driving a clapped-out Trabant and not a decent car. I hope things are not going to get messy. I want to see the forensic report on the car. You had better find out if that rupture was wear and tear or deliberate, and I want everything you can find out about this character Volkov. I want to know where he fits in, if at all.'

In the Bronze Dragon, the lunchtime diners were beginning to leave. Greg and Nicky had enjoyed their meals. Despite the recent day's events, Travers was starting to get back into thinking about a slightly more normal way of life, a decent meal, and companionable conversation. It had been good to have an honest discussion about how he was feeling with someone who knew him; he respected her judgement, and what was more, she might be right. Deep down, he knew she was right. He wasn't grieving for Cassandra anymore; he'd not done that for weeks, and he had been using that as an excuse for wallowing in an alcohol-fuelled pity party. Nicky would be walking into work tomorrow, back to the area he knew so well, where his desk was still waiting for him, with all the familiar furniture and décor and friendly faces. Greg thought about what it would be like to just be able to walk in with her and pretend that the last four months hadn't happened, but he knew that it wasn't quite that simple. He would need to speak to management first and convince them that he was mentally and emotionally ready, then get the official ok from the medical team. At least he was now more open to the idea.

Having paid the bill, Greg and Nicky finished their drinks and then left the table. By now, there were only a handful of people left in the restaurant, including the woman Travers had studied so closely earlier. She was now drinking a cup of coffee and deeply engaged in conversation with the other woman sitting opposite her, and didn't look up as he walked out. Travers walked Nicky to her black Audi, which was parked in the car park of the now almost deserted restaurant.

Nicky unlocked her car, before getting inside, she turned to Travers.

'Let me know what you decide to do about work, and don't forget, if you want to chat, pick up your phone. That's what friends are for.'

'Thanks, Nicky, it was lovely to see you again, and yes, I will keep in touch,' replied Travers.

With that, they hugged and kissed each other on the cheeks. Then Travers stepped back and watched as she pulled out and sped away.

Travers had had a pleasant time; he had worked with Nicky for many years and always enjoyed her company. She was fun, but she also made a lot of sense. He made his way down to the embankment and watched the fast-flowing ebb tide for a while, and the array of boats passing across his vantage point. He cast his mind back to the woman in the restaurant. Was it just his imagination? As he stood there, he looked at all the other people around him; were they all secretly watching him, or just minding their own business, as he should be? If he didn't get a grip, he would become suspicious of his own shadow. He turned away, frustrated by his inability to rationalise his insecurities, and began the walk back to his car.

Travers headed off across the Battersea Bridge and the A3220 towards Wandsworth and then Wimbledon. The traffic was fairly light, and Travers hoped he would get home before the rush hour kicked in. The road followed the Thames until the Wandsworth roundabout before turning south away from the river. It was a forty-minute drive before he reached the familiar long Church road, driving past the All England Club on his way up the steep hill to the Village and home.

Travers sat back in his comfortable leather chair and reflected on a very positive day. The morning business had gone well, and his lunch with Nicky had been both relaxing and thought-provoking. The last week had put him through the wringer, but the light at the end of the tunnel seemed to him to be brighter than it had been previously when viewed through his alcohol-induced stupor and the idea of actually going back to work was gaining traction. He looked across at the beautiful portrait of Cassandra that hung on the wall opposite his chair. He knew exactly what she would say: "Stop wasting time, get out of that hog wallow you've been in, and get back to work".

After several hours of rather listless sitting around, a restless Travers decided to pop round to Warren House for a light snack, a drink, and a chat with Jasper, his favourite barman. Perhaps the night air and a walk would do him good. His conversation with Nicky earlier was still rattling around in his head. The next best confidant to a barber was a bartender, and he had gotten to know quite a few over the last few months. He walked across the common, which was still bathed in now rapidly diminishing evening sunshine, and into the busy hotel car park. He walked through the reception area, smiling at the receptionist as he passed, and made his way down a couple of steps into the main bar area. The bar was bustling. Travers wondered if there was a function there tonight; he wasn't inclined to be psychoanalysed by fifty complete strangers. He stood at the bar and quickly caught the eye of one of the bar staff.

'Hi, busy tonight?' asked Travers.

'Yes, sir, it's a fiftieth birthday party, they'll be moving into the main function room later for a meal. What can I get you?'

'I was hoping to see Jasper, is he not on tonight?'

'Jasper's on duty in the function room, prepping everything.'

'I see. Champagne cocktail, please.'

As the bartender opened a fresh bottle of champagne, Travers glanced around at the milling crowd to see if he recognised anyone. They were certainly a well-heeled group, a black tie affair, most of whom clutched the stems of Champagne flutes whilst the occasional cocktail glass could also be spied. Travers took his drink and slowly eased his way through the group to the far corner of the room. He considered stepping out either into the Orangery or outside onto the patio. Given he could not readily speak to Jasper, he opted to enjoy his cocktail and people-watch for a while. While he would not describe himself as a card-carrying fashionista, he could pick out the odd Dior and Alessandra Facchinetti dresses as they were amongst his wife's favourite designers and she had worn several when they had been out together. The last time he had seen such a glitterati gathering was during one of his visits to Les Ambassadeurs before his wife's death, a far cry from some of the less salubrious establishments he had frequented in the four months since then.

He sat and watched the party-goers for a while, refilled his glass, and managed to catch a fleeting glimpse of Jasper as he dashed out of the function room, too busy to do anything other than offer Travers an acknowledging wave. Travers looked out of the window; the day had finally passed into night, and with the birthday revellers moving off now into the adjoining room, Travers decided to move on too. He thanked the bar staff as he walked out and climbed the steps leading to the reception and exit. As he walked through the crowded car park, he could only admire the array of expensive sports and luxury cars on show.

As he left the hotel entrance, the lane ahead was unlit with little moonlight to guide him. He decided not to walk across the common in near darkness; if there was a hole or a ditch, he was bound to walk into it. There were no oncoming vehicles, so Travers began walking along the short, darkened road that bordered the common and led to his house. As he walked, he heard what he thought was a car coming. He stopped and turned round, but all he saw was the dark outline of a large car, parked on the verge as many regularly were. He continued walking towards the end of the lane, dimly lit by a moon partially obscured by clouds.

Then, without warning, a large car swept up behind him, its full-beam headlights came on, dazzling him. He barely had time to think, but just enough to react. Travers flung himself to his left towards the common a split second before the inevitable impact. Too late! The car slammed into him, throwing him high into the air.

He landed heavily on the grass and rolled along the rough ground before coming to a stop. He looked up briefly to see the car speed away before it soon left his sight. He sank back on the grass, not knowing how badly he had been injured. He hadn't lost consciousness, but his whole body was shaking as he struggled to control his rapid, shallow breathing. As he lay there, shocked, dazed, and disorientated, he heard footsteps coming towards him.

Moments later, Travers saw two men appearing out of the darkness running across the road and onto the grass where he lay prostrate. Were they coming back to finish him off? He tried to crawl away, but they quickly restrained him. In his semi-conscious state, he stared up at the two men looking down at him.

'Get on with it then,' said the breathless and confused Travers as he waited for the expected coup de gras.

'Don't move,' exclaimed one of the men urgently.

'What's your name, mate?' said the other.

Travers had braced himself for the end, but the end didn't come.

'Just lie still, we're calling an ambulance, you'll be ok, we saw the whole thing, what's your name?'

Chapter 9

Charles Stanley's phone rang. It was late into the evening, and he was still working, co-ordinating the latest Constable Investigation intelligence with the Metropolitan Police. However, this time, it was not Deery on the phone; it was a Registrar from the A&E department at the Royal Victoria Hospital. He reached across his laptop to his phone and picked it up.

'Hello, Charles Stanley.'

'Mr Stanley, this is Dr Patel at the Royal Victoria. We've had a patient brought in. He says his name is Greg Travers. He was involved in a hit-and-run case tonight. I should say at this point that he is ok, a bit shaken up, but we have given him an MRI scan and he seems ok. He asked us to call you and advise you of the situation.'

'Thank you, Doctor. Are you keeping him overnight?'

'No, I don't think that will be necessary, there is nothing broken, as I said, he's had an MRI, there doesn't seem to be any internal damage, I'd say he has been very, very lucky.'

'Would you ask him to stay there, doctor, and I will be straight over. I should be there in 30 minutes or so.'

With that, Stanley thanked the doctor for his call and ended the conversation. He then rang Detective Deery's mobile number.

'John, I've just had the Royal Victoria on the phone. Travers has been run over.'

'Shit! Is he dead?' asked a shocked Deery.

'No, the doctor says he'll be ok. I'm going over to the hospital to see him now. Listen, it happened close to his house. Can you send someone over there tonight, just in case?'

'I'll get someone to keep an eye on it. Let me know what Travers has to say. I'll catch up with you tomorrow,' said Inspector Deery.

Stanley left immediately, and traffic permitting, he should be there in about twenty minutes. He didn't believe in coincidence, not in his line of work; it was obviously attempted murder, and he needed to talk to Travers as quickly as possible to get as much information as he could whilst it was fresh in his mind.

Given the lateness of the hour, Stanley was able to find a parking spot close to the entrance of A&E with relative ease. He couldn't see Travers as he walked in, so he went straight to the reception desk, showed his credentials, and asked to speak to Doctor Patel. The receptionist briefly looked at a notepad on her desk before pressing a four-digit extension number on her phone keypad. After a brief conversation, she advised Stanley that Doctor Patel would be out shortly. Stanley waited by the desk, momentarily, when a tall, strikingly handsome man in scrubs came around the corner and addressed the receptionist, who motioned towards Stanley.

'Mr Stanley? I'm Doctor Patel.'

'Good evening, Doctor. Thank you for calling earlier. I have come to see Mr Travers. Do you have anything to add about his condition?'

'No, not really. I would say that he has been extraordinarily lucky. It was more of a glancing blow rather than a full impact, and landing on the grass rather than the road probably saved his life. He was pretty shaken up, and he will be black and blue and very stiff for a few days, but other than that, he hasn't sustained any serious injury,' concluded the doctor.

'Thanks, Doctor, may I see him?' asked Stanley.

'Yes of course, would you follow me please,' said the doctor.

The two men left the waiting room and walked along a short corridor containing several curtained cubicles. The doctor stopped at the last cubical on the left and drew the blue curtain back. Stanley walked in to find Travers sitting down pouring a half glass of water from a hospital jug.

'Hello Greg, it sounds like you had a lucky escape tonight. I'm glad to see you're still in one piece.'

'Good evening, sir. Yes, I really thought I'd had it.'

'The doctor tells me, apart from a few bruises, you're ok and free to leave.'

'That's great,' said Travers, who was desperate to go.

'Come on, let's go and sort out the paperwork,' said Stanley, as Travers gingerly rose to his feet and stepped out of the cubicle.

Within thirty minutes, Stanley's car pulled up outside Travers' house in Wimbledon Village. The two men walked up to the front door. The porch light was on, and so was the living room light. As Travers opened the front door, it became immediately apparent that they had had visitors. Drawers and shelves had been emptied, and the contents strewn across the floor. What could they possibly have been looking for? Travers knew he didn't have any sensitive work-related documents at home, and they had been trashed. As he paused and surveyed the mess, he spotted the remains of his glass-framed wedding photograph on the floor. He bent down and picked up the broken frame containing the now torn image of him with Cassandra. He had been run over, his home ransacked, and a picture that reminded him of his happiest day needlessly ruined. Stanley immediately called the police. Where had been the Police cover that Deery had promised earlier? Fifteen minutes later, a patrol car arrived accompanied by DCI Deery in an unmarked Police vehicle. As Stanley saw the police cars pull up, he opened the front door to let them in, while Travers looked around the wreckage of his living room.

'Evening Charles, phew, quite a mess,' said the Chief Inspector. 'Where's Travers?'

'In the other room. What happened to the policeman you were sending?' asked Stanley.

'He checked in from his car forty-five minutes ago; he should be around somewhere,' commented Deery.

The Chief Inspector turned to one of his team. 'Rogers is around somewhere; he's not picking up his receiver, but his car's in the road. Look around, see if you can find him.'

Deery began walking through the house, and he found Travers in his kitchen.

'Greg, you seem to have poked a hornet's nest, haven't you? First, you get banged by a car, then they come and rearrange your home furnishings, what have you got mixed up in?'

Stanley came around the corner and joined them. The three men stood in the hallway as the team of detectives examined the upturned contents of Travers' home.

'What happened tonight? Did you see the car or the driver?' asked Deery.

'No, John, I went down to Warren House for a drink, that's all. When I came out, it was dark, and I walked along the road. I didn't see any cars apart from one parked on the side of the road. I thought I heard something, I looked around but saw nothing. Then there was a sudden whine, the headlights came on, and before I had time to do anything, it was right behind me. I tried to dive out of the way when it hit me. They must have thought they'd nailed me because they just drove on,' added Travers.

'And the car?' asked Deery.

'Large 4x4, black and electric. I didn't see the driver or the plates.' said Travers.

'Pity. We questioned the men who called your ambulance; they saw the impact, unfortunately, they didn't notice the licence plate either, only that it was large and probably black.'

As they discussed the events that had taken place earlier in the evening, another police detective entered the house and rushed to join the group.

'Boss, we've found Rogers. He's in the garden.'

Deery, Stanley, and Travers followed the officer out of the front door. To the right of the house was a pathway obscured by tall shrubs leading to the back garden. Approximately five yards along the path, the detective's torchlight picked out the black boots and ankles of a body lying behind some shrubbery. Deery's heart sank; he had only lost one team member in the line of duty during his time at the MET, but it was a harsh and painful reminder of just how dangerous the job could be. He shone his torch onto the bloodied body. A jagged cut ran across Rogers's throat, his contorted face covered with blood, glistening and still oozing from the fatal wound. The pathologists would be able to tell him if it was the same knife used to dispatch Lisa Scott.

'Fucking hell, this investigation is becoming a bloody blood bath. Greg, you had better pack an overnight bag.' Turning to one of his subordinates, The Inspector continued.

'Tape it off, get forensics round. I want every inch of this place covered, with no shortcuts. We need to find some evidence; we need to find something. I want this bastard.'

The following morning, Travers left his temporary accommodation in a MI5 safe house, and his destination was Thames House. As he was on extended leave, his ID and electronic pass were suspended. On reporting to the reception desk, he was signed in, given a temporary pass, and escorted up to Stanley's office.

'Good morning, Greg, did you have a good night's rest? Have you had breakfast?'

'Yes, well, not bad, sir, considering. It's fair to say that almost everything hurts, and what doesn't hurt aches. I'm stiffening up a bit. Apart from that, I'm ok,' said Travers.

'Forensics have been in your house all night, and the police pathologist has got the detective's body for post-mortem examination and …' Stanley didn't have the chance to finish his sentence.

'Sir, I want to return to work. I want to help. I've spent years tracking people like this, and I've given this a lot of thought over the last few days. You've already read me into the MI5 operation, and I am right in the middle of the police's Constable and Scott murder investigations. Please, sir, let me help.' pleaded Travers.

'Greg, I am well aware of your experience and expertise. I also know why you were given extended leave. Do you seriously think you are ready? I have a duty of care for the people who work here, and that includes you. You will need to demonstrate that you are mentally and emotionally ready and fit to work. You are not just a government employee by the way, you are a government employee in the middle of an ongoing operation who just survived attempted murder and could well be targeted again until we catch these people.'

'Sir, I am aware of my shortcomings and the current circumstances, but I don't want to sit around when I know I can make a difference.'

Stanley, whilst not completely convinced, was nonetheless moved by Travers' sincerity.

'I'll tell you what I'll do. I'll endorse your request to return, provided you are cleared by medical and you pass your psychological evaluation. Fair?'

Two days later, Travers reported to Charles Stanley's office again. He had been confident that he would pass the physical examination despite his altercation with a 4x4, since the hospital had carried out a complete and thorough examination when he had been brought in, and apart from cuts and bruises, he was fine. He was more concerned that he might be tripped up by an overzealous shrink's trick questions.

'Come in, Greg.'

Travers walked in and stood in front of Stanley's desk. He could see two folders lying in front of him bearing the medical department stamp. What was in them would determine how the meeting went and his immediate future.

'All right, I'll put you out of your misery. You have been cleared as fit to return to work, if that is still what you want to do?'

'Thank you, sir,' said a relieved Travers.

Stanley handed Travers an envelope.

'Here is your new ID and all your system access passwords, you know the drill. You will report directly to me until this mess is cleared up. Welcome back. I presume you remember where your desk is? I suggest you go and do a full system check. There is a briefing at midday, I'd like you to be there.'

Forty-eight hours later, Travers felt emotionally renewed and revitalised. He had a sense of purpose and a feeling of belonging once more. It seemed impossible to believe that even a week ago, he could have felt so different. Drifting through life as he had been, like flotsam floating aimlessly, carried by the currents and tides, with no sense of self-determination or personal responsibility. With his enhanced system access restored, he had immersed himself in McKenzie and Hunt's client records. He was looking for the imperceptible crack that might lead to a significant breakthrough and give them hope of bringing the killers of Constables Rogers and Lisa Scott to justice.

Travers gazed at the centre monitor of the three sitting on his desk. On it was the list of McKenzie and Hunt clients, and the screen on the right showed the police report on the death of Igor Volkov. On his desk was also a notepad on which Travers scribbled his musings. With names of possible persons of further interest, most of whom had subsequently been crossed out as they became superseded by more interesting candidates. However, the fog of confusion was beginning to clear, and Travers was beginning to see the semblance of an idea. It was only a supposition at this stage, but it made sense to him. As he stared intently at the screen, he was completely unaware that Charles Stanley had arrived and was standing next to him.

'Good morning, Greg.'

'Good morning, sir, sorry I was miles away,' said an apologetic Travers.

'Are you making any headway? I've just been on the phone with your friend Detective Deery. The report on Volkov's car has come back. The fuel line was definitely tampered with, no doubt about it. Someone wanted him out of the way,' said Stanley.

The news that Volkov's death wasn't accidental added another piece to the ever-more-complicated jigsaw puzzle that Travers was now trying to fit together.

'I've been going through the list of clients of McKenzie and Hunt and also William Constable, looking for any linkage and possible motives. Now, the late Igor Volkov was a former Russian military. When the Soviet Union collapsed at the end of 91, he initially went into the export business in Russia, then set up a company in London in 2005. He made a small fortune. Last year, Constable investigated his company, which was suspected of laundering money from Russia. As a result of that investigation, his assets were seized, and several people were prosecuted, but Volkov avoided prosecution, turning King's evidence and ratting on his comrades,' said Travers.

'So he had a motive and a score to settle,' concluded Stanley.

'Perhaps, but that raises several awkward questions. Firstly, he had underworld connections. Why wait so long to collect on his debt, and secondly, if he had been given immunity, why risk that by committing murder? Also, if McKenzie and Hunt were tipped off about Constable, and as a result of that tip-off, Constable was killed, then whoever murdered him must have had contact with McKenzie and Hunt. Either that or it was an amazing coincidence.'

'Are you suggesting that Volkov isn't our man then?' queried Stanley.

'Volkov certainly had a motive, but he is not on McKenzie and Hunt's list of client names, and there is no mention of Volkov or his company listed on McKenzie and Hunt's phone records. Of course, there could always be a personal connection; we'd need to look into that.'

'The other conundrum,' continued Travers, 'is that if Volkov did kill Constable and perhaps Lisa too, then who killed Detective Rogers and tried to run me down? Because that obviously wasn't Volkov, because by then, he was chargrilled. My guess is that someone connected to McKenzie and Hunt somehow got the Russian to hit Constable, then had him killed to tie up loose ends.' added Travers.

Stanley then handed a piece of paper to Travers.

'Well, I have a small spanner to throw into your theory. The police pathology report on Rogers says that both he and Miss Scott were killed using the same knife, both right to left, both showing faint signs of bruising over the left-hand side of their mouth.'

Travers pondered the new information for a moment before adding.

'It would take quite a setup to have somebody on the take in the treasury, arrange for a professional hit to eliminate Constable, and then have them killed. That takes planning and money. I have been going through all the companies listed on McKenzie and Hunt's books and cross-checking them with Companies House. There were several shell companies listed, and the interesting thing is that they all link back to the Albatross Group,' said Travers.

'Interesting. Is that the same Albatross that includes the Albatross Foundation? Asked Stanley.

'Yes, the corporation was founded by Robert Devereux; he controlled all their commercial activities, and the Foundation was largely the brain-child of his wife, Olga, as a charitable organisation after he died,' replied Travers.

'Olga Devereux is a formidable woman,' said Stanley. 'When her husband died in 2002, she took control of the business, and today, it's worth billions. As for the Foundation, she sponsors NGOs all over the world; she has the ears of government ministers and a hand in their wallets, both in this country and abroad. I once attended one of her charity dinners here in London. There were several members of the Treasury, some MPs with vested interests, and a few city high rollers there. You would be amazed how many men went weak at the knees when they were introduced to her.'

Travers stared at his computer screen, with the discussion about Olga Devereux and the Albatross Foundation whirling about in his head, and suddenly a penny dropped.

'Sir, do you remember what Lisa Scott said William Constable said to her when he collapsed in Covent Garden? The exact words?'

'Exactly? No, it was along the lines of 'Albe's got me' or 'it was Albe,' or something like that, wasn't it?' replied Stanley.

Travers turned and looked directly at Stanley.

'Constable was desperate, he was gasping for breath, he may well have suspected that he had been poisoned and possibly going to die. With his last breath, he wanted to tell her who it was. Suppose Albe wasn't a man, what if it was Albatross, and someone in the Albatross organisation was responsible? I'll bet that Constable found something out when he was in McKenzie and Hunt that made him suspicious. Even if we are meant to believe Volkov did the poisoning for personal revenge, I believe Constable thought it was the Albatross group.'

Stanley was astounded at the bombshell that Travers had just dropped into his lap. It was bad enough when the Oxfam scandal broke a few years ago, but if Travers' suggestion was true, the result would be seismic.

'Alright, Greg, Deery's team is still checking everyone else out. I want you to concentrate on the Albatross Foundation and Olga Devereux. Discreetly for now.'

Chapter 10

Olga Devereux's maid knocked on her bedroom door. It was eight o'clock—late, by Olga's standards—later than usual. She didn't usually linger in bed unless she had a particular reason, but this morning, she had a reason. A few moments later, Olga opened the door and allowed the maid to enter. She was still in her silk peach-blush Botan kimono, which hung provocatively over her shoulders and was tied at the waist with a long black silk cord, leaving little of her figure to the imagination.

'Good morning, Mary,' said Mrs Devereux.

'Good morning, ma'am,' replied the maid as she walked across the polished rosewood floor to the large tinted windows and opened the blinds, flooding the room with morning light. As she turned to leave, out of the corner of her eye, Mary caught sight of an arm protruding from beneath the scarlet duvet that covered the enormous emperor-size bed.

'Mary, would you bring in fruit juice and a pot of tea for two, please?'

'For two?' There was a short pause. 'Yes, ma'am,' said Mary as she left, closing the bedroom door behind her.

Devereux walked towards the windows and looked out over the water before opening the French doors that led to a large balcony. She stood at the entrance for a few minutes, taking in the fresh morning sea air, her shoulder-length hair gently blowing against her face in the soft sea breeze. As she looked out, her young companion stirred, slowly rolling onto his side, facing the now open window where Devereux stood with her back to him, her naked form clearly visible through her almost translucent silk gown.

'Hi.' His eyes were still not fully open as they strained to get used to the sudden brightness.

'Good morning,' said Olga as she came back towards the naked figure lying in her bed. She sat beside him, allowing the folds of her soft silk gown to rest on his exposed thigh as she put her left hand on his chest and kissed him passionately on the lips before allowing her hand to slowly and deliberately move down his body and rest provocatively on the inside of his thigh as they kissed again. She untied the black silken cord that encircled her waist, causing the material to open and expose her voluptuous figure. Then she wound the tasselled cord around both her lover's wrists, raising the bound limbs over his head and hooking them over the heavy brass headboard behind him. The man writhed in ecstasy as she continued to stroke his chest, her tongue caressing his nipples.

He found her provocative sexuality intoxicating; every nerve and fibre of his body was alive, tingling, and aching for relief. Despite the difference in their ages, he couldn't remember a night like it—one incredible sensation after another—as he willingly succumbed to her seduction. For Olga, sex was both a passion and a weapon. A powerful, attractive, sexually assertive, mature woman—irresistible to so many men, especially those with younger blood and fire in their loins, even if some were young enough to be her grandchildren. Her appetites were insatiable, and her conquests were almost without number.

A few moments later, there was a knock on the door. The young man frantically tried, unsuccessfully, to free his hands from the restraining cord and pull the duvet over his body to conceal his highly aroused state. The door opened, and the maid walked in, carrying a silver tray containing the pot of tea and two glasses of fruit juice that Devereux had requested. She placed it on a table. As she left the room, she couldn't help but glance at the bed and smile at the handsome young man, blushing with obvious embarrassment, lying naked but for the duvet covering his ankles, with his hands still bound to the bed.

Olga poured a glass of fruit juice and put it on the bedside table before releasing the man's hands.

'Drink up. I have things to do—I have to get dressed and go to work,' said Olga. Her mind had already moved on from the amusement of having this twenty-something lapdog satisfy her sexual needs to focusing on the day's business.

Her lover stretched out his now free hand, his tanned, toned torso and erection still prominent and glistening with anticipation.

'Can't we…?'

'No, we can't. The bathroom's in there. I suggest you take a cold shower instead, then get dressed. The boat leaves in thirty minutes. If you're not ready, you'll have to swim.'

Olga removed her dressing gown, laid it over the Chippendale chair by the window, and walked naked across the floor to her dressing room, closing the door behind her.

Within an hour, Olga Devereux strode into Albatross House, waving to the reception, they pressed the release button on the security turnstiles to allow her to pass without her having to use her electronic I.D. pass. The daily rush hour bustle between eight and ten had passed, and she called a lift to take her up to her office suite on the seventh floor.

'Good morning, Mrs Devereux,' said her personal secretary, Maxwell Jarvis.

'Morning, Maxwell, any calls? I have a meeting shortly with Hector and Mr Rackman, see that I am not disturbed, please.'

'Yes, Mrs Devereux,' replied Jarvis.

Olga sat at her desk and opened her computer, checking her emails, video messages, and phone calls. It wasn't long before her intercom buzzed; it was Jarvis.

'Mrs Devereux, I have Mr Hector and Mr Rackman here to see you.'

'Thank you, Maxwell, show them in, and no interruptions please,' ordered Olga.

A moment later, the heavy wooden door opened, and the two men walked in and over to her desk.

'Good morning, gentlemen, shall we sit over there?' suggested Devereux.

They walked across to the window and made themselves comfortable on the white leather sofas. Olga began the discussion by first turning to her son, who was sitting opposite her.

'Hector, I hope you have some good news to tell me.'

'I spoke to Graham McKenzie last night, and he confirmed that Igor Volkov has been taken care of. The Police are doing what the police always do, asking lots of questions, shaking the tree hoping a rotten apple will fall into their laps.'

'What about the other matter?' asked Olga.

'The man who was with Constable in Covent Garden? The Op's team took care of him as well, searched his house and found nothing … but,' said Hector.

'But what?' said Olga, her eyes tightening as she stared intently at her son.

'Well?' Hector paused again, looked across at Rackman, then back to his Mother.

'We might have a problem. The man they hit, well, he may be MI5.'

'Christ!' Olga didn't swear often, but when she did, she meant it. 'What do you mean, might be, is he, or isn't he?'

'They found some personal papers when they were searching the house. It looks like he was on some kind of extended leave. There was some medical stuff and letters. I think he worked there.'

'Did they confirm this man's termination?' asked Olga.

'They were pretty sure they killed him, but they didn't go back to check, in case they were spotted. However, there is another problem. After the hit, when they searched the guy's house, they were disturbed by a policeman, who was in the garden. They had to deal with him.'

'So, now we may have a possible witness, who, far from being eliminated, may still be alive, and working for Military Intelligence, and now you tell me that we also have a dead policeman on our hands too. How much worse can it get? Special Operations are supposed to be professional. What the hell were they thinking of.' said the irritated matriarch.

Olga sat back, running her hands through her hair as she stared at her son for a moment, while she thought.

'Alright, Hector. We can't have the police apprehend them now, recall them all, at once, and get them out of the country. We'll deal with them later, in the meantime, get a replacement team in place as soon as you can,' demanded Olga. 'Are McKenzie and Hunt still under surveillance, Richard?'

'The police are still trawling through their accounts and list of clients. I've not heard anything from our man at the Treasury, but I think it would be sensible to assume that either the Fraud Squad or

MI5 will try again. If we start shifting funds, it might just draw attention to us,' said Rackman.

'Agreed. I'll speak with Sir Giles and remind him what is expected of him,' said Olga Devereux.

'And if he doesn't remember?' asked an unconvinced Hector.

''I've had his balls between my fingers, Hector, he'll remember,' said Olga, fixing Hector with a steely and determined stare.

Rackman was still concerned about the unwelcome attention of the police over the McKenzie and Hunt killing and turned to Mrs Devereux.

'Olga, the authorities are circling over McKenzie and Hunt like starving Vultures. I know McKenzie has said it will blow over, but don't you think it would be prudent to delay the Graf operation?'

'Richard, this is not like cancelling a cocktail party. Graf is one of the richest men in Germany and is expected to be the next chancellor, which will make him the most powerful man in Western Europe. Do you really think that I am going to stand by and watch the grandson of that German butcher lord it over us? He slipped away after the war, avoided the retribution he deserved and made his fortune off the backs of the thousands he had murdered, many of them Russian Jews,' Olga opined.

'I understand that, Olga, I'm just saying ...' continued Rackman. He knew he was swimming against the tide, and it was not an argument he was going to win.

Olga stood up, clearly displeased, and walked a few steps to where a large portrait of her parents hung on the wall. She stared at it for a few moments, then turned to the two men.

'Richard, this is not business, this is personal. This is very personal. You're English, you couldn't possibly understand what it is like to see your parents dragged out of their homes, beaten and shot, dumped by the roadside, and left to rot. My Mother told me what it was like, how she pleaded with the commanding officer for her parents' lives, how he looked at her and laughed as he gave the order to shoot them. Then he and two of his men dragged my distraught mother into a garage by her hair, raped her, and left her for dead. No, Richard, you couldn't possibly understand. Otto Graf must die. Plans are already underway. Graf is due to visit England very soon for preliminary talks with interested parties, including the government, to pave the way for policy agreements to be announced if, as expected, he is elected.'

'My contact in the Bundestag says that the timetable and itinerary will be released very soon. When that happens, our friend from Israel will move. In the meantime, if there are any developments from either the Monica Stein leak or McKenzie and Hunt, I want to be told immediately. That's all, gentleman. Thank you, Richard. Hector, will you stay please? I'd like a word.'

With that, the two men stood up. Rackman walked to the door and let himself out while Hector joined his mother in front of the portrait of her parents.

'You're taking a terrible risk, Mother. This is not an anonymous clerical worker that no one will miss. This is a very high-profile political figure. If this blows up in our faces, there will be nowhere to hide, and everything you have worked for will be finished,' said Hector.

'You worry too much, Hector. What kind of a fool do you take me for? Have you learned nothing all these years?'

Her tone was severe; it was a raw nerve that would never heal until the Germans' family had atoned for the misery they had caused.

'We have almost unlimited resources and reliable contacts in every corner of the globe. This has nothing to do with the Foundation. David Rubin is a former Mossad operative; he has no connection with either the Foundation or any NGOs we have operating in Israel, and there is no linkage of any kind. Moreover, his own grandparents were sent to the gas chambers in Treblinka. He's experienced. He's available and for four point two million shekels in gold, he is willing. Leave this to me, Hector. I want you to make sure that you focus on the other issues. Have you had any results of the back trace on Monica Stein? Has she been sending out any other messages? Was she working alone, or is there another in-house malcontent for us to deal with?' said Olga.

'As far as we can tell, she was working alone. Security hasn't found anything suspicious apart from the email that was sent out. We checked her mobile and found nothing, but she may have had access to another device we haven't found,' replied Hector.

'Alright, Hector, keep at it, we can't afford any slip-ups and we don't want anyone sniffing around here.'

With that, Hector left his mother and returned to his own office. Olga sat down at her desk and looked at a photograph of her late husband, Robert. As an Englishman, he, too, like her own Chief of Staff, would have frowned on the unnecessary risk to the hugely successful business empire she had created by allowing personal feelings, however acute, to influence her judgement. She turned her gaze away from the man from whom she had learned so much. Her decision had been made as soon as the true identity of Otto Graf had been revealed to her; such was the pain and anger that languished in her subconscious. It festered such that no amount of wealth could vanquish it. She would not rest until the slate had been wiped clean, the scales of justice re-balanced, and her grandparents and her mother avenged.

Chapter 11

Greg Travers stared out across the grey, choppy waters, watching the many boats plying their trade back and forth across the River Thames. The tide was ebbing, the water flowing out of London towards the estuary. It had been an early start for him and a busy morning, but his latent instincts, dulled by several months of chronic alcohol abuse, had kicked in. Despite the events of recent days, he no longer felt as though he was the hunted. Now, he was the hunter. He had a name, and he had a location. The Albatross Foundation was now firmly in his sights.

He didn't yet know what the connection was or why they might be involved, but they were linked to several dummy corporations held by London-based accountants McKenzie and Hunt, who were already under investigation. From what Charles Stanley had told him, the Foundation was a well-funded, well-respected global enterprise owned and run by the charismatic Olga Devereux, whom Stanley himself said had a reputation for making grown men who met her 'weak at the knees.'

It was hard to imagine that someone so respected for their philanthropic work could be involved in corruption, let alone murder. He was going to have to dig deeper, much deeper, to get to the bottom of it all. He finished the cup of tea he had taken with him, turned away from the bustling river, crossed Millbank, and returned to Thames House.

He had barely had time to settle in for the afternoon when his phone rang. It was Stanley.

'Good afternoon, Greg. It's Charles Stanley. Listen, I've got Detective Chief Inspector Deery here. Can you pop in for a few minutes?'

'Yes, sir. I'll be right over,' said Travers.

Travers grabbed his file as he left. He felt sure that one or both of them would ask him for an on-the-spot update, even if it wasn't a scheduled briefing, and he wasn't going to be caught sucking his thumb.

A few minutes later, Travers arrived at Stanley's austere office. He knocked twice on the door and walked straight in.

Stanley was sitting behind his rather plain and functional wooden desk. DCI Deery was sitting in a chair facing him, slightly to his left. The Chief Inspector stood up and greeted Travers with a warm handshake.

'Greg, it's good to see you back at work. No after-effects from your aerobatics the other night, then?'

'Hello, John. Actually, it's really good to be back. The doctors say I'm okay. I still have some bruised bones, and when I get up in the morning, I'm as stiff as a board, but they say it will ease up over the next week,' said Travers.

'The Chief Inspector and I have been going over what we know, what we suspect, and how best to proceed. Pathology has come back. They say it was definitely the same knife used to kill Lisa Scott and Detective Rogers at your place. They found a tiny nick on the blade, which was replicated on both wounds. Much more importantly, they found skin cells under the fingernails of both Miss Scott and Rogers. We have a DNA match. If we catch them, they'll go to jail, and we can throw away the key. But as to their identity and finding them, that's another matter,' commented Stanley.

Travers took a seat next to the Chief Inspector. The DNA results had proved, if nothing else, that this investigation was much broader in scope than initially thought.

'Sir, these were not random stabbings. It was efficient, ruthless, and professional, and it was linked with the murder of William Constable. Don't you see? This is all connected. As I was telling you yesterday, I have spent hours trawling through Constable's clients and McKenzie and Hunt's. The dummy corporations on their books trace back to the Albatross Foundation. That Foundation is worth billions.

Sir, you sent Constable in because you suspected McKenzie and Hunt. If the Albatross Foundation is using McKenzie and Hunt to launder money or circumvent the authorities, and they thought they were about to be exposed, they have the resources. Especially if you're right and they were tipped off,' said Travers.

'Greg, you are talking about one of the biggest charitable organisations around. Mrs Devereux has had dinner at Number Ten and the White House, for goodness' sake. Before I march in with a search warrant, I'll need to be damn sure we have something more to go on than even one of your hunches, or my next job will be litter-picking in Hyde Park if I'm lucky,' said the Chief Inspector.

Stanley turned to Travers. Although they had never worked together, he knew of Travers' reputation. If there was anyone capable of finding a needle in a haystack, it was the man he had just reinstated.

'All right, Greg. There is no other way. We, and by that I mean you, need to find evidence to prove that a hitherto unimpeachable symbol of humanitarianism is a crook and a murderer. Given what you have already experienced, it could very well be dangerous. If you are right and she is the mastermind of a criminal organisation, you are going to need help from someone used to being at the sharp end of things.

You're back and in at the deep end. Are you still willing to go through with this?' asked Stanley.

'Yes, sir, I am.'

'Good man,' said Stanley, who picked up his phone and tapped in a four-digit extension code.

'Would you come in, please, Alicia?'

'Sir?' said a slightly bemused Travers.

There was a knock on the door. Travers turned to see who it was that Stanley had summoned. He wondered what exactly she was supposed to do.

The door opened. In walked a slim young woman, probably late twenties or early thirties, with shoulder-length blonde hair, dressed in a smart black two-piece suit.

'Greg, allow me to introduce you to Intelligence Officer Alicia Downes.'

Travers stepped forward to shake her hand. 'Miss Downes, Greg Travers. How do you do?'

'Well, I've not been run over yet! Alicia Downes, nice to meet you,' she responded.

Sensing Travers' confusion, Stanley interjected.

'Alicia will be working with you. She has spent a lot of time operating in the field, and she's not afraid to get her hands dirty if necessary. Part of her brief will be to try and stop someone from killing you.'

'I certainly hope she's successful, sir,' observed Travers wryly.

'Alicia, you have been briefed. You will report directly to me. DCI Deery's team will be working with us as a combined operation. I want you two to come up with a plan of action. When you are ready, report back to me.

Any questions?' asked Stanley.

'No, sir,' said Downes in a matter-of-fact manner as she turned to face Travers.

'You, Greg?'

'Well... err, no, sir.'

'Then I'll not keep you. Go and get acquainted. Greg, bring Alicia up to speed with your latest theories.'

With that, Greg and Alicia turned and, with a nod to Deery, left Stanley's office.

'Let's grab a coffee,' said Downes.

'Good idea. Let's go to the restaurant,' suggested Travers.

After collecting their drinks, they made their way to a quiet corner. Sitting opposite each other, Travers looked intently into his new partner's blue eyes as she sipped her coffee.

Downes met his gaze as she put her cup down.

'You're staring,' she said.

'I'm sorry, Alicia, but have we met before?'

Downes laughed. 'Oh dear, I've not heard that one for at least a week. Do you use that one on all the girls you meet, Greg?'

'I'm sure you've heard them all. I just have this funny feeling—you just look familiar,' said Travers.

'No, we've never met before, exactly. However, I do know that you like your Pimm's by the jug and that you are partial to Chinese food.'

'Then it was you following me at Warren House and the Bronze Dragon. Orders from Stanley?'

'Yes, he asked me to keep tabs on you,' revealed Downes.

'Really? Well, where were you when I was cartwheeled over the common last week?' asked Travers.

'I wasn't on the job then. Still, I'm glad you weren't killed.'

'Me too,' said Travers.

'We are going to need a secure place to work. You're still at a safe house, aren't you?'

'Yes. Well, my place has been full of people in hazmat suits—it might be a little crowded.'

'OK, here's what we'll do. We'll swing around to where you're staying and pick up your stuff. You can move in with me for a while—I have a spare bedroom.'

'Do you always order people around?' said Travers.

'Only when I have to. You are a potential witness to a murder. Someone has already tried to kill you once, and they may try again. My job is to keep you alive. There are a lot of people in Thames House who can do what you do, but no one can do it as well as you. Didn't you wonder why Stanley allowed you back so quickly? You should have had a phased return to work. He's been asking questions—he knows your reputation. He even had to get authority from the Director to reinstate you straight away.

'Stanley believes you can crack this case. You're running point on this one. He has great faith in you,' said Downes.

'I see. Well, under the circumstances, I guess I'll go to your place,' said Travers.

Greg Travers stopped outside his temporary accommodation, collected the few personal items he had managed to gather in the limited time afforded him by the police, and shoved them into his overnight bag. Alicia Downes waited for him in his car. Travers placed the small case into the boot before rejoining her.

It was a relatively short trip to Alicia's two-bedroom flat in Kensington. Travers parked outside, retrieved his bag, and followed Alicia up a small set of steps to the main entrance, passing through the door into a large, well-lit hallway, at the end of which was a switchback staircase leading up to the higher floors.

'Come on, this way,' said Alicia as she led the way up the first flight of stairs. 'We're on the third floor,' she continued.

'I'm glad I only have a small case—I'd hate to have to stagger up with an armful,' commented Travers.

Once they reached the third floor, Travers watched, intrigued as to what kind of taste this woman had. She had a sense of style and refinement that belied her occupation. Alicia unlocked her apartment door and walked in. Travers followed her into the light, airy flat.

'Very nice. This must have cost a small fortune.'

'I did have a bit of help from Mum and Dad,' replied Alicia. 'Your bedroom is in here,' she continued.

Alicia led Travers into a double bedroom filled with pastel shades and bespoke furniture. Travers looked around the room admiringly before following her back into the living room.

'I must say, someone has very good taste, Alicia. It's lovely, it really is.'

'Product of a good education, I suppose. You would probably have to thank my parents for that,' she replied.

Alicia walked across to her living room windows, where a pair of French doors opened out onto a small balcony overlooking Holland Park.

'Would you like a cup of tea or coffee, Greg? Make yourself comfortable.'

'Thanks. Tea would go down very nicely—strong, with a couple of sugars,' replied Travers, who picked out a particularly comfy-looking armchair.

After a few minutes, Alicia brought a small tray into the room with the drinks. Travers took his cup of tea and sat back in the chair.

'Where shall we start?' asked Alicia.

'I think we should start with you. I presume Charles Stanley has already told you all about me, including the last few colourful months. Up till then, I spent most of my time in MI5 sitting in front of a computer screen, scouring the universe for information on dodgy people doing their best not to be found. That was about as exciting as it got.

'In the last two weeks, I've seen someone poisoned, a friend has her throat cut, my home ransacked, and someone tried to run me over. And now I am sharing a roof with a secret agent. So, it's not been a typical few days for me.'

'Well, the boiled-down version is I'm 28, single, and I don't much like working in an office. My parents sent me to Marlborough College, then Oxford, where I did a BSc in Criminology. Career-wise, I couldn't think of anything worse than being stuck behind a desk all the time. I applied to MI5 and hey presto.'

'And what precisely do you do? Kill people?' asked Travers.

Alicia laughed. 'You gather intelligence through your laptop, I gather it out there,' she said, pointing to the window. 'Sometimes you have to go into some dark places and turn over some slimy rocks to get the answers. Greg, your instincts are leading you in a certain direction, but they will only take you so far. Sooner or later, you have to take your instincts and theories out into the real world and test them. That's what I do. Stanley believes you can crack this, but we are going to have to get out of the office to find the proof.'

Travers unpacked and turned on his office laptop. Resting the laptop on her coffee table, he logged on, opened his case folder, and sat on the sofa next to Alicia.

'OK, I've spent days trawling through McKenzie and Hunt's books. A number of their accounts belong to dummy corporations, and they all trace back to the Albatross Foundation. Their headquarters are in Poole, Dorset. The day William Constable was killed, there was a news report of a woman's body being fished out of Poole Harbour. Dorset Police are still investigating, but guess who she worked for… The Albatross Foundation,' said Travers.

'All roads lead to Rome. Sounds like we'll be packing our bucket and spades,' added Alicia. 'We'd better get all the information we can on that headquarters and Mrs Olga Devereux. It's beginning to sound like the answers to your puzzle are in that building.'

'Well, Charles Stanley may be able to help there. He's actually met her,' said Travers.

Detective Chief Inspector Deery sat back in his chair and stared ruefully at his mug, now full of cold tea. He had been looking forward to his tea for ages, subconsciously aware of it when it was brought in, but his focus and mind were elsewhere. Now, the steam had been replaced by an unsavoury-looking film over the surface of the liquid. He was up to his eyes in paperwork. Everyone wanted answers, including the Chief Constable. News of the William Constable case had reached the top of the tree, which both increased the pressure for results but also gave him a bit more muscle, particularly with MI5's involvement. Given the circumstances, he was sure that if he needed more resources, he would have no trouble getting them. There was a knock on his door.

'Come in,' said the Chief Inspector.

'Boss, have you heard of an Olivia Hunter?' asked the detective.

'Olivia Hunter? Can't say I have. Who is she?' asked Deery.

'She's an investigative journalist—freelance. Writes about all sorts of stuff: financial, political, and big business exposés. She likes to poke the mud to see what comes out.'

'What about her?' asked Deery.

'Well, she was involved in a hit-and-run a few days ago. Killed.'

'And how is this relevant to the investigation?' queried Deery, trying to stir up some enthusiasm.

'The police in Bournemouth were checking her details and looked at her mobile phone records. She'd received five phone calls from Monica Stein, the woman fished out of Poole Harbour. The last one was the day before she died,' said the detective.

'That's more like it. Hit and run, you say? Any witnesses? You'd better get down there. I want to know what she was working on, get copies of everything, and keep me informed. If anyone gives you any trouble, refer them to me. I'll ring the Chief Superintendent there and tell him you're on your way,' said Deery.

Maybe this was the lucky break Deery was hoping for. He rose from his chair, picked up his cold mug of tea, opened his door, and called out to one of his staff.

'Get rid of this swill, will you, and bring me a fresh cup?'

One of his colleagues respectfully took the mug. Deery walked back to his desk, a spring now in his step, and picked up the phone to update Charles Stanley.

Chapter 12

There was a knock on his bedroom door. Travers, half-dressed, acknowledged the call, got to his feet, and quickly reached for his shirt, buttoning the middle two before walking across and opening the door.

'Good morning, Greg. How was your night?' said a bright and breezy Alicia.

'Very comfortable, thanks. Is something up?'

'Just had a call from Stanley; we need to report to work for a special briefing at 10:00.'

'Did he say what it's all about?'

'No, just that they have received some new information regarding Olga Devereux and there is a rush on to get some particular documents prepared before we go,' said Downes.

Downes and Travers walked along the corridor leading to Charles Stanley's office. Downes knocked on the door before opening it and walking into the room. Stanley was standing by an open window, looking out across the River Thames.

'Ah, there you are. Come in and sit down.' 'I'm sorry about today's delay, but I've had a long discussion with the Director, and we have agreed on a change of approach,' said Stanley, adding, 'There is a major black-tie event in Poole to celebrate Olga Devereux's charity work and the twenty years of the Albatross Foundation, which she founded. There will be several hundred people there, civic dignitaries, charity bigwigs, and some members of relevant government departments, and you two.'

'And what are we two going to do there, sir?' asked Travers.

'Alicia, you are going to be attached to the onsite security team, which means you will have a direct comms link, access to all areas, and the ability to wander around as much as you want, being as nosey as you like,' said Stanley.

'And what about me?' probed Travers.

'This is your lucky day, Greg. You've got a new job, a very desirable new job, particularly from Olga Devereux's point of view.'

Travers was immediately suspicious and didn't like where this conversation was heading.

'You have a new job title too, Greg, or I should say a new cover, Senior Government Procurement Officer,' said Stanley.

'What, or who, am I procuring, sir?'

'In your role as Senior Procurement Officer, you would have access to government contracts, contracts worth tens of millions, in some cases hundreds of millions of pounds, to approved companies and organisations. We're going to bait a trap for Mrs Devereux. We want to dangle you under her nose. I don't think she will be able to resist having someone on her payroll who is holding the government's debit card in their wallet,' Stanley continued.

'Pick up any glossy celebrity magazine, and you will see Olga Devereux with a handsome young man on her arm. Her private life may be a bit of a mystery, but her social life certainly isn't. She has a well-known passion and appetite for men, especially younger, good-looking men, and according to Miss Downes here, you tick all the right boxes.'

Travers looked across briefly at Alicia, who blushed slightly before winking at him.

'Go on,' said Travers suspiciously.

'The reason we delayed your trip down to the south coast today is that our accounts department has been working non-stop, with the full co-operation of your bank and Credit Card Company, I might add, to, shall we say… put a few question marks around your character,' declared a smiling Stanley.

'You've done what?' exclaimed Travers, who was liking the idea less and less.

'Yes, I'm afraid your gambling debts have maxed out your credit card since your wife passed away. You really should have left home without it. Your bank and Credit Card Company are busy updating your statements from the beginning of this year to better reflect a lavish, reckless, but unsupported lifestyle. You know your bank manager is very concerned about you defaulting on your extended overdraft facility,' added Stanley.

'Overdraft? I don't have one,' said Travers.

'You do now, Greg. A big one,' said a smiling Stanley.

From his in-tray, Stanley produced an A4 letter from the Human Resources Department, which he handed to Travers.

'This is a copy of a letter that Personnel has placed on your file. It's a final written warning as to your future conduct. You might like to keep that in your wallet for the time being. It may come in handy should you feel the need to leave it lying around for any reason!' said Stanley. 'Yes, everyone has been surprisingly helpful in flushing your reputation down the toilet, but don't worry, once the operation is over, your good name and financial standing will be restored,' after a short pause, Stanley sardonically added, 'I expect.'

'Well, now that my job prospects and credit score are disappearing down the pan, what actually is the plan, sir?' said Travers.

'We want you to make a particularly favourable impression on Mrs Devereux at this event.'

'Suppose she is not favourably impressed?'

'Don't worry, she will be. Quite apart from your charming personality, as soon as you tell her about your job and your money troubles, you will find she becomes very attentive,' commented Stanley.

'Like a boa constrictor, I expect!' chipped in Downes.

'I see, and what am I supposed to do then?' said Travers.

'She's a cougar with a thing for younger men. Use your imagination,' Stanley quipped. 'We just want to get you on the inside. Just go with the flow, let her make the running and see where it leads.'

'That's what I'm worried about,' said Travers.

'Oh my god, you are such a wuss!' piped up Downes.

'Alicia, she's older than my mother!' comented an exasperated Travers.

'Let's see your watch, Greg,' requested Stanley, as he opened one of his desk drawers.

Travers took his old but trusty Omega Seamaster off and handed it to Stanley. He looked at it dismissively for a moment before handing over a small wooden box, which Travers then opened.

'That's a Rolex. It's gold and very expensive. It was a present from my wife, and if it doesn't come back in pristine condition, two things will happen. Your pension pot is going to take a very big hit, and my wife will probably put your balls through her mincer.'

'Now, I presume you have a half-decent tuxedo and shoes, etc.? You need to look like a man of means, or at least a man who wants to look like a man of means. I don't want to have to stretch my modest budget any further than I have to. All the details of the black-tie event are in this envelope, along with background cover details of your procurement role. I'm sorry, Greg, but we must explore or exploit every avenue, every opening, and every weakness,' said Stanley.

'As long as I don't end up as fish food in the harbour,' said Travers.

'That's not going to happen, Greg. You have too much to offer her financially, quite apart from any more personal attributes that might tickle her fancy,' added Stanley acerbically.

'Well, I've no desire to tickle her fancy, or anything else, sir,' Travers said.

'All right, you had better cut along, you'll leave for Poole in the morning. If there are any changes or updates, I'll let you know. Remember, if the Albatross Foundation is a front for major organised criminal activity, as you suspect, they'll have the resources to check up on you. That's why we're doctoring your financials, remember that,' said Stanley.

After the meeting, Travers, accompanied by his new 'bodyguard', travelled the few miles back to Wimbledon Village. His house was still festooned with crime scene tape. Opening the front door, Travers was both dismayed and disheartened at the mess and the thought that someone had broken into his home and ransacked it. He couldn't even bear to think about the murder of Detective Rogers in his garden. For the present, he was grateful to stay with Alicia for a while. Travers made his way to his bedroom, where he proceeded to pack a large suitcase. As he walked back through the hall, Downes was standing, admiring a photograph.

'This looks like it was taken in the garden at No. 10?'

'Yes, it was, a few years ago,' replied Travers.

'I remember now. It was while I was with MI6. I was away in South Africa at the time, so I missed all the excitement. You cracked a terrorist cell at the 11th hour and foiled an assassination attempt on the PM.'

'I got lucky, very lucky, but the Prime Minister was most gracious; he invited Cassandra and me to No. 10 for drinks after things quietened down,' added Travers.

'Didn't you get a commendation—'a brilliant piece of deductive reasoning,' as I recall? I don't think luck had anything to do with it.' Downes' praise and admiration were fulsome.

Travers had slept remarkably well, considering he would shortly be working 'in the field' for the first time, with all the latent hazards that might accompany such an experience. Not to mention the potential jeopardy of being propositioned by man-eating Olga Devereux. With that in mind, he was determined to enjoy his hearty breakfast. Whatever Alicia Downes merited as an intelligence officer, there was no doubting her competency in the kitchen, providing him with tea, toast, and a magnificent full English breakfast. Travers felt ready for anything. Downes had already had a long telephone conversation with Charles Stanley, who had brought her up to speed with the latest developments from the Dorset Constabulary.

'Stanley had a call from DCI Deery last night. He sent someone down to Dorset yesterday to follow up on a hit-and-run incident.'

'What's that got to do with us?' asked Travers.

'Stanley said the victim was a journalist doing some work on the Albatross Foundation. She was in contact with the woman who drowned in the harbour. The Chief Inspector's man is looking for the journalist's notes now. With a bit of luck, we'll get a few more pieces of your jigsaw by the time we get there,' she added. 'It'll take a good couple of hours to get down to Poole.'

'How long do you think we'll be down there?' asked Travers.

'That depends on what happens.'

'Grab your gear, Greg. Let's be on our way.'

With that, Travers picked up his case, as well as one of Downes' two Samsonite suitcases, and passed through the front doorway to the landing, where he waited as Alicia shut the door behind her and joined him as he began walking down the stairs. After loading the bags into the cavernous boot of Travers' BMW, they sat silently inside the car for a moment. Travers briefly turned and looked at Downes, who looked directly ahead, ignoring his glance.

'All set?' said Travers.

She turned her head slightly towards him. 'Let's go.'

Travers depressed the brake and turned the ignition key. The engine growled and roared into life, and they were on their way. It would probably take two and a half hours or more to get to Poole, depending on the traffic. Once they had negotiated the busy London streets, it should be plain sailing, barring hold-ups for the inevitable roadworks, with motorway or dual carriageway covering most of the 110 miles. At least the weather was still holding.

Detective Deery was walking back to work and halfway through a well-stacked cheeseburger when his phone rang. He could never understand how his phone always seemed to know when he was in the middle of something important. He struggled to hold his rapidly disintegrating burger in one hand while fumbling in his pocket to retrieve his phone with the other. Trying not to drop the contents of either hand, he swiped across the still-ringing phone.

'Deery,' he said brusquely.

'Boss, it's Evans, down in Bournemouth.'

'Yes, Dave, what have you got?' asked the Inspector.

'Nothing really relevant yet, boss. The police have been searching Miss Hunter's house in Corfe, but it looks like someone got there first. They found papers strewn all over the place. They've been sifting through it all, and the lab boys have got her laptop,' said Evans.

'Well, at least we can rule out accidental death now. I want you to stay on down there. MI5 are sending two of their personnel down there today to nose about. I'll send you their details.'

'Yes, boss,' said Detective Evans.

Deery ended the call, and with his focus now away from the phone conversation, he looked down at his feet, cursing under his breath. He watched the remains of his lunch slide down the side of his black Oxford brogues onto the pavement.

Greg Travers and Alicia Downes' drive had been remarkably uneventful, with no traffic jams, even through Newbury, which had been notorious for delays. A significant portion of the M27 passed through the New Forest, the 219-square-mile National Park, and one of the largest areas of forest and heathland in southern England. New Forest ponies could frequently be seen roaming the open land. Shortly before midday, they saw the 'Welcome to Bournemouth' signs.

'We'll be in Poole in 20 minutes. Where exactly are we going?' asked Travers.

'Just follow the signs for Sandbanks. Stanley's got us a couple of rooms in The Harbour Heights Hotel,' said Alicia.

'Sandbanks is one of the most expensive places around. I don't suppose you mentioned that when you got him to authorise your expense account for this trip?' enquired Travers.

'Don't tell me your conscience is troubling you, Greg.'

About twenty minutes later, they drove up the steep tarmacked driveway that led to the front of the whitewashed hotel. Travers found a parking bay close to the entrance, and the pair got out and walked around to the rear of the car, where they retrieved their bags. It was only a few short steps to the dark wood-framed glass double doors that marked the entrance to the hotel. They walked across a narrow foyer to the reception desk, where they checked in. A smartly dressed porter emerged from a nearby room and was asked by the receptionist to take Alicia's bags up to her room.

'Would you follow me, please, madam,' said the porter as he picked up Alicia's two grey suitcases and led the way towards the main staircase.

'Come on, Greg, we are on the top floor; the porter's got the keys,' said Downes as she turned to follow the rather stout man as he began the journey up the stairs. On reaching the top landing, they proceeded down a short corridor until they arrived at their allocated rooms. The porter inserted the electronic key card and opened the door. He put the bags down next to the king-size bed, then turned and gestured for Greg to follow him. Travers' room was next door. Once the porter had departed, Travers went back into Downes's room. She was standing on her balcony, staring out across Poole Harbour.

'My god, look at that view, Alicia,' Travers said, turning away and looking round at Alicia's elegant deluxe room. 'This must be costing a fortune.'

Downes walked across to her handbag and picked out her mobile phone.

'I'd better check in with Stanley, he may have some news for us.'

Travers picked up one of the maps in the hotel welcome pack and sat on the bed, acquainting himself with their surroundings while Downes spoke to Stanley. Five minutes later, she replaced her phone in her bag.

'Do you want the good news or the bad news, Greg?'

'There is some good news, then?' Travers replied.

'Oh, did I say good news? Perhaps I should have said it's not all bad news,' said Downes wryly.

'The police have searched the journalist's house, but they haven't found anything yet related to the Foundation or Olga Devereux, and as for her laptop's hard drive, they looked, but it hasn't just been wiped—it's been physically removed.'

Travers considered that news for a moment before replying.

'Someone is going to a great deal of trouble to cover something up. Was this journalist freelance or working for someone else? She may have passed on her information to a third party before she was killed, or she might have been so concerned about what she was uncovering that she shared it with someone else. I presume the police have questioned her neighbours and close friends?'

'I think that we should go over to her house this afternoon and have a look ourselves,' suggested Downes.

They promptly left her room and walked down the carpeted staircase to the ground floor and into the bar, where they briefly stopped to order drinks before continuing to a set of double doors that led down to a large multi-level patio area. Walking to the far end of the expansive patio, they selected a table under a large open cream-coloured umbrella. Travers stepped across to the short glass balustrade, interspersed with potted palms and conifers that enclosed the patio and looked out across the spectacular vista. From his high vantage point, he could see the whole of the Sandbanks Peninsula, the harbour, and the Purbeck hills in the distance. He could now understand why this was such expensive real estate and a magnet for the rich and successful.

'Alicia, look at this view, it's incredible.'

Downes left her seat and joined Travers, resting her hand on the wooden handrail and gazing across the blue waters of the harbour, with only the sails of yachts and windsurfers breaking up the blue canopy.

'Do you know why we are staying here, Greg?' Before Travers had time to answer, Downes pointed to the opposite end of the mouth of the harbour. 'You see the town over there? That's Poole; it's less than a mile away. That's where the Albatross Foundation headquarters is, and out there in the harbour, less than a mile away, is Devereux's private island. This is their world, and we are right in the middle of it.'

They returned to their table. Travers now knew that if the Albatross Foundation was responsible for Lisa's savage murder, the other deaths, and the attempt on his own life, the answer would be found here, and he was now at the sharp end of things. Travers picked up his glass; this time, he had to forego his favourite Pimms and settle for something non-alcoholic in the form of orange juice and lemonade.

'Here's to success,' toasted Travers. Downes raised her glass of Prosecco and offered a toast of her own.

'Good health and long life.'

'I'll certainly drink to that,' said Travers. 'Alicia, what made you want to do fieldwork, really?'

'I suppose it's in the blood. I know that sounds like a cliché. My father spent thirty years in the army, including ten in the Special Air Service. His mother worked for the SOE in Europe during the war, so it was probably inevitable. They both served behind the lines. It was just a lifestyle that I grew up with and accepted. As I said, the thought of a regular office job was never part of my thinking, and my parents understood that and didn't try to influence me one way or the other.'

'So you have no regrets?' asked Travers.

'Regrets? No, not yet. Every day is different. I had two years seconded to the SIS. I've been all over the world and only got shot at twice! Now I'm back on my home patch. I wouldn't swap it for a desk job,' said Downes. 'What about you, Greg? Are you happy?'

'Is that a loaded question, Alicia?' said Travers. 'You know about my wife?'

'Yes, Stanley told me all about it. I'm sorry, but you must have thought about the future, whether you want to carry on or not, or even have a complete change.'

'To be honest, I hadn't got close to making a decision. Then all of this blew up. People started dying around me. I couldn't walk away. I knew I could make a difference, and besides which, I wanted to get the bastard who murdered my friend and tried to run me over.'

'You've never thought of a different environment, swapping a desk for fieldwork?' asked Downes.

'Like you?' replied Travers. 'Running around, jumping off rooftops, working undercover, even killing people? No, I couldn't do it. I think you have to have a particular aptitude for that sort of thing. I don't know what I'd do if I came face to face with someone who wanted to kill me—probably crap myself. I beg your pardon.'

After enjoying a quick lunch, Travers and Downes returned to their rooms. The first order of business was to get the exact location of Olivia Hunter's address. Deery had texted the contact details of Detective Dave Evans, who had been briefed to liaise with the local Dorset Police and make himself known to Downes and Travers when they arrived on the scene. Downes spoke briefly to Evans, arranging to meet him at the journalist's address later in the afternoon. There was a knock on her door; it was Travers.

'Come in.'

'Hi, got the address?' he asked.

'Yes, it's a cottage in Corfe. Deery's man, Evans, will meet us there to show us around. You ready?'

They walked down the stairs, through the foyer, and out of the entrance into the bright sunshine. Downes put her handbag into the rear bucket seat and handed a piece of paper containing the address to Travers to input into the car's satnav, just in case.

'I hope you don't get seasick, Greg?'

'What!?'

'Corfe is the other side of the harbour, so we'll be crossing on the Sandbanks ferry. When we get out, turn left down to Banks Road, then turn left again and follow the signs for the ferry.'

Travers started the engine and pulled away slowly down the steep drive until he reached the kerb, then, following Downes's instructions, drove down the steep road that led to the harbour and Banks Road. As he pulled up at the junction, Travers looked ahead across the choppy water and watched scores of windsurfers, with their multi-coloured sails—some skimming across the waves with complete mastery, and others simply trying to master standing up. As he followed the road leading to the peninsula, he cast his eye across the harbour and the many sailing boats—some making their way to the mouth of the harbour and the open water of Poole Bay, whilst others were content to navigate the small islands within the security of the harbour itself.

As they approached the ferry slipway, a queue of cars appeared in front of them. Now, it was just a question of waiting until they reached the slipway itself.

Thirty minutes later, their time had come, and Travers drove his car down onto the slipway, up the ramp, and onto the chain ferry. A steward directed him towards one of the lanes painted on the deck, and he soon found himself facing the water on the seaward side of the ferry, with the only thing between him and the swiftly flowing current being the slightly raised ramp and a metal gate. The ferry made the three-minute crossing every 20 minutes. At the appointed time, the gates on the landward side were closed and the ramp raised. Slowly, the ferry started to chug away from the slipway and moved inexorably across the three hundred metres of open water towards South Haven Point. During the short passage, some people got out of their cars and went up on the decks to look out across the harbour.

As the ferry approached its destination, those drivers who had left their vehicles returned, and many started their engines. Once the ramp had been lowered onto the slipway, the stewards opened the gates and directed the cars off the ferry and onto the road. As one of the cars on the front row, Travers was soon instructed to move off the ferry, across the slipway, and onto the road. Turning to Alicia, he commented:

'On your left is Shell Bay, absolutely pristine sands. Did you know that Diana, Princess of Wales, used to walk here, just over there? She told her bodyguard to wait and just went off for a walk; she loved it here. Of course, you know what else Shell Bay is famous for, don't you?'

'Of course I do, there's a naturist beach here, and no, I am not going to try it. We have more important things to do,' said Downes.

After paying the toll for the ferry, they proceeded along Ferry Road, through long stretches of sand dunes that morphed into heather and gorse-filled heathland as they moved further away from the sea. It was open, unspoilt countryside. The journey to Corfe was about six miles, passing through Studland before turning west across the Purbeck hills, which saw them climb ever higher until they had a superb panoramic view across the whole of Poole Harbour and the surrounding countryside.

Before long, they began a slow descent as they approached the village of Corfe. As they traversed the narrow, snaking road towards the castle, Travers caught tantalising glimpses of the famous ruins until finally, the whole castle came into view. Standing on top of a fifty-five-metre hill, the castle dominated the surrounding area. Built initially by William the Conqueror in the 11th century as a fortress, Corfe became a royal palace until being sold by Elizabeth I. As a royalist stronghold, it was captured by the Parliamentarians during the English Civil War and slighted to prevent its further use. Now, it was a very popular tourist attraction. Travers followed the signs to nearby Corfe Village until they arrived at the address of journalist Olivia Hunter. Parking the car, Travers and Downes looked around for Detective Evans.

A few minutes later, a short, slightly chubby man walked across the road towards them and introduced himself as their contact.

'Hello, Detective Evans? I'm Greg Travers, this is Alicia Downes.'

'Hi, yes, I'm Dave Evans. Good trip?'

'Fine, thanks, pretty impressive,' said Travers, looking back at the castle. Evans led Travers and Downes towards a pretty thatched cottage, opened the gate, and walked through to the front door.

'Have the local police finished here?' asked Downes.

'Basically, it's just a hit-and-run incident, so they don't have any reason to lock it down. However, after my governor's call, they agreed to search the property,' said Evans.

'And found nothing?' asked Travers.

'When they entered the house, they found that someone had already been in there, and that certainly tweaked their interest, but no, I'm afraid they found nothing of interest,' added Evans.

'Did they interview the neighbours?' asked Travers.

'I believe so,' said the policeman.

While they stood in the front garden, an elderly grey-haired woman walking past the property leaned across the gate.

'There's nobody there now,' said the woman.

Alicia moved forward towards the woman.

'Hello, we're with the police. Did you know the lady who lived here?'

'Not really, I live next door, but she kept herself to herself mostly. She rented the cottage, you see. She was only here a few months, it's such a shame,' added the woman.

'Did you talk to her much?' asked Downes.

'Now and again, I can't believe what happened to her,' said the neighbour.

'Did you notice her having any visitors or deliveries recently? Anything out of the ordinary?' said Travers.

'Well, no, not really. Well, she did have one—it was actually the day she had her accident. A man went to her door with a parcel. I said she was out and asked if he wanted to leave it with me, but he said that she wanted it left by her back door if she wasn't in. So, I left him to it,' said the woman, who continued, 'There have been a lot of police around. I thought it was a car accident?'

Detective Evans moved to reassure the elderly woman.

'It's just routine, madam. You know what police work is like these days. Someone stubs their toe on a pavement, and there has to be a report. So, when someone gets run over, we have to be seen to investigate it thoroughly. It's nothing to worry about. Do you remember what this delivery man looked like?'

'No, I'm sorry, officer. I think he was tall. He had one of those bright, high-visibility jackets on. I didn't pay much attention to him, I'm afraid.'

With that, they thanked the neighbour for her assistance, and Evans walked to Hunter's front door, opened it, and allowed Travers and Downes to enter. The three walked into a rather minimalist living room. They looked around; nothing was out of place, however.

Travers looked at Detective Evans, who seemed to anticipate the question Travers was about to ask.

'There was paperwork and box files strewn all over the floor. It was all collected up, and there was nothing that related to the current investigation.'

'Did you search upstairs as well?' asked Travers.

'Yes, we looked everywhere. We didn't find anything,' added Evans.

Travers sat back in his chair and stared ahead, his mind working overtime. Something was missing.

'Our delivery man took Hunter's laptop hard drive; we don't know what else he found, if anything. She may have backed up her digital files in the cloud, but that may take time to find. It may be the 21st century, but I don't know a journalist or reporter who doesn't have hard copies of their work. She made her living exposing malpractice and dodgy companies. She was used to threats. If she thought this was a really big story, she would make sure she kept whatever evidence she had safe. She wouldn't risk her family or close friends, and probably wouldn't trust associates or loose friends. Where would she hide it?' Travers muttered.

'For all we know, it could be hidden under the mattress, but it could be backed up as a micro SD card, Flash Drive, anything,' said Downes.

'No, it won't be electronic. It will be a hard copy, and if the delivery man didn't find it, it's because she has stashed it for insurance.'

'Alicia, you've bought your flat? Where do you keep your deeds?' asked Travers rhetorically; he already knew the answer.

'My solicitor has them.'

'Exactly. Detective Evans, can you get hold of Miss Hunter's solicitor and ask if she made any special provision to store documents with them, or if they are aware if she had any Safe Custody facilities anywhere else? You'd better try her bank as well.'

'A shot in the dark, Greg?' asked Downes.

'Not quite. If you wanted somewhere safe and secure, somewhere she trusted, not connected to anyone personally, but in the event something happened to you, they would have access to your final instructions. I wouldn't bet my bottom dollar, but that's what I would do if I were her. We'd better have a look around here before we go, just in case anything was missed,' he added.

Chapter 13

Olga Devereux walked straight into her Chief of Staff's office, making no attempt to disguise her displeasure. Richard Rackman had seen that expression recently and knew what it meant. There had been a succession of mishaps since the Monika Stein incident, and Olga Devereux's patience was now wearing thin. He immediately dismissed the meeting he was chairing. The three men attending rose from their chairs and walked swiftly out of the room without making eye contact with their employer, who maintained her intense glare towards the Chief of Staff.

'Did I misconstrue your message, Richard, or did you actually say that a member of our Special Ops team has gone AWOL despite being recalled?'

'I'm afraid so. They were told to check in immediately for reassignment. Four of them have come in, but one hasn't. As far as we know, he is still in London,' said an apologetic Rackman.

'Who is it?' demanded Devereux, her eyes narrowing as the intensity of her anger grew. She would not tolerate disloyalty in her organisation, and those culpable could expect punitive penalties.

'Nikolay Petrov.'

'Him again! Richard, I told you to get rid of him. He's unreliable, a psychopath, and nothing but trouble. Deal with him properly this time. Do you understand?' Devereux's meaning could not have been clearer.

'Olga, he has been involved with McKenzie and Hunt,' said Rackman nervously, knowing that it was likely to enrage Olga's mood still further.

'Explain?' Routine day-to-day matters were often delegated to her Chief of Staff, including extracurricular matters officially 'off the books.' However, when incompetence, ineptitude, or disloyalty were involved, she made her feelings known in no uncertain manner.

'I'm sorry, Olga, but he's up to his neck in it. The woman from Covent Garden, the policeman, the journalist. He's been involved with all of them. If he's picked up, there's no telling what he'll say. If they offer him a deal with immunity, they won't be able to shut him up,' said Rackman.

Devereux, usually a model of restraint and decorum, was furious.

'For God's sake, Richard. You are responsible for personnel. Find him, find him now, and Richard, I don't want any excuses this time. Has the new team arrived?'

'Yes, they flew in two days ago.'

'Right, send them in. Focus on London. I want Petrov found and taken care of, and tell them they had better not cock it up, or they will answer to me personally. You had better hope they find him before the police do. Keep me informed,' said the Albatros matriarch.

With that, Olga turned and walked out of the chastised Rackman's office. She was expecting an update from Berlin today regarding the travel arrangements of German politician Otto Graf. The last thing she needed was an unstable, psychopathic killer running around London with links to the Foundation, with blood on his hands, and wanted by the police.

Chapter 14

Detective Chief Inspector Deery's office door burst open.

'Guvnor…!' called out an enthusiastic young detective as the door banged against the frame.

'For God's sake! Didn't your mother teach you to knock before bursting in?' shouted Deery, causing the man to stop in his tracks.

'Sorry, boss. I think we've got a lucky break with the case. I've just had Rachel Stewart from Pathology on the phone.'

'And?' said the Chief Inspector angrily, still annoyed at the unannounced interruption.

'You remember that bar brawl a few days ago? It was all over the news.'

'Yes, some guy got knifed. What about it?' commented Deery.

'The man who was killed had multiple stab wounds and a slash across the throat. Well, Doctor Stewart was reviewing the post-mortem report. Guess what? It's the same knife that was used in the two murders in our case.'

'Is she sure about that?'

'Yes, boss. They found the same tiny nick on the throat wound from the blade. There's no doubt about it.'

'Good work. Do we have eyes on the killer?' asked Deery eagerly.

'There's CCTV footage and eyewitness accounts, boss. Seems the guy was out of control, either drunk or drugged up. Just came in spoiling for a fight. Eyewitnesses said he was tall, fit-looking, white, spoke with an East European accent, and had a large hunting-type knife. He disappeared before the police arrived.'

'Right, get hold of the CCTV footage. I want a picture of this man. Check the street cameras too, and go back to the witnesses and try and nail down the accent,' requested Inspector Deery.

Deery's mood improved immediately. If they could get a decent image from the security cameras, facial recognition might be able to identify him. Certainly, his MO on Lisa Scott and Detective Rogers suggested military training, which gave them another avenue to explore. Perhaps the net was closing, just a little.

Within a matter of hours, Deery had his wish granted. A good-quality picture had been obtained from the bar's security camera and sent to all allied law enforcement agencies, in the hope that his face was on record somewhere.

The Detective Chief Inspector's luck was about to change as he sat in his office, looking out of the window. The news from the pathologist and the fact that they now had a picture of the assailant had given him fresh hope that a breakthrough was only a matter of time. His phone rang. He desperately hoped it was good news.

'Deery here.'

'Chief Inspector, this is Stuart Richards at the National Central Bureau in Manchester. We've got a match to your photograph enquiry. He popped up on our SLTD Travel and Identity Database. We have his name as Nikolay Petrov. He's Belarusian. Nasty piece of work, his passport was revoked. I'm sending his details to you now. There's also a European arrest warrant out for him.'

'Fantastic. We strongly suspect he has been involved in at least two murders here, including one of my own team, and serious organised crime. We need to find this character. Please let us have everything you have on him. Thanks, Stuart, I appreciate it.'

As soon as Deery finished his call, he went to speak to his team to pass on the new information.

'Listen up, everyone. I've just had a call from Stuart Richards from Interpol NCB in Manchester. We've got a name for our face. He's Nikolay Petrov, a Belarusian. Check your inboxes for his details. His passport's already been revoked, so God knows what name he's using now. Send his photo off to all the UK forces to arrest on sight and get on to the press office. I want his photo out there, top priority. Pass it on to all the airports, Transport Police, Border Force, and all related London units. Tell the Press Office I want this distributed to all the television and news outlets. I don't think this guy is going to blend into the background; someone is going to see him.'

Deery returned to his office as his team scurried around. Getting a positive result on their search for this killer's identity so quickly had been a much-needed shot in the arm, not just for the Inspector himself but the whole team. It was close-knit. Most of them had known Detective Rogers for many years, and his brutal death at the hands of this man had hit them hard. Now there was every chance Petrov would be picked up.

The next day, Petrov's picture appeared on the front pages of all the daily newspapers and also on all the TV news broadcasts. There was nowhere for him to hide. He knew that sooner or later, someone was going to finger him. He could lie low for a while, but without help, he didn't have much of a chance. He also knew that, having ignored the Foundation's recall request, they too would be looking for him, especially in light of the recently instigated police manhunt. It was a simple choice. He couldn't get out of the country on his own. It was either give himself up to the police and accept a probable whole-of-life sentence, or make contact with the Foundation via their usual third party and risk their displeasure and possibly severe consequences as well. Petrov hoped that he would be given some credit for past services rendered, and as such, they might overlook the hot-headed behaviour that had got him into such a mess.

Richard Rackman sat at a table on the roof garden of Albatross House, with a glass of wine in his hand. Nearby, palms fluttered in the gentle breeze. It was a small oasis where he could, at least for a few minutes, escape the rigours and demands of his job. As Olga Devereux's chief of staff, his responsibilities included both the legitimate day-to-day operations of the Foundation as well as all the off-the-books activities. Initially, he had found the arrangement fractious. He knew full well that this was a lifetime appointment. The rewards were tremendous; Olga had seen to that. But it wasn't a job you resigned from. Should he ever fall out of favour, with everything he knew, it was likely that he would end up being found floating face down in the harbour, like Monica Stein. However, this was a consideration he swiftly dismissed.

There was no one he admired more than his employer. He had been an excellent and respected manager for an international brokerage firm until the shadow of temptation crossed his path, and he was caught with his hand in the till. His hitherto untarnished reputation now in tatters, he escaped with a substantial fine and a suspended prison sentence but became a pariah in the business community until he met Olga Devereux. Like so many men before him, he was seduced by her beauty, her confidence, and her charisma. At the time, she needed someone to manage the day-to-day business after the death of her husband — someone competent and efficient, but also someone who understood the need for a more flexible approach to the constraints of rules and regulations.

That was more than fifteen years ago. In the public domain, the Foundation had become a byword for global philanthropy, yet behind the façade, the avaricious fingers of greed stretched into every dark corner of the world. The Devereux's were not racist, nor did they discriminate; they were opportunists who took whatever they could, wherever it was, regardless of the consequences, as long as there was a profit in it. What little conscience Rackman had left when he accepted the role of Chief of Staff had long since departed this world. Now, his loyalty to Olga and the Devereux family was unwavering. He had seen the news headlines this morning. Petrov's face had been all over them. He knew that Olga Devereux would also have seen it and would be expecting prompt action. The McKenzie and Hunt mess was starting to unravel. If he wasn't careful, the authorities would tease out one thread somewhere and start pulling. Just as he contemplated returning to his office, his mobile phone rang — it was Petrov's handler.

'Rackman.'

'Good, right, where is he now?' said Rackman, continuing.

'Tell him to stay where he is. We'll send someone to pick him up within four hours.'

'Tell him we'll have him offshore and on his way to a non-extradition country by tomorrow. Just tell him not to go running around showing his face… or bloody killing anyone else before we get there.'

Rackman terminated the call and immediately got up, walking out of his temporary sun-drenched oasis and back into the real world. It took only a few minutes to reach Olga Devereux's office.

'Afternoon, Max. Is Mrs Devereux in?'

'Yes, sir,' replied Maxwell Jarvis, Olga's personal secretary. Jarvis pressed his intercom and announced Rackman's request to see her.

'Send him in, please, Maxwell,' said Mrs Devereux.

He didn't wait to be told and walked straight in, across the floor to where Olga was sitting.

'Yes, Richard?'

'We've found Petrov. He is still in London. I've told our contact to tell him to keep his head down, and we'll have him picked up later this afternoon,' said Rackman.

'Right, contact our team, get them to pick him up and take care of him. Tell them not to leave a mess behind; make sure they understand that,' ordered Devereux.

Chapter 15

At Metropolitan Police Headquarters, Detective Chief Inspector Deery's phone started ringing again. He was starting to think that his was the only phone in the building that actually worked, either that or everyone had deliberately put their phones on call-forward to his number as a practical joke. Despite his annoyance, he did his best to put on his best professional voice.

'DCI Deery, how can I help you?'

'This is Sergeant Hubbard at Southwark Police Station. We've had a sighting of that man Petrov you're after. He was spotted coming out of a convenience store by an ex-copper who saw his picture in a newspaper.'

'Great work, Sergeant. Did he see where he was heading?' asked the Chief Inspector.

'There's a hostel close by, bedsits mostly, I think. We get a lot of students, backpackers, and the like round here. He disappeared into the main entrance.'

'Thanks, Sergeant. Can you put me through to your governor?' asked the increasingly animated Chief Inspector.

A few minutes later, Deery rushed out of his office, calling three of his team to follow him.

'What's up, boss?' said one of the officers.

'Follow me! Petrov's been spotted in Southwark. I've got the local lads to keep an eye on the building till we get there with reinforcements. MO 19 are on their way just in case we need armed support, but I don't want him getting shot till I've had the chance to get my hands around his neck first.'

Twenty minutes later, Deery's car pulled up in a side road close to the suspect's hostel. After consulting with the Southwark police, The Inspector dispatched two of his men to the rear of the building, joining two local constables who had been keeping watch since the alert was raised.

'If he comes your way, remember he is extremely dangerous. If you have to use your Tasers, don't hesitate,' said Deery.

The Chief Inspector, a junior detective, and two constables entered the hostel and walked across to the reception desk. Holding up a photograph of Petrov, he asked the receptionist where the man was staying. The receptionist provided the room number, adding that it was on the ground floor towards the rear of the building. Deery radioed his colleagues at the rear of the hostel that they were about to move in and to be ready. The Chief Inspector and his entourage moved swiftly to the room number provided by the man at the desk. Knocking on the door, Deery announced himself and instructed Petrov to come out quietly. As expected, there was no response. He sent one of his men to the front desk to get the master key. When he returned and put the key in the door to unlock it, the detective could hear a tremendous commotion from behind the door.

The door burst open, and Deery saw the back of a man disappearing through the ground-floor window. He ordered a colleague from his own team to remain in the room and secure it, and whatever evidence it contained, while he and the two constables ran back through the front of the building and around the side to the rear, where he hoped to find the suspect subdued and in custody. One of the police constables was lying in a pool of blood, being tended by another member of the team. Petrov, was out violently of control, wildly lashing out with his hunting knife in a frantic attempt to escape the clutches of the police. His arms flaying in all directions as he grappled with Deery's men. Running to the scene, the arriving reinforcements quickly subdued the ferocious onslaught, pinning the murderer to the floor before handcuffing him behind his back.

'Get an ambulance quick, get this piece of shit out of here, and read him his rights before I kick his fucking head in, and get that knife into an evidence bag,' demanded Deery as the adrenaline surge of the moment slowly began to subside.

Nikolay Petrov was bundled handcuffed into the back seat of a car and driven away to the police station. An ambulance had arrived, and the wounded PC was being treated for multiple stab wounds before being taken to the hospital. With their prime suspect now in custody, Deery returned to Petrov's bedsit, which was now a hive of activity, as the search for further clues to help them with their investigation continued at pace.

'I want everything photographed and bagged up, then the rest of you head back to the office. I'm going to have a chat with Mr Petrov. Rob, you're with me.'

Within a few minutes, the Chief Inspector was walking into the police station and straight up to the front desk.

'Afternoon, Sergeant, has Petrov been booked in yet?' he asked.

'Yes, sir, he's in a holding cell in the custody suite,' said the sergeant.

'Has he made his phone call? Asked the Detective Chief Inspector.

'Oh yes, his solicitor is on her way,' replied the sergeant.

'Then I think I'll go and introduce myself to the little shit.'

The sergeant rose to his feet and joined Deery via a side door. The men walked along a short corridor and down several steps before entering the custody suite, where the custody officer directed them to the holding cell where Petrov was being held. The heavy metal door swung open, and the detectives walked in to find the Belarussian lying on his back on the rudimentary single bed.

'Mr Petrov, I am Detective Chief Inspector John Deery. This is my colleague, Detective Inspector Rob Taylor.'

'I have nothing to say until my solicitor comes,' said the churlish Belarussian.

'You don't have to say anything, you just have to listen to what I have to say. You're up to your neck in shit, mate: two murders, one attempted murder, possession of a deadly weapon, assault with a deadly weapon, resisting arrest, illegal entry into the country, and heaven knows what else we'll find. By the time you get out of prison, you'll be on your third set of teeth. You're going to take the fall—and a mighty big one—while the others just walk away. Is that what you want? You're not an idiot, you know what's coming. Look, you help me out, and perhaps we can help you,' said the Chief Inspector through gritted teeth, as personally, he would have liked nothing better than to see the man swing for the murder of Detective Rogers.

'I have nothing to say,' replied the recalcitrant man, who lay back on his bed and ignored the police presence.

There was a knock on the door; it was the custody officer.

'Mr Petrov's brief is here,' he said, handing Deery a business card.

'My, that was quick,' the Chief Inspector looked at the card. 'Well, you had better not keep her waiting.'

The custody officer departed and returned a few moments later with a very striking, professional-looking woman: tall, slim, with long blonde hair, and wearing a smart, dark business suit.

'Miss Rodrigues, I presume? My name is Deery, Detective Chief Inspector John Deery. You were quick out of the blocks; just passing, were you?' said the Inspector with a hint of sarcasm.

'I was with another client nearby when the call came. I came straight here,' said the solicitor. 'I hope you have not been acting improperly with my client, Chief Inspector.'

'By no means, Miss. Just making small talk till you arrived,' said Deery.

'Now, I wish to consult with my client privately, please, if you don't mind, Chief Inspector.'

'As you wish. Come on, Rob, let's get a cup of tea and leave them to it,' said Deery, as he turned and began to walk away.

'Mmmmmm, well, she can consult with me privately anytime,' whispered Taylor as he watched her turn towards the door, briefly meeting his gaze and smiling before closing it.

'Down, boy. I don't think your wife would approve,' said Deery as they walked up the stairs and out of the custody suite.

In the custody cell, Petrov sat up, staring at his newly acquired solicitor.

'Who are you? Did the Foundation send you?' asked Petrov.

'Listen to me very carefully, Nikolay. We have a plan to get you out. You must do exactly what I tell you,' said Rodrigues. Pulling up her navy blue skirt, she removed a small package containing a tablet concealed in her stocking top.

'This will make you feel sick and vomit. When you do, call for help and pretend you have stomach pains or cramps. They will get you medical assistance or paramedics, but they will have to take you to hospital for a proper assessment. They will put you in an ambulance under guard. When they transfer you, we will be waiting. A private jet is ready in Bournemouth; you will be out of the country and on your way to South America by breakfast. Say nothing to the police. I shall tell them that I will be back in two hours, and they can interview you then. Wait about twenty minutes, then take the tablet.'

Having imparted her instructions, Rodrigues stood up and knocked on the door before leaving the custody suite. She stopped as she saw the inspector walking towards her.

'Detective Inspector, I have instructed Mr Petrov to say nothing until I return. I was on my way to see another client when I called here. I'll be about an hour.'

'All right, Miss Rodrigues, I dare say we can wait till then,' said Deery.

'You do that,' said Rodrigues as she smiled and walked away from the Chief Inspector and headed for the station exit.

'Goodbye, Sergeant,' the young woman said as she passed the front desk and headed out the door towards the adjoining side road, where her 4x4 was parked. The glamorous solicitor had certainly turned a lot of heads during her short visit, with many of the officers no doubt now considering what pretext they could use to secure a personal visit.

Miss Rodrigues reached her car, opened the passenger door, and sat down. The man sitting in the driver's seat turned to her.

'Everything set?'

'Yes, as long as he follows my instructions. I'd like to be here to see that Chief Inspector's face when he finds out what a fool he has been,' said Rodrigues.

'We'd better get going. We need to be out of the area when the shit hits the fan,' said the driver as he started the engine and drove off.

The Detective Chief Inspector had returned to his office to update his report on the day's events and call his boss, Superintendent Barclay. Keeping an eye on his watch, he made sure he returned to Southwark in good time to question Petrov. He walked through to the Custody Suite and checked in with the Custody Officer on duty.

'Has that blonde solicitor come back yet?' asked Deery.

'No, sir, not yet,' replied the Custody Officer.

'Heard anything out of Petrov?'

'Not a peep, sir.'

'Well, come on, let's wake the bastard up,' said Deery.

The two men walked across the corridor to the Custody Cell where Petrov was being held and unlocked the steel door.

Lying half on his bed and half on the floor, Petrov lay face up, his eyes wide and staring blankly into space. Deery rushed forward to check for a pulse—Petrov was dead.

'Fucking hell, that bloody bitch,' raged the infuriated Chief Inspector.

Chapter 16

Travers walked across the room from his bed, opened the window, and looked out across the harbour. A sea fret obscured much of the activity on the water, but it was early yet. It would take some time before the sun gathered enough strength to burn its way through the fine mist that swirled across the water. Travers returned to his bedside cabinet, picked up his watch, and snapped the stainless steel clasp around his wrist. It was 8:15 a.m. He rang Alicia, who answered almost immediately.

'Morning, Greg. Sleep well?'

'Yes, thanks. Very. You?' replied Travers.

'Until some hungry seagulls woke me up.'

'What time are you going to breakfast?' Travers asked.

She glanced at her watch. 'Give me 15 minutes. I'll see you outside at 8:30.'

Just before 8:30, Travers picked up his phone and electronic key card, left his room, and waited in the corridor for Downes to join him. A few minutes later, they walked into the restaurant. After providing their room numbers to the restaurant manager at the door, they chose a table by a window. They then made their way to the breakfast buffet. Before them was a rich selection of either Full English or Continental breakfast options, together with a range of breads and cereals.

After an enjoyable breakfast, they stepped out onto the patio area and strolled over to the far corner, where they stopped and sat at a table. In two or three hours, this would be a veritable suntrap, packed with locals, hotel guests, and passing tourists. But for now, it was quiet, cool, and relaxing.

Alicia picked up her phone. Travers glanced across at her with an enquiring expression.

'I'm ringing Stanley.'

A few moments later, his familiar voice answered.

'Good morning, sir. It's Alicia Downes.'

'Ah, Alicia. How are things down there, and how is 'Agent' Travers shaping up?' asked Stanley.

'Like a cat on a hot tin roof, sir. He's been prowling around like a caged lion. I don't know who I feel sorrier for, Greg or Devereux,' laughed Downes.

'How did you get on with the journalist's house?' asked Stanley.

'Not much progress yet, sir. Nothing turned up at the house. We are checking in with the local police today to see if they have any updates regarding Greg's inquiry. If we could just find Olivia Hunter's notes, it would give us something to go on. Failing that, we'll need to get a lot closer to Devereux's organisation to find our answers. Did DCI Deery get anything out of Petrov?'

'Nothing at all. He's dead, murdered,' said Stanley.

'Murdered?' said a shocked Downes, who turned and glanced across at Travers, whose face mirrored her own astonishment at Stanley's news.

'Afraid so. Someone turned up claiming to be his solicitor. She insisted on speaking to him alone, as she's entitled to, then left, saying she'd be back in an hour or so for the interview. She must have slipped him something. When Deery went to question him later, he was dead. The woman never showed up, of course.'

'Sir, I've arranged to accompany one of the local detectives here on a visit to see Olga Devereux in her office,' said Downes.

'That's a bit risky, isn't it? Especially after what happened to Greg?' questioned Stanley.

'No, it should be OK. One of Devereux's staff has died under unusual circumstances. It's just routine for the police to provide an update and ask some follow-up questions to the employer. I'm obviously not going to identify myself as MI5. Greg's got me a dummy police ID, should it be necessary. I just want to get inside the building, meet her, and get a feel for the place,' said Downes.

'All right, but for heaven's sake, be careful. Good luck tomorrow night at the charity gala, and try and keep an eye on Greg, I don't want him to get into any trouble. Fill me in on the details later,' said Stanley.

'I'm sure he will be fine, sir,' added Downes with an air of reassuring confidence.

'OK, keep in touch,' said Stanley before hanging up.

'When do you propose to visit Albatross House, Alicia?' asked Travers.

'Maybe tomorrow. I've got to set up the meeting with the police, and it is dependent on Devereux being there. We'll see.'

'Well, I think we should take a look at Devereux's Island. We can go down to the quay. There are plenty of boats that tour the harbour,' said Travers.

'Yes, that sounds like a good idea. When we get back, I want you to get hold of the blueprints of Albatross House,' said Downes.

An hour later, they drove down to the quay, parked the car, and walked along the busy quayside. There was a line of pleasure craft tied up, some of them being used to take passengers on short cruises either around the harbour or further afield, while others were just secured to mooring bollards. The quay itself was lined with numerous public houses, bars, and restaurants that catered for the thousands of tourists who flocked to the area.

With forty minutes until the next sailing, Travers and Downes had time to kill. They spotted an empty table outside one such pub.

'It will be useful to orientate ourselves and see what Parkson Island is like up close. Unless we get a break, we are going to have to have a closer look at both the island and her office. Whatever is going on, the answers are going to be there,' said Alicia.

'You mean break in?' said an alarmed Travers.

'You're the digger, Greg. Come up with some conclusive evidence against Devereux or someone in her organisation that we or the police can use. Otherwise, we are going to have to go in and find it ourselves.'

Travers looked across admiringly at Alicia as she took a drink. Even after such a short time, he had developed great respect for her. She was well-educated, articulate, had a dry and cultivated sense of humour, excellent taste, and darned attractive to boot. But she also had more balls than a lot of the men he'd worked with.

'Don't you get worried, Alicia? What happens if you get caught? You know what they are capable of,' said Travers.

'It's my job, Greg. I'm a professional. What does a professional in any walk of life do when something goes wrong? You fall back on your training, your experience, and your instincts, and you find a way to get through it the best way you can.'

'Alicia, this is not like sorting out somebody's dodgy plumbing. These are ruthless people. Look at the body count since Constable was killed. I don't like it. It's very risky.'

'Oh, Greg, I've been doing this for years. It's not nearly as dangerous as you think. It's mostly just another way of gathering intelligence,' said Downes.

Thirty minutes later, they left their rustic seats and made their way along the busy quay. The warm sea air was now infused with the stench of landed fish. The *Sea Dragon* had now tied up alongside, with the passengers still disembarking.

According to the tour guide, this particular harbour cruise included Parkson Island. It was better to use a regular tourist trip than to draw any additional attention to themselves by hiring a private boat and cruising the island alone. They stepped aboard and made their way to the bow, which would afford them the best possible vantage point.

Ten minutes later, the captain ordered the crew to cast off, and the boat slowly moved away from the quay and into the open water of the harbour. There were innumerable pleasure craft of all shapes and sizes on the water. The *Sea Dragon* pressed on, following a south-easterly course towards the Sandbanks peninsula before turning southwest past the famous Brownsea Island and heading towards the smaller islands.

Before long, Parkson came into view. Alicia Downes reached into her bag and produced a miniature monocular. Putting it to her left eye, she focused intently as the *Sea Dragon* passed the south end of the island, bringing the landing jetty and boathouse into view before moving away.

'What do you think?' asked Travers.

'Getting onto the island isn't the problem; getting on undetected is the problem. She probably has night vision CCTV, infrared beams, pressure pads, and all manner of electronic surveillance. I think we'll have more chance with the office. When we get back, I'm going to try and set up this meeting with Devereux for tomorrow. Can you try and get your hands on the blueprints of the building and anything else you think might be useful?'

'That shouldn't be a problem. And if I can hack into their mainframe, I should be able to see what security systems they have. It might be handy if you have a sudden urge to do something daft,' said Travers.

With the motor launch moving away from the island, today's reconnaissance was complete. Travers and Downes strolled off to find the bar on the upper deck. The enclosed bar area was heaving, and it took some time for Travers to be served. Brandishing the drinks like a prized trophy, Travers gestured to Downes to move away from the bar and back onto the deck, into the fresh air and away from the bustling throng of people.

'May the wind be always at our backs,' said Travers, raising his glass towards Alicia.

'Cheers,' said Downes as their glasses chimed.

The *Sea Dragon* slowly wended its way across the far side of the harbour and back to the quay. With their harbour tour completed, Travers and Downes returned to his car and then to the hotel, where there was still much work to be done before tomorrow.

Dinner that night was booked at the on-site Chinese restaurant. Travers had arranged to meet Alicia in the bar at 7:30 for a drink before heading into the restaurant. As he sat at the bar with a cocktail in his hand, he contemplated what tomorrow might bring. He had known Alicia for such a short time, but he still felt anxious—it was potentially very dangerous.

As he sipped his drink, he looked at the clock on the wall. It was 7:30 precisely. Knowing how punctual Alicia was, he turned towards the entrance to the bar—and there she was, dressed in a soft yellow midi slip dress with narrow shoulder straps, looking sensational. As she walked towards him, his eyes were transfixed. What a woman!

'Good evening, Alicia. You look amazing. Is that a D&G?' Travers asked, eyeing her dress.

'Thank you. No, Ted Baker.'

Gently taking her hand, he led her to the bar.

'What can I get you?' he asked.

'I'll have a Kir Royale champagne cocktail, please, Greg,' said Downes as she perched herself on the stool next to Travers, her dress cascading gracefully from the seat.

I spoke to Detective Inspector Roberts in Poole this afternoon to discuss setting up a meeting with Devereux tomorrow. He'll ring Olga Devereux's secretary in the morning to make sure she'll be there. If she is, I'll meet Roberts there, and we'll see Devereux together—it will give me a chance to look around her office.'

They continued chatting for another fifteen minutes over their cocktails before moving on to the restaurant, where their table awaited them.

'I must say, it's much more fun to have a Chinese meal with you sitting in front of me than to have you surreptitiously spying on me from another table,' commented Travers.

'Stanley asked after you this morning and wished us good luck for tomorrow,' said Downes.

'I bet he did. Why didn't he step up and volunteer to entertain Mrs Devereux? Why did it have to be me?' said Travers.

'He's too old. And in any case, with the best will in the world, I don't think he could pass himself off as a playboy. Besides, what are you complaining about? I'm told she is very desirable. You'll just have to grin and bear it. King and Country, Greg, King and Country, remember? Besides, from what you've been telling me, you can't even remember much of the last few months anyway.'

'I was usually hammered back then,' reflected Travers.

The meal had been a great success. Travers had enjoyed Alicia's company immensely, and both had felt sufficiently comfortable to share confidences that would not normally be offered in so short an acquaintance. The wine had flowed almost as freely as the conversation, and as Travers looked at Alicia on the other side of their small table, he found himself drawn more and more to this remarkable woman.

The low-cut dress, which scarcely covered her breasts, her dark blonde tresses lying softly across her shoulders, and her blue eyes sparkling like diamonds in a flawless face—she was indeed a very desirable woman.

Downes looked at her watch. It was late, and she needed to be on her toes tomorrow.

'We had better be going, Greg. We have a lot on tomorrow.'

'I'm just hoping I still have a lot on by the end of the tomorrow,' said Travers dryly.

Travers looked around and signalled to one of the waiters that he wanted to settle the bill. A few minutes later, the young Chinese man returned and placed a small stainless steel tray containing the bill on the table.

'Mr Stanley's treat, I believe,' said Travers as he picked and looked at the slip of paper.

With the bill paid, Travers and Downes left the restaurant. After such a good meal, Travers thought it far too testing to walk up the stairs to their rooms, and so, when they reached the staircase, he paused. To the right was the lift.

The elevator bell chimed, and the doors slowly slid open. As they stood in the mirrored elevator, Travers couldn't resist casting approving glances at Alicia from every conceivable angle. The view of the two of them dressed in their finest did nothing but reinforce Travers' conviction that they made a very handsome couple.

Then it was only a short walk before they reached their rooms. Travers's conscience wrestled with his swelling libido as he followed her along the corridor to her room. Her flowing, figure-hugging dress leaves nothing to his imagination.

After reaching for her key card and unlocking the door, she turned to Travers. His conscience and better judgment had won the day. Putting his hand on her upper arm, he gave her a gentle kiss on the cheek and wished her goodnight.

'Thank you for a lovely dinner, Alicia. See you for breakfast?' said Travers.

After breakfast, Downes and Travers returned to her room to discuss the plans for the day. She had received a call from Detective Roberts—a meeting with Olga Devereux had been arranged for 11 o'clock that morning. As the investigating officer, he had already been to see Chief of Staff Rackman regarding the initial report on the death of Monica Stein. Today, Downes would accompany him under the guise of a fellow officer. Armed with her dummy police identification, she asked Travers to drop her off outside Albatross House, where she waited for DI Roberts to arrive.

Once he arrived, he briefed her on the latest developments, and then they both walked up the stone steps to the glass-fronted entrance, speaking to a woman at the reception desk. She asked them to wait for a moment while Mrs Devereux's secretary came to take them upstairs.

Five minutes later, Jarvis, Devereux's personal assistant, walked across the slate-tiled floor and introduced himself before leading them towards the lift area. The lift swiftly arrived and took them up to the top floor, where Jarvis showed them into his office. He knocked on Olga Devereux's door, opened it, and announced that the police were there to see her.

Devereux, who had been sitting at her desk, stood up and walked to the open door. Roberts led the way and was first to greet Mrs Devereux, briefly holding up his ID. Alicia Downes followed him through the doorway and fleetingly waved her identification.

'Mrs Devereux? DI Roberts and Officer Downes. It's regarding the death of your employee, Monica Stein,' stated Roberts.

'Oh, I see. Then you had better come in,' said Devereux, leading them towards her desk. 'I was led to believe that she drowned.'

'Yes, seawater was found in her lungs, and there were no obvious signs of violence. However, we have received the results of a full toxicology report. Apart from seawater, the lab found minute traces of Flunitrazepam in her body,' reported Roberts.

'Excuse me?' questioned Devereux.

'Rohypnol, Mrs Devereux—commonly used as a date rape drug. In high doses, it can cause incapacity and unconsciousness. It's possible that Miss Stein's death was not accidental. We are now treating her death as suspicious. As her employer, I thought you should know,' said Roberts.

Devereux stood motionless for a moment, staring at DI Roberts, her head in her hands.

'I can't believe it. Are you suggesting that she may have been murdered? I just can't believe it,' she repeated.

'It's a possibility that we are looking into, Mrs Devereux. Our investigations are ongoing.'

As DI Roberts continued to question Mrs Devereux, Alicia Downes wandered over to one of the windows. She made a point of commenting on the view to Mrs Devereux. As she did so, she made a mental note of the layout of the suite and, in particular, likely locations where a safe might be concealed. It seemed probable that Devereux would consider her office suite on the seventh floor of the building as virtually impregnable.

'Mrs Devereux, I would like to talk to Miss Stein's line manager and her colleagues, please,' asked DI Roberts.

'Of course. I'll ask my Chief of Staff to take you down and introduce you,' said Devereux, immediately picking up her phone to call him.

'Thank you. I think that is all for the present,' said Roberts, who then turned to Downes. 'Anything you want to add?'

Alicia thought for a moment—she really wanted to elicit more information from Olga Devereux before they left her office.

'Mrs Devereux, Miss Stein worked in your accounts department, didn't she?'

'Yes, that's correct. She was a junior accountant,' answered Devereux.

'Did she deal with or have access to any sensitive information?' Downes continued.

'I wouldn't have thought so, but you will have to ask her manager for specific details,' replied Devereux.

'Albatross House is the international headquarters of both the Corporation and the Foundation, is it not?'

'Yes, it is.'

'So, you must have to deal with a great deal of extremely sensitive information, particularly on the corporate side.'

'Naturally, as would any large corporation,' retorted Devereux.

'I presume you have a safe in your office, Mrs Devereux?' asked Downes.

'Of course,' responded Devereux. 'It's on the third floor.'

Downes was sure that Devereux would not keep any potentially incriminating documents in a safe that was not under her personal control. Devereux explained that access to the main office safe was restricted to senior management and a small number of authorised staff members.

'Is it possible that someone was trying to blackmail Miss Stein into corporate espionage?' asked Downes. 'Is that the only safe, or is there another in the building?'

'Well, yes, naturally, I have one in my office here,' said Devereux, faintly nodding her head towards one of the walls on which hung a large oil painting of her parents.

'I see. And how many people have access to it or know the combination?'

'Just myself, my eldest son, Hector, and my Chief of Staff, Richard Rackman,' revealed Devereux.

'I see. And no one else?'

'No,' insisted Devereux.

Downes turned to Roberts and indicated that she had finished her line of questioning. Roberts leaned across to Mrs Devereux and extended his hand.

'Thank you, Mrs Devereux. I think that will be all for the present. I'll keep you updated with any developments, of course. Now, if I could see Miss Stein's line manager,' added Roberts.

DI Roberts and Alicia Downes walked out of Olga Devereux's office and waited with her personal assistant, Maxwell Jarvis, until Rackman arrived and escorted them down to the accounts department.

It was another two hours before Downes finally returned to the hotel. After dropping her coat and bag in her room, she knocked on Travers' door before entering. He was sitting at the desk by the open window, the sun streaming in. She flung herself onto his bed and let out a prolonged sigh.

'How did you get on?' asked Travers.

'I'll tell you one thing—she is as guilty as sin.'

'Come on, let's get a drink. I've got some news for you,' she added.

'A drink? OK, I'll grab my shades.'

They stopped at the bar to order their drinks on their way out to the patio, where they managed to find a spare table. By mid-afternoon, it was packed, and vacant seats were at a premium. A few minutes later, a waiter brought out two large glasses of Pimms with ice.

'Cheers,' said Travers.

Downes needed no second invitation and downed at least a third of her glass before pausing for breath.

'Thirsty work, spying!' said Travers. 'Well?'

'What do you know about Rohypnol?' asked Downes.

'Same as you, probably. Date rape drug, fast-acting. It has no flavour, so it can be easily slipped into someone's drink. Depending on the dose, it can either give you a feeling of euphoria or knock you out—or pretty much anything in between. Why?'

'The police found traces of it in Monica Stein's system.'

'Really? That's interesting. I wonder how it got there,' said Travers cynically.

'We spoke to her colleagues, and none of them ever saw or heard of her taking anything like that recreationally.'

'Which leaves two possibilities then, doesn't it? Both deliberate—sex and murder. Given the circumstances, it's just too coincidental to be a random sexual assault,' suggested Travers.

'So what you're suggesting is that someone drugged her, killed her, or dumped her in the harbour to shut her up. But who?' asked Downes.

'Speaking of 'who, how did your meeting with Olga Devereux go? Did she live up to your expectations?'

'Well, the good news is she does have a safe, and it's in her office—but I didn't see it. Only three people know how to open it. I must admit, she does have a certain magnetism. And she's very attractive.'

'Do you think you'll be able to open it, or do we need to get a cracksman in?' asked Travers.

'That's the sixty-four-million-dollar question. How did you get on with the building blueprints?' asked Downes.

'No problem there—they're all on my laptop. I managed, with some difficulty, to hack into their mainframe as well. We can monitor their security feeds or shut down individual cameras—or the whole lot—remotely, if necessary. Since the Foundation rents out space in the building to other charities, it would probably be a lot easier to access her suite from inside rather than try to gain entry into the building after hours,' said Travers.

'I have to give Stanley a report on tonight's operation—assuming all goes well. I'll tell him what we might have in mind. I don't think he's going to like it much, and I'm going to need some more gear. Did you have any luck with that journalist's notes?'

'Well,' said Travers, 'the solicitor and the bank didn't have any record of a safe custody request. However, I did manage to get hold of one of her publishers. He said that when Olivia Hunter last worked with him, she mentioned maintaining an account at a private storage facility where she kept some of her records. He pinged me the address. I'm going to check it out tomorrow.'

Chapter 17

Downes and Travers returned to their hotel rooms to prepare for the evening ahead. For Downes, fieldwork was the most exciting part of her job and the one that gave her the most satisfaction. For Travers, the prospect was rather more daunting. The thought of having to ingratiate himself with a woman who may have been directly or indirectly responsible for so many deaths, including his friend Lisa, and the attempt on his own life was difficult to grasp. Just how far did Stanley really expect him to go to curry favour with this woman in the hope that she might give herself away?

Travers showered, then stood for a moment, looking in the large mirror at the naked figure staring back at him and wondering what the next few hours would bring. At that moment, there was a single knock on the door before it swung open. It was Alicia. Travers scrambled for a towel to cover his lower half, much to her amusement.

'Oh, sorry, did I interrupt you?' she said with a mischievous smile.

'No, you just gave me near heart failure. I thought it was room service,' said Travers as he calmed down.

'I thought I would come and see how you scrubbed up.' Downes' eyes studied the glistening contours of Travers' body. 'I think Mrs Devereux will think all her birthdays have come at once when she sees that! See you later,' she smiled.

With that, she left the slightly red-faced Travers and closed the door behind her. Travers removed the towel from his waist, continued to dry himself, then dressed. His Armani tuxedo was undeniably impressive, even if it was a few years old. By the time he had donned the accessories, including Stanley's gold Rolex, he started to believe he might actually pull it off—or at least give a good account of himself.

Having been rattled by Downes' unexpected entrance, Travers looked in the mirror one more time before walking out of his room. Taking his duplicate key, he knocked twice before opening Alicia's door.

She was sitting in her underwear, applying her makeup. Noticing Travers in her mirror, she turned round and looked him carefully up and down. She liked what she saw.

'Very impressive. I have a feeling you are going to pull tonight.'

'If you mean it's grab-a-granny night, that's not funny,' said Travers.

'Right, got your wallet, bank cards, your new business cards, and your glowing reference from HR?' said Downes.

'Yes, all present and correct.'

'Clean underwear? Or are you going commando to save time?' she joked, making sure to make the most of Travers' obvious embarrassment.

'Do you want to check?' retorted Travers as he turned to look at something that had caught his eye lying on the bed. 'What's that? Have you adopted a stray cat?' he joked.

'So much for your powers of observation. I'm disappointed you don't recognise it—I wore it at Warren House, the first time I saw you.'

Travers wandered across, sat down on the edge of the bed, and picked up the long dark wig.

'Why the headdress?' he questioned.

'It's just part of my alter ego in case I bump into Mrs Devereux or any of her team tonight after seeing her yesterday.'

'I'll be twenty minutes, Greg.'

'Don't you have a slinky LBD to wear tonight?' asked Travers.

'I'm working—in plain sight, in case you had forgotten. We'd better take your car, Greg. It might be difficult to pick up a taxi later, especially if you are otherwise engaged. I don't want to be sitting around twiddling my thumbs all night whilst Olga Devereux is chasing you around her bedposts.'

Thirty minutes later, Downes and Travers began to drive the short distance from the Harbour Heights to Compton Acres, parking in the large car park. Before getting out of the car, she reached into her bag and produced what appeared to Travers to be a small lipstick holder. Unscrewing the bottom, two small earpieces dropped into the palm of her hand.

'Right, put this into one of your ears. It will allow me to hear your conversations. Don't forget, this is as much about networking as anything else. There will be a lot of names flying around, and yours needs to be one of them. So when you meet someone, introduce yourself, and don't forget to mention your job title. Apart from Devereux, many of her business associates and close associates will be there. If we're lucky, someone in her inner circle will hear about you and arrange an introduction. If not, you'll just have to engineer one yourself. One more thing—if you get into an awkward situation, lose the earpiece. Otherwise, just start saying, 'I beg your pardon,' and perhaps they will think you are hard of hearing.'

Downes reached into her handbag again and produced a small gold-plated Colibri cigarette lighter.

'Here, put this in your pocket. It has a tracker in it. Make sure you hang onto it. It means I will still be able to locate you if we get separated.'

Travers took the lighter, admired it briefly, and placed it in his trouser pocket.

'I presume it will still light a cigarette?' he joked.

'Don't worry, you'll still be able to enjoy a puff with Olga… afterwards, if you have any left,' laughed Downes.

'I wish you wouldn't keep saying that,' said Travers with just a hint of nervousness.

With that, Downes and Travers left the car and walked to the entrance of the famous gardens, described as one of the finest in England. The soirée was taking place in the Grand Italian Garden and the Italian Villa. As they entered the magnificent Italian Garden, it was already clear that it was going to be a very popular night, as there must have been at least a hundred finely dressed people already in attendance.

'I need to check in with the head of security. Wander about and get your bearings, and I'll see you at the foot of the steps to the villa in ten minutes.'

Travers watched as his partner, dressed immaculately in a dinner jacket and trousers, strode swiftly away from him in the direction of the villa. He walked towards one of the uniformed waiters handing out glasses of champagne and gratefully took a glass when it was offered to him.

In front of him was a long rectangular stone-clad pond surrounded by classical statues and columns, with a small temple at one end containing a statue of the god Bacchus, which seemed oddly appropriate given the quantity of champagne and fine wine that was going to be consumed during the course of the evening.

He turned around and headed back to the villa, where Downes was already waiting for him. He hadn't recognised her from a distance, with her dark wig and reflective glasses.

'What a great place for a party,' observed Travers. 'Is she here yet?'

'No. As a guest of honour, she'll probably be one of the last to arrive. I've got the itinerary and the expected guest list. It's champagne and canapés whilst everyone arrives, then there's a grand buffet served inside the villa, followed by some back-slapping, sycophantic speeches. After that, it's every man for himself till carriages at midnight,' said Downes.

'What about the guest list? Apart from Devereux, is there anyone we need to look out for?' asked Travers.

'Other than Devereux and her associates, there are the usual dignitaries and a gaggle from various civil service and government departments, along with the press corps, of course,' added Downes. 'All you have to do is circulate and look for any opportunity to make contact with Devereux or any of her cronies.'

'And what about you? Where will you be whilst I am doing all this circulating?' asked Travers.

'Watching you and listening in. You had best be on your way; I don't want to cramp your style.'

Before they parted, they heard cheering and a round of applause coming from the Villa. A number of those who had been wandering around the gardens turned and hurried back to see what the commotion was, with the probable arrival of the celebrated Olga Devereux.

'I think that's our cue. Good luck, Greg.'

Travers left Downes and joined those latecomers rushing up the steps of the Italian Villa to pay homage to the guest of honour. The room was packed, and it was impossible to get a clear sight of her, but the night was yet young. Travers backed away and made his way to a slightly less crowded spot where he could enjoy another glass of fine Champagne and clear his thoughts. He could just make out some words of welcome from the master of ceremonies before, a few moments later, the assembled audience started to make their way out of the villa again, whilst Olga Devereux enjoyed a glass of Champagne and had the chance for a quiet conversation with some of the luminaries and civic dignitaries before the buffet began.

About thirty minutes later, the MC announced the start of the buffet, and a steady flow of people again walked up the steps and into the Villa, where the buffet was arranged. An array of silver salvers spread across a dozen or more tables, each table covered by an ornately embroidered white lace tablecloth and a beautiful floral decoration, no doubt taken from the gardens themselves. Guests moved from table to table, sampling a wonderfully diverse selection of food to cater for every possible taste, before moving away to either find a table to sit at or, for many, the open space and balmy night air that the open garden offered.

Usually, Travers needed no second invitation to free food, but his mind was not on his stomach tonight. Besides, with the butterflies already in there, there was precious little room left for food, even if it was free.

He spent a few minutes looking around at the other guests stuffing their faces, presumably thinking that, having paid a hefty ticket price for the privilege of being there, they were entitled to eat as much as they could. In the far corner, Travers could see Devereux, surrounded by a cluster of middle-aged men drooling over her as they desperately vied with each other for her attention and favour. Travers walked out of the Villa and down the steps back into the Italian garden, still grasping the glass containing what remained of his Champagne. He heard footsteps behind him; a middle-aged man hurried down the steps to join him.

'It's a free-for-all in there,' the exasperated man said.

'Yes, I think I'll pop back in when it quietens down a bit. My name is Travers, Greg Travers, by the way. Are you connected with the Foundation?'

'How do you do, Greg? Ryan Jones. No, I'm a writer. I had an interview with Mrs Devereux recently for a business magazine. My publishers managed to get me a press pass for tonight's bash.'

'Really? That's interesting. I'm hoping to meet her tonight. How did it go, and what did you make of her? What's she like?' asked Travers, anxious to acquire as much insight as he could

'She's got a really interesting background, you know. Her family came across from Germany during the war. She's a real powerhouse. Her British husband, Robert Devereux, was a brilliant businessman and obviously taught her well. She's doubled the corporate empire he created, and that doesn't include the Foundation. An amazingly single-minded and driven woman,' said Jones.

'but what about her personally? What's she like?' asked Travers.

'Very confident and self-assured. She has a magnetism, an aura. You can almost touch it. It's in the air all around her. It's no wonder that she enjoys the reputation she has. When she looks you in the eye, in a certain way, you get goosebumps, and the hairs on the back of your neck go up. It's pretty erotic, if I'm honest,' said Jones.

'Wish I'd read it,' said Travers.

'It's not been published yet. They were holding it back for the Foundation anniversary.'

As the two men talked, Jones's attention was drawn to a man standing in a doorway at the Villa. Noticing Jones's preoccupation, Travers asked him what he was looking at.

'When I went for my interview with Olga Devereux in Poole, I saw someone I didn't expect to see there, a civil servant, I think, a big one, but for the life of me, I just couldn't remember his name. I've just seen him again, following Mrs Devereux into that room,' said Jones.

Travers turned and took several steps back, and looked through a French window. At the far end of the room, beyond, he could see Devereux talking to a tall man. Travers wasn't able to see his face, but he could see that he towered over his interlocutor. After a few moments, the conversation ended. Mrs Devereux left the room through another door. The man turned his head slightly as he watched her walk away. Travers spun round and re-joined the writer at the base of the steps.

'That's Sir Giles Mulholland. He's a very senior official at the Treasury. I wonder what he was doing there?' confirmed Travers.

'Of course it is! It's been really annoying me,' said Jones. 'It seems to be thinning out a bit in there. I think I'll see if they have anything left. Nice to meet you, Greg,' said Jones as he started his short journey back up the steps into the villa.

'Yes, you too.'

Thirty minutes later, the buffet was drawing to a close. Travers stood by the doorway while the Minister for Overseas Development eulogised about the charitable achievements of Olga Devereux and the Albatross Foundation. Travers mused and thought, *If only they knew what she was really like.*

With the official meet and greet over, the assembled audience dispersed, and, as Alicia had put it, it was every man for himself now. Easy listening piped music was now the order of the day as guests headed to the bars and kept the stewards fully occupied. Travers, armed with a fresh glass of Champagne, continued to circulate amongst the other guests, offering his name and job title to anyone and everyone that he bumped into.

As he walked along one side of the large ornamental pond, he caught sight of Mrs Devereux at the far end of the garden, talking to an enthusiastic young couple of admirers. A few minutes later, they parted. This was his chance. Travers stiffened his back, raised his head, and hoped that his nerve didn't desert him when he needed it most.

He walked as nonchalantly as he could towards Mrs Devereux, who was dressed in an alluring full-length black satin gown, with three-quarter sleeves and a square top that barely covered her fulsome breasts. Her dark hair falling loosely on her shoulders.

'Mrs Devereux, my name is Travers, Greg Travers. May I offer my congratulations? It's been a lovely evening and richly deserved.'

'Thank you, Mr Travers. I don't think we have met, have we?' said Devereux.

'No, I'm based in London. I'm only here for a few days,' said Travers.

'London? What do you do, Mr Travers?'

'I'm with the Government, a Senior Procurement Officer in Whitehall,' Travers, hoped that Devereux would be sufficiently impressed by this fact alone to extend the conversation.

'Procurement Officer, really? How interesting,' she said, already physically attracted to the tall, ruggedly handsome man now standing in front of her. 'You must tell me more. Come, let's get some more champagne. I've met a number of Whitehall officials through the Foundation, but they are usually pot-bellied, balding men in their sixties. You, however, are different – rather young for such a responsible position,' said Devereux, as she looked him up and down.

'I was an early riser,' said Travers, looking directly into Devereux's lustrous eyes and testing out her boundaries. Would she flirt with him?

'I like a man who rises early,' she offered tantalisingly, as she casually touched his hand and looked into his eyes.

Travers was in business. He could sense that she was physically attracted to him.

'As you know, the Foundation is a huge worldwide organisation. I've found it's often mutually beneficial to work very closely with officials, to cut through some of the red tape,' said Devereux.

'I can imagine. It must be very frustrating for a woman as confident and successful as you to be tied up with red tape… or anything else for that matter,' added Travers with perfect timing. 'Can I get you some more champagne, Mrs Devereux?'

'Thank you. I think I will. How long have you been a civil servant?'

Travers found it surprisingly easy to converse with Devereux, who was adept at both making polite conversation and drawing confidences from complete strangers. He had to remind himself that she was the number one suspect in a murder investigation. He also had to remember Stanley's instructions to 'ingratiate' himself with her. However, she seemed as keen as he was to continue the conversation. To that end, Travers suggested that they meet up next time she was in London – an offer that seemed to find a great deal of favour.

'I should like that. Perhaps you have a business card I could have, Mr Travers?'

Travers reached inside his jacket for his wallet and pulled out his new business cards. As he opened it, he ensured – as he had practised in his hotel room – that the letter from HR, which Stanley had given him, dropped out onto the floor in front of Devereux. She resisted the urge to open it and instead simply smiled at her young admirer as she returned it.

'A love letter?' commented the inquisitive Devereux, as she picked up the paper and handed it back to Travers.

The door had been opened; all he had to do now was hold his nerve and have the courage to walk through it.

'I wish it were. Unfortunately, it's a letter I received from my management today. My wife died a few months ago, and I got into some bad habits and quite a bit of debt. They are not very happy about it,' said Travers.

'I'm sorry to hear that,' replied Devereux, who stretched out her hand, reassuringly taking hold of Travers' hand while at the same time studying him, as a cat might study a mouse before pouncing on it and sinking its teeth into the rodent's neck.

'I'm sorry, Mrs Devereux. It was wrong of me; I shouldn't have mentioned it. It must be all the champagne that's gone to my head.'

'Think nothing of it. We all go through difficult periods in our lives. I would hate to think that your life and career might be blighted by such a tragedy. Would you excuse me for a moment? I must go and freshen up. I'll be back in a few minutes,' said Devereux.

Mrs Devereux rose from her chair and walked around the pond, acknowledging well-wishers before turning and briskly continuing towards her destination. As she reached the building, she paused to speak to her Chief of Staff, who had been watching the encounter from the steps. During the conversation, he told her that he had witnessed

Travers peering through the window during Olga's private meeting with Sir Giles earlier and would probably have recognised him. Olga's relaxed expression changed to one of concern as Rackman gave her the news. Mulholland's attendance at the event had been unexpected and certainly not something that Olga wanted to be made public. She handed him Travers' business card.

'He says he is a procurement officer for the Government. Check him out, Richard. Thoroughly. Find out everything you can about him, including his financial status. If he does have access to government funding, he might prove to be very useful. I think some initial cultivation is called for over some more champagne,' said Devereux, as she walked past him to the nearby bathroom.

As Travers sat waiting for Mrs Devereux to return, Downes walked around the ornamental pond towards him.

'Well done, Greg, that's fantastic.'

'Thanks. Did you hear that conversation I had with the writer?' said Travers.

'Yes, I did. I think Stanley is going to be very interested in that. What was Sir Giles Mulholland doing in Devereux's office anyway? He isn't on tonight's guest list either. You know he suspects someone in the Treasury tipped off McKenzie and Hunt about Constable. I wonder what he'll make of that.'

'What do I do when Devereux comes back? How far do I play along?' asked Travers.

'All the way. Let her call the shots. You heard what Stanley said; it's vital that we find out what she is up to. This is what working undercover is all about. She now knows you are in debt and possibly vulnerable. She'll target you for either blackmail or bribery. Suck it up, Greg, just close your eyes and think of England. Don't forget, if you need to, dump the earpiece. You don't want to be caught with that. I'd better be off. Good luck.'

With that, Downes walked away slowly, exchanging a few words with another guest as she passed them. Meanwhile, Travers looked around and tried to calm his rapid breathing. In the distance, he could see Olga Devereux returning, now with a white shawl covering her shoulders. She stopped a couple of times to chat with other guests before continuing towards him. Travers stood up to greet her as she re-joined him and took her seat next to him.

'I thought you might need this,' she said, handing another glass of champagne to him.

'Thank you, that's very kind of you. I don't think I'll be able to drive back to my hotel tonight at this rate. I'm going to have to find a taxi,' said Travers pointedly.

'Oh, I think we can do better than that. I don't think there are enough taxis around to cater for everyone. I'll drop you off; it's no trouble. Anyway, now that that is sorted, tell me, what does a Procurement Officer actually do?'

This was going to be awkward. The background that Stanley had given him about his cover was limited, to say the least. Travers was going to have to wing it and change the subject as quickly as he could without looking as though he was being evasive or trying to dodge the question.

Travers and Olga Devereux continued their animated conversation for the next twenty minutes. Perhaps it was the insidious effects of the constant flow of champagne starting to affect him, but Devereux's seductive company was intoxicating. She was a very tactile woman, frequently touching his hand as she spoke to him. Travers could feel the hairs on the back of his neck rise up. His erogenous zones were on red alert as he looked into her deep blue eyes.

The spell was momentarily broken when Devereux's Chief of Staff interrupted them to advise her that the Minister for Overseas Development was about to leave.

'I'm sorry, Mr Travers, will you excuse me for a moment whilst I pay my respects to the Minister? We'll continue our discussion when I come back.'

Travers rose to his feet and watched as Devereux, accompanied by Rackman, left and walked back towards the Villa, where the Government Minister and his party waited to take their leave. Within 10 minutes, Olga returned, behind her a waiter carrying an ice bucket and a fresh bottle of champagne.

Alicia Downes had maintained a discreet distance as she carefully observed Travers and Devereux's interaction. Thanks to the earwig still in his ear, she was able to hear both sides of the ongoing conversation and was relieved at how well it had gone thus far. She walked down the steps from the Villa and around the ornamental pond, now illuminated by flaming torchlight. There were still a sizeable number of people either sitting at outside tables or milling about, so she was able to wander around without attracting undue attention. She had noticed in recent exchanges that Travers was starting to slur his words a little, no doubt as a result of all the champagne Devereux was encouraging him to drink. Downes walked around behind her and across Travers' line. He was definitely showing signs of alcohol fatigue. As she caught his eye, she tapped her ear and gestured that it was time to remove his earpiece, while he still had the wherewithal.

Thirty minutes later, Devereux signalled Rackman, who had taken closer order after she had re-joined Travers, with a wave of her hand. He called to one of the stewards and asked him to have her car brought to the door and to advise her son Hector that she was shortly leaving the event.

'Richard, look after Mr Travers. I need to go and thank our host and make my apologies before we leave.'

Devereux then rose again from her chair, leaving Travers, as she made her way to the Villa. For him, it was a job nearly done, albeit at the cost of consuming an inordinate amount of champagne. True, his fingers were tingling, and he was feeling mildly intoxicated, but it had gone better than he had expected. There was no denying the potency of her seductive personality, and he had to constantly remind himself that she was the subject of a murder investigation. However, with Charles Stanley's words still ringing in his ears, Travers had accepted Olga's invitation to continue their discourse in her apartment in Albatross House.

Travers and Devereux walked slowly back through the Italian garden to the entrance where her limousine was waiting. Moments later, it pulled away. Downes, who had followed the couple, ran to the car park and swiftly into Greg's BMW. She activated the onboard tracking app on her mobile phone, which immediately picked up the homing signal from the tracker she had given to Travers. Devereux was heading for Poole.

Ten minutes later, the Devereux limousine pulled into the front car park of Albatross House. The group walked up the wide stone steps and through the main entrance. Passing through the turnstiles, Olga Devereux called a lift and from there to her private suite adjoining her office on the seventh floor.

'How are you feeling?' she asked as she helped him walk across the floor of her suite.

'A bit groggy, actually. It must have been all that champagne. I'm sorry if I have inconvenienced you.'

'Not at all. I think we have a lot to talk about. I'd like to help you. So I thought it would be much better to continue our chat in private, away from prying eyes,' suggested Devereux.

'I, too, was devastated when my husband passed away, so I understand how you must have felt when your wife died. But there is no reason why you have to lose your career over this. Everyone needs help sometimes. All it takes is money and a change in perspective,' said Devereux.

'Perspective? I'm not sure I follow you, Mrs Devereux,' said Travers, who was all too aware of where the conversation was going. He just hoped he would be able to maintain the façade.

'Please, call me Olga. I think we have a lot to offer each other. You are a young man with ambition, but also a taste for the finer things in life. Expensive clothes, expensive watches, that doesn't come cheap. They are not mutually exclusive, though. I am in a position to help you. I have worldwide corporate interests as well as the charity work done by the Foundation. I employ thousands of people. You are in a position to influence Government contracts worth hundreds of millions. There is no reason why we can't help each other. For a start, I could clear all your debts; it would mean a clean slate for you.'

'What about you, Olga? What would you expect from me in return?'

Devereux looked into Travers' glazed eyes as she moved her hand on his knee.

'Shall we discuss that later?' she said, as she began to slide her hand slowly along his thigh to the centre of his groin, making him flinch nervously. She untied and removed Travers' bow tie and began unbuttoning his shirt.

'I think you would be more comfortable if you took your jacket off.'

Despite the increasing effect of the evening's alcohol, Travers had to fight his instincts to resist her advances, remembering Alicia's instructions to let Devereux call the shots and submit to whatever she wanted. He would just have to 'suck it up,' as Alicia had put it.

Soon, Travers had been divested of both his jacket and shirt as Devereux's relentless fingers caressed his bare chest, toying with the dark hair as her lips caressed his nipples. For Travers, the line between awkward embarrassment and erotic pleasure was beginning to blur with every stroke of her hand. She kissed him several times on the neck and lips before probing the inside of his mouth with her snake-like tongue. With their lips passionately locked together, her right hand slowly ran down his chest as far as his waistband and lay there momentarily before disappearing beneath his trousers. A few moments later, Mrs Devereux's hands had unfastened Travers' belt and trousers and pulled them down as far as his knees.

'An early riser indeed, Greg, very impressive,' said Devereux, who pulled her satin gown up around her waist, swung her right leg over Travers, and planted herself on his lap.

After a few seconds of manoeuvring, she was fully impaled and began moving her body slowly up and down rhythmically, with both hands resting on Travers' chest. Travers' hands grasped Devereux around her slim waist. As the intensity of the moment increased, his hands wandered across the folds of her satin dress until he reached her stocking-covered thighs and the bare flesh above them. As her pace quickened, she ground herself down onto Travers with ever greater force. He had long since given up any thoughts of closing his eyes and thinking of England, as beads of perspiration began to trickle down his temple. Travers' heart rate surged, and his muscles tightened as his body raced towards an inexorable climax. The bare-chested and now satisfied Devereux sank onto Travers' chest with her arms around his neck. He had submitted to Olga Devereux's physical excesses under duress for duty's sake, but now he had been carried along by a raging torrent of sexual ecstasy provided by this formidable force of nature. A woman old enough to be his mother, alluring and undeniably seductive, highly intelligent, confident, rich, powerful, and dangerous – very, very dangerous.

Alicia Downes sat in Greg's car less than a hundred yards away from Albatross House. She could see the building lights on the seventh floor, which had been on for over two hours since she arrived, suddenly go out. She reached into her handbag for her monocular and focused on the building entrance. After twenty minutes, there was still no sign of Travers. There was nothing to do but wait for news or instructions.

She had rung Stanley as soon as she arrived at Albatross HQ and updated him with the news about Sir Giles Mulholland and his potential connection with Olga Devereux. He was delighted when she told him that Travers had left the black-tie event with Mrs Devereux and returned to Albatross House with her.

Chapter 18

It had been a very long night for Alicia Downes. She had waited and watched the seventh-floor lights of Albatross House go on and remain on for over two hours. When they went off, Downes had hoped that Travers would emerge or contact her. Stanley had told her to wait and watch. Her instincts told her that he was all right; Devereux had no reason to harm him. If he had held his nerve and managed to maintain his cover, she had every reason to cultivate a relationship with him for her own advantage. Yet she was still worried. Travers was an analyst. He was not used to the lies and deception that had to be second nature to someone who often spent their time infiltrating criminal organisations, living a double life, where the slightest slip could result in exposure and possibly death. When he didn't appear, she contacted Stanley again. This time, she was instructed to return to the hotel and wait. Despite reservations, she reluctantly complied with Stanley's order.

She had barely slept last night, and as the morning light crossed her pillows, she buried her head in the soft white Egyptian cotton, in a desperate attempt to avoid nature's wake-up call. If only she could shut down her brain as easily as she could shut her eyes. There was a knock on her door. Downes had no idea what time it was. She hadn't returned to the hotel until the early hours. She couldn't remember if she had put out the Do Not Disturb sign on her door, but she just wished they would go away. There was a second knock. This time, she reluctantly got out of her bed, put on the white towelling hotel dressing gown, and walked slowly to the door, opening it, preparing to tell the room service staff to come back later.

'Greg!' said an elated Downes, unable to conceal her relief at seeing him back. 'Where have you been? I've been so worried about you.'

'Fieldwork?! Whatever they're paying you, Alicia, it isn't enough,' said Travers as he brushed past her and sat on her bed.

Before last night's assignment, she had made a point of downplaying his apprehension and never missed a chance to poke fun at his embarrassment at the approaching liaison. She knew he was anxious, and with the investigation's body count mounting, it was a risky encounter for someone with no experience. Despite repeatedly attempting to justify to herself that everything would be all right, she couldn't stop worrying, particularly when she watched Travers and Devereux leave the function together last night. At least now her troubled and sleepless night had been rewarded by his safe return.

'Why didn't you ring me?' griped Alicia, as an anxious mother would with an overdue child.

'Sorry, I must have lost my phone during the night,' said Travers.

'You look shattered. Want some tea?'

'Tea? A lobotomy and some DDT would probably be more useful.'

'What happened?'

'You mean apart from spending the night tied up by a raging nymphomaniac?' said Travers.

'You mean you actually had sex with her last night?'

'Close your eyes and think of England. Let her call the shots, I believe you said.'

'Well yes, but …' she began, before being quickly interrupted by Travers.

'Well yes, no buts. I followed your instructions, I played along, consumed enough champagne to sink an aircraft carrier, and then had my clothes ripped off and had our principal suspect treat me like some kind of sex doll. Apart from that…'

Travers' colourful commentary was interrupted by Downes, who, no longer able to contain herself, burst out laughing. Born as much out of her own relief that the only misfortune he really suffered was wear and tear from a middle-aged nympho, a few missing buttons, a dry cleaning bill for his suit, and the knowledge that the episode would soon be the talk of the department.

'I'm sorry, Greg. If it's any consolation, I've been really worried. Apart from getting your leg over, what did you find out? Anything new? Anything that could help us?'

'I think she believed my story. She proposed to put me on her payroll and bail me out if I put a few sizeable government contracts her way. She wants to see me again. I don't know if that's to discuss business or just to firm up our relationship,' commented Travers sardonically.

'If your relationship gets any firmer, you'll need hospital treatment,' remarked Downes sarcastically.

'Where are you meeting?' asked Downes.

'She wanted another meeting in her suite, but I said I was busy tonight.'

'Tut tut, can't keep up with a woman twice your age, Greg? There's a chemist up the road if you need some help.'

'Very funny. Why don't you go then?'

'In case you hadn't noticed, I bat for the other side.'

'Frankly, I don't think that would make any difference to her,' said Travers. 'She suggested meeting at the Haven Hotel, by the Ferry. I said I would need to confirm the date later,' he continued.

'If it's in a public place you'd better wear a wire; at least you'll probably be keeping your close on, the more information we have, the better,' said Downes.

'What did Stanley have to say about Giles Mulholland?' asked Travers.

'The investigation is ongoing with McKenzie and Hunt. I'm pretty sure that Stanley wants to get someone else on the inside. He was talking about trying to flush out the traitor with a bogus email about another Trojan Horse exercise on McKenzie and Hunt. After last night, though, he's focused on Sir Giles. He's spoken to the Home Secretary; they are going to tap his phone and monitor all his electronic communications. He'll be given plenty of rope. It's only a matter of time before he trips himself up, and we'll be waiting,' said Downes.

'In the absence of something stronger, I'll have that tea, please. Alicia, do you mind if I use your bath? I feel like I need a good hot soak after last night, and to be honest, I'm still feeling a bit shaky.'

'Sure, I'll go and run it,' said Downes.

The small tea service kettle came to the boil, and Alicia proceeded to make two cups of tea, which she brought back to the bed.

'Thanks, Alicia,' said Travers, as he took the cup and saucer of hot tea from Alicia and placed it on the right-hand bedside table.

'What was it like last night, really?'

'Initially, I was pretty nervous, especially when I saw Olga Devereux on her own, just talking to a young couple. I knew this was the opportunity, and perhaps the only opportunity I would get, and I had to act—physically walk up to her and initiate a conversation, pretending to be somebody else, knowing who and what she was. The adrenaline rush was massive.'

'I followed you to Albatross House and waited there for several hours, but you didn't come out again.'

'She started asking me questions about my job and lifestyle and offering to clear my debts. She made it very clear that if I joined her organisation, I could pretty much name my price. Stanley was right. Once she knew what I had to offer, she was all over me.'

'Sounds like she bought it,' said Downes. 'What happened then?'

'What do you mean, then?'

'Greg, I need to debrief you for my report. Stanley is going to want to know everything.'

'Debriefed? I think one debriefing is enough for me right now. Although to be fair, she was rather more demanding about it,' said Travers, with a hint of irony.

'Oh, I see. Well, I don't think we need to go into the 'ins and outs' of all that.'

'Just as well,' said Travers.

'Greg, you've done a great job. It's not easy out there in the field on your own.'

Travers felt better after a hot soak and with a full English breakfast inside him. They sat out on the patio after breakfast. The tranquillity was broken when Downes's phone rang. It was Charles Stanley.

'Good morning, sir.'

'Good morning, Alicia. Has Don Juan recovered from his adventures last night?' asked Stanley quizzically.

'Yes, sir, I think so,' said Downes. 'Although he's been pretty sheepish about it.'

'No, sir,' called out Travers across the table. 'I'm knackered. With respect, you have no idea how hard it was. I was up half the night ingratiating myself with that woman.'

'Yes, so I hear, Greg. Still, you've done a grand job,' said Stanley. 'I appreciate the sacrifice.'

'Listen, Greg, I've had a call from your credit card company. Someone has run a credit check on you this morning. We are trying to trace the originator, but the important thing is they are checking out your cover. Your bank has been given instructions to cooperate with anyone posing as an authorised person or company requesting information on you. We don't want to make it too hard for Devereux or her associates to put a noose around their necks. When you meet her again, it's essential that you maintain your cover and go along with anything she suggests, however distasteful it seems.'

'Yes, sir, I'll try to remember that, and thank you for the vote of confidence,' said Travers reluctantly.

Downes ended the call, took a sip of her black coffee, and turned to Travers.

'By the way, there's a courier on the way with a replacement phone for you.'

'Thanks, Alicia. I don't know how I lost it, but if someone is checking my accounts, they must have lifted my wallet when I was in Devereux's suite,' said Travers.

'Well, if they took your phone too, they're going to be very disappointed.'

'Why's that?' asked Travers.

'Because it's a company smartphone. We use them when we are working in the field. If we're caught or the phone gets lost, there's a programme installed which fries the circuits and wipes the memory if anyone unauthorised tries to access it,' said Downes.

Detective Chief Inspector Deery muttered to himself as the daily briefing concluded at New Scotland Yard. He had been in a bad mood ever since Nikolay Petrov, his one strong lead and prime suspect in the Constable case, was assassinated right under his nose by a woman posing as his legal representative. His team had been scrutinising all the CCTV footage they could find, both within the station and the surrounding streets. A fuzzy video had shown the woman, who had called herself Anabela Rodrigues, leaving the Police Station and walking along a side road before getting into the passenger seat of a large dark 4x4. After a few minutes, it drove off.

Deery's mood had improved momentarily when traffic cameras picked up the car driving out of London heading south before losing it. Now, at last, some good news. Hampshire Police had found the car, or at least what was left of it, outside a small village in the New Forest.

'Well, what's the news on the car?' asked the Chief Inspector.

'Burnt to a crisp, plates gone, and the VIN number under the bonnet has been chiselled off,' said the Detective.

'The plates were stolen. Now, I presume that smile you're wearing means you do have some good news for me,' said Deery.

'How did you guess, boss? They missed the VIN under the door panel. We've been onto the DVLA, the car's registered to a Milton Rex, criminal enforcer, spent ten years in Belmarsh for manslaughter.'

'Where is this character now?' asked the Chief Inspector.

'Steady, boss, you've had the good news.'

Deery growled and muttered under his breath in dismay, then called out to his team.

'Listen up, everyone. Milton Rex, I want him, I want his friends, if he has any, and his known associates, and I want him found PDQ! His picture and details are on file, and if he has a good-looking girlfriend who gets off pretending to be a solicitor, I want her too. Contact the Dorset Police, we'll start with his last known address,' said Inspector Deery.

Less than an hour had passed before Detective Inspector Roberts called from Poole with the news that Deery had hoped for. Rex had been spotted with a young woman close to his last confirmed address near the harbour. Deery had requested the Detective detain Rex and his girlfriend on suspicion of murder until he arrived to question him personally. Having been humiliated once by losing a key prisoner in custody, the Chief Inspector was determined not to make the same mistake again. Once the locals had Rex in custody, he would make the two-hour-plus trip to Poole.

An hour later, Detective Roberts rang from Poole. Milton Rex had been arrested, although his girlfriend wasn't with him at the time and was still at large. Deery grabbed his trench coat and together with his colleague Detective Williams, walked briskly out of the building to his car to begin the journey to the south coast town a hundred miles away. The trip passed without incident or delay, and it was a relaxed but determined Detective Inspector who walked into the local Police Station, introduced himself to the desk sergeant, and asked to speak to Detective Inspector Roberts, who emerged from a back office following a call from the duty sergeant.

'Good morning, DI Roberts. Did he give you any trouble?' asked Inspector Deery.

'No, sir, I think we caught him by surprise. I'm afraid his girlfriend wasn't with him when we picked him up,' replied Roberts.

'Shit! Has he phoned anyone yet?'

'Yes, he did make a phone call, but it wasn't to a solicitor,' said Roberts.

'So, he hasn't asked for legal representation then?' asked Deery.

'No, sir, not yet.'

'I want to talk to him, so you'd better get the Station Duty Solicitor in here. The last thing I want is for some liberal leftie lawyer to march in here waving the Human Rights Act and getting the bastard off on a technicality before I've had the chance to ring the truth out of him or ring his neck, whichever comes first. Right, let's see him,' said Detective Chief Inspector.

Five minutes later, Deery and DI Roberts entered the interview room. Already seated were Milton Rex and, beside him, the Police Station Duty Solicitor. Having started the interview recorder, the Chief Inspector introduced himself and Roberts.

'Mr Rex, I believe you own a black 4x4 electric Mercedes?' asked Deery.

Rex stared blankly back at the Inspector without answering the question.

'You needn't deny it, we know you do. We found it in a country layby, burnt out, with the plates removed. Any comment?'

Rex turned to his legal counsel for advice before replying.

'No comment.'

'Does anyone else have access to your car, Mr Rex?' asked Deery.

'No comment.'

'Your girlfriend, for instance?' asked Deery. 'Mr Rex, your car was used during the murder of a man in police custody in Southwark a few days ago. We suspect it was also used in a hit and run in Wimbledon Village a week ago. You've quite a record, recently released from HMP Belmarsh after spending ten years at her late Majesty's pleasure. If you don't co-operate, you'll soon be booking in again, mate. After the hit-and-run, the house of the victim was ransacked, and a police officer there had his throat cut. If your car is linked to all three incidents, well, you can see how this looks. Now, if you help us, perhaps we can help you. Which is probably more than can be said for the organisation you're working for. Let's go back to Southwark, shall we? Who was the woman with you? Was it your girlfriend?' asked Inspector Deery.

'No comment,' mumbled Rex.

The exasperated Chief Inspector pushed his chair aside and stood up, taking a moment to allow his rising frustration to subside before returning to the question Rex further.

'Mr Rex, a woman got out of your car, walked into the police station posing as a solicitor, and passed a substance to her client who thought she was there to help him. She wasn't, and she didn't. It was cyanide. She then got back into the passenger seat of your car, which then drove away. If the people you're working for send someone to help you, my advice would be to tell them to piss off,' said Deery. 'Now, are you going to cooperate with us or take your chances with them?'

'No comment,' said an increasingly surly Rex.

'No comment, is that really the best you can do? Rex, these people don't care about you. If you're lucky, you'll go to jail; if not, you'll end up in a body bag or worse, and you won't get a choice. Is that really what you want?' added an infuriated Deery.

The Chief Inspector turned to the voice recorder by the desk.

'Interview terminated at 11:35.'

Deery and Roberts left their seats and walked out of the interview room. Rex had been completely uncooperative, but with his record, it was only a matter of time.

'We need the girlfriend,' said Inspector Deery.

'We've got the place staked out, sir. As soon as she comes back, we'll bag her.'

'Have you got a picture of her, Inspector?'

'We found one in his wallet; we're presuming it's her.'

'Let's have a look at it,' said Deery as he reached into his pocket for the black-and-white image of Rodrigues taken from the Southwark Police Station CCTV.

On reaching his desk, Roberts thumbed through his file for the photograph of the young woman and handed it to Deery for comparison.

Holding the two images side by side, he studied the two faces carefully. The girl in Roberts's photograph had shortish dark hair, while his had long blonde wavy locks, but despite the shortcomings of the CCTV, he thought the similarities of the two faces and general build warranted the conclusion that they were the same woman.

'Alright, DI Roberts, you say you have Rex's house under surveillance?'

'Yes, sir. If she puts in an appearance, we'll arrest her. We've circulated her picture.'

'Can I use your phone, Inspector?' asked Deery.

With a nod from DI Roberts, he picked up the Inspector's landline telephone in one hand and checked for a number in the contacts from his mobile. His finger stopped at 'S.' He selected the desired name and began dialling. Four rings later, the familiar voice of Charles Stanley answered.

'Good afternoon, Charles. It's Deery here.'

'Hello, John, how are you?' replied Stanley.

'I'm fine, thanks. I have some interesting news for you on the Constable case. We've made an arrest— the man involved in the murder of Nikolay Petrov. After the killing, they made off in their car before torching it in Hampshire. It's a large black electric 4x4 Merc; does that ring any bells?'

'Sounds like the one that tried to flatten Greg Travers, John.'

'It's in a bit of a state, but we've got forensics crawling all over it. It's definitely the one used in the Southwark killing and may well be the same one used in the hit and run with Travers. At the moment, the owner, Milton Rex, is not commenting. After the events in London, he knows he's living on borrowed time. The local police are still trying to trace the woman he was with. I thought you'd like to know,' added the Chief Inspector.

'Where did you pick Rex up, John?'

'Poole.'

'Poole? You can tell Travers yourself. He and Alicia Downes are down in Sandbanks now working on the case. I'll text you their contact numbers; I'm sure they'd like to see you,' said Stanley. 'If you get anything further out of Rex, please let me know.'

'Will do, Charles, I'll be in touch,' added Deery as he closed the call.

An hour later, DCI Deery was enjoying a drink at the Haven Hotel with Greg Travers and Alicia Downes. After the aggravation of the Rex interview, it was good to unwind, at least briefly. It was the Chief Inspector's first visit to the area, but if the first impressions were anything to go by, it wouldn't be his last.

'This is wonderful; I could just sit here for hours watching the world go by,' said Londoner.

'I understand from Charles Stanley that you may have arrested the man who tried to run me over,' said Travers.

'It's not definite yet, but we know Petrov killed your friend Lisa Scott at her house and my colleague, Detective Rogers, at your house. You described the car that tried to kill you as a large black electric 4x4. Milton Rex, who is currently resting in a police cell here, drives, or I should say drove, a large black electric 4x4, and he was driving it in London when his accomplice murdered Petrov. I'm confident there is a connection there. Once we pick up his girlfriend, I think they will be easier to break, and one of them will talk. How are things at your end of the puzzle?' asked the detective.

Downes caught the detective's eye, then gave an obvious, knowing look toward Travers.

'Greg's been busy working undercover, Chief Inspector, or perhaps I should say under the covers.'

The detective looked quizzically at Downes, assuming that a fuller explanation was imminent.

'We attended a local black-tie event last night in honour of Olga Devereux and her charity work. Stanley got Greg to pose as a vulnerable government official and ingratiate himself with Mrs

Devereux. It's fair to say that he took the job of ingratiating to a whole new level, wouldn't you say, Greg?' said Downes as she smiled at Travers.

'Alicia, I'm sure John doesn't want to hear all the gory details,' said a slightly embarrassed Travers.

'You mean you and Olga…' Deery, could now barely contain his amusement as he smiled back at Downes.

'Can we change the subject here?' pleaded Travers.

'What's your next move, then, apart from furthering your flourishing undercover experience with Mrs Devereux?' asked Deery.

'Stanley confirmed that someone has been doing background checks on my story. Assuming it holds up, the next move is Devereux's, and Alicia plans to break into Devereux's safe in her suite in Albatross House,' said Travers.

'Well, one of us needs to come up with something, and fast, if we are going to crack this case,' said Deery. 'Let me know how your lunch date goes, Greg, and do try and stay out of trouble this time.'

'At least it's a public place, Greg, you should be safe,' laughed Downes.

The Inspector's mobile phone interrupted the laughter.

'DCI Deery.'

'Chief Inspector, it's DI Roberts here. We have spotted Rex's girlfriend heading for his house.'

'Right, I'm on my way,' said the Inspector.

Deery paced nervously around the operations room like an expectant father as they waited for news of the arrest of Rex's accomplice. She had made a proper monkey out of him, and it was payback time. He walked towards one of the duty officers.

'Any news yet?'

'No, sir, not yet.'

'Do we know where she is now?' asked the Chief Inspector.

'Heading towards Rex's house in Studland, sir. An unmarked car spotted her coming out of a pub with an unidentified man. They separated, and she drove off in a red Ferrari 430 Spider Convertible. The surveillance team is aware and on the lookout for her.'

'Well, that shouldn't be hard to spot,' said Deery. 'Did they get a look at the plates?'

'Yes, sir, the car is registered to Penelope Vasilakis, a Greek national.'

The Ferrari pulled up outside the detached house in Studland, and the young woman, dressed in pale blue jeans and a white T-shirt, got out and started walking the short distance towards the house. As she reached the gate, the two detectives, who had been keeping Milton Rex's house under observation, got out of their unmarked police car and walked towards the suspect.

'Excuse me, miss. May we have a word?'

The woman stopped and turned to see who had spoken to her.

'Miss Vasilakis?' said one of the detectives.

'Who are you?' she replied.

The detective held up his identity card, then stretched out his hand towards the woman's arm.

'Would you come with us, please?'

'Why, what is this about?' she replied.

'Miss Penelope Vasilakis, we have a warrant for your arrest on suspicion of murder,' the detective said.

'Murder! That's crazy!'

'You have the right to remain silent, but it may harm your...'

The detective had barely started to read Vasilakis her legal rights when she produced a small cylindrical object from her bag and, without warning, discharged pepper spray into his face. He recoiled in agonising pain as his eyes and face suffered the full effects of the burning sensation of the Oleoresin Capsicum. As the detective doubled over into the arms of his colleague, Vasilakis turned and ran to her nearby car, speeding away into the distance. The unaffected detective immediately contacted the control room for medical assistance and provided the team with an update on the Greek woman's escape. Roberts and Deery looked at each other, dismayed that, yet again, she had slipped through their fingers.

'Roberts, can we get a chopper over there? We've got to stop her getting away. If we lose her now, we might not get another chance.'

Roberts picked up the phone and spoke to his superior for the necessary authority.

'The NPAS Operations Centre at Wakefield will dispatch one from Bournemouth International Airport,' said Roberts.

'Do you have any local units in the area?' asked Deery.

'Yes, they are closing in on her last known position, but with a car like that, I'm sure she will dump it as soon as she can and steal something less conspicuous,' said Roberts.

They scarcely had time to lament their lack of good fortune when an urgent call came over the radio. A regular police patrol vehicle had spotted the Ferrari heading southwest in the general direction of Lulworth and was in pursuit.

'They'll never catch it, not a Ferrari,' said Deery.

'She's not on a motorway now, sir. These are small country roads. Besides, she might do us all a favour and wrap it around a tree,' said Roberts.

Word soon came through that the police helicopter had been dispatched from Bournemouth and was en route to the Isle of Purbeck. It would be there in a matter of minutes. With air support, a pursuing car, and others joining the chase to intercept Vasilakis, there was now every chance of apprehending her before she had the chance to ditch a car that would stand out like a scarlet Belisha beacon.

Penelope Vasilakis fought desperately to control the powerful car as it sped around the tight corners of the Purbecks' minor country roads. She had seen the police car in her rear-view mirror in between the twists and turns of the narrow roads but had not seen it now for some time and believed she had outrun it. Then, looking over her driver's window, she saw the police helicopter, some distance away at this moment—it hadn't found her yet. She slowed down as she passed through a stretch of tree-lined road, hoping that the thick canopy would conceal her presence from the police's roving eye in the sky.

The helicopter continued moving forward ahead of her without hovering, but as she welcomed the fact that it had not yet detected her, less welcome was the sight of the pursuing police car, its flashing lights now occupying a place in her rear-view mirror. She slammed her foot down on the accelerator. The wheel-spinning car shot forward and lurched to the left as Vasilakis took a sharp turn, the rear of the car swinging wildly to the right, almost into a ditch as she frantically turned the wheel to correct the spinning vehicle before she completely lost control. She had not lost the pursuing car, though, which had gained ground since her rear end wobbled. She had to get clear before the helicopter picked her up, and could then guide other police units to intercept her.

The V8 engine screamed as the rev counter went into the red. Time was running out; the flashing lights behind her were getting brighter in the mirror. She turned again onto another road, not one that she was familiar with. The road climbed along a fenced embankment, her speed over 80 miles an hour and climbing as she pushed herself to the limit and beyond. She took a brief look in her rear-view mirror, then, seemingly out of nowhere, the police helicopter appeared directly in front of her. Instinctively, she thrust her foot hard down on the brakes. They screamed like wounded banshees. The car whirled like a Catherine wheel, spinning across the road and hurling the unrestrained woman out of the car, which then plunged down the embankment before crashing into a tree and exploding.

A few moments later, the police car arrived on the scene. The officers rushed out of their car and found Vasilakis impaled on the iron railings that bordered the roadside, her body suspended several feet above the ground. Three iron posts transfixing her lifeless corpse. Her blood streamed down the length of the bars and pooled on the ground at the bases of the heavily rusted metal rods. Her arms were outstretched, her face still beautiful, gazing down at the ground with her eyes wide open, staring, as though in shock that her life was about to come to such an abrupt and violent end. It was a dreadful sight; even the experienced police officers at the scene felt their stomachs churn.

Word quickly reached the police control room. The suspect had been pronounced dead at the scene. Chief Inspector Deery had seen his fair share of dead bodies, but he didn't envy the emergency services recovering the body on this occasion.

Chapter 19

Charles Stanley had received an update from Alicia Downes detailing her and Greg Travers' recent activities in Poole. Stanley was far from happy with her proposal to enter Albatross House covertly, locate and attempt to open Olga Devereux's safe, then copy any relevant evidence and get out safely. At best, it was risky, very risky, and at worst, well, he didn't want to think about that, given how many bodies this case had already provided the police pathology lab with. However, with the death of Petrov, their one definite lead, he needed a breakthrough, and with Downes' experience and expertise, he felt it was a risk worth taking.

Whilst he had reservations about her proposal, he had followed her career with interest and knew her to be an outstanding intelligence officer. He had even persuaded her to return to MI5 after her successful years in the Secret Intelligence Service. However, he had approved her plan and agreed to her request for additional specialist equipment, which would be sent to her by courier. Even though he was focusing on just the Constable case, his in-tray was overflowing. The afternoon had been a busy one, with two meetings, a Home Office briefing, and finally signing off several intelligence reports. He was tired and longed for a hot meal, a bath, and a good night's sleep. Then his desk phone rang. What now?

'Good evening, Charles Stanley,' he said wearily.

'Hello, Charles.'

'Hello, sir,' said Stanley, who visibly braced as he recognised the voice in his ear. Although they had known each other for several years, when the Director General of MI5 rang, it didn't pay to sound tired, regardless of how one felt.

'Listen, Charles, I've just had the Deputy Director of the NSA on the phone. Are you familiar with their decryption programme Bullrun?'

'Yes, sir, it's a classified US government programme used to crack encrypted online communications, like our own Edgehill programme at GCHQ,' confirmed Stanley.

'They've got hold of some intelligence that could help us, but there might be a sting in the tail,' said the Director General.

'What's that?' asked Stanley.

'Be in the briefing room at 1 o'clock tomorrow, bring your best analyst—your man Travers—and be on your best behaviour, the Home Secretary is coming.'

'Travers is in Poole, sir, investigating the Albatross Foundation,' said Stanley, who fully expected the Director to then request someone else.

'Pull him out! Get in touch with him, and see that he's here tomorrow morning.'

'What about Alicia Downes? She's there too, sir?'

'No, she can stay there; we need to keep someone on-site.'

'Very good, sir, we'll be there.'

Stanley put the receiver down—that was a call he wasn't expecting. What could the Americans know about his case that he was not aware of, and what did the Home Secretary know? He only turned up when the shit was about to hit the fan. First, he had to ensure that Travers was on parade tomorrow. The Director had expressly asked for him to be present. Downes would have to contain herself for a day or two until either Travers was able to return there or someone else could be freed up to provide support. After contacting Travers and informing him that he had to report back to Thames House in the morning for a high-level briefing, Stanley could finally shut down his laptop and leave his office.

Dense grey clouds were building up over London. What little blue sky there had been in the morning had now been completely covered as Travers walked through the entrance to Thames House and headed for his desk. He had just enough time for a coffee and to sit at his desk and contemplate the forthcoming meeting. Stanley had told him very little, except that both the Home Secretary and the Director General would be there, and that the Director had requested he be present. Travers hadn't met either man before, so it was going to be interesting, to say the least. Travers had studied his online meeting request; other than Stanley, the Director, and, of course, the Home Secretary, he didn't recognise many of the attendees' names.

At 12:45, Travers walked across to the large briefing room. Stanley was already there, along with probably a dozen other people, one or two he knew, and a few faces that looked vaguely familiar. Just before 1 pm, another door on the opposite side of the room opened, and the Director walked in, accompanied by the distinguished figure of the Home Secretary. After the Home Secretary had taken his seat, the Director stood up to address the briefing.

'Good afternoon, everyone, take your seats, please. The Home Secretary has asked me to convene this briefing as a result of a video call I received from the Deputy Director of the National Security Agency in Maryland last night. The Home Secretary has spoken personally with the NSA Director this morning. Home Secretary.'

'Director General, ladies and gentlemen, as you may be aware, the NSA runs a number of global surveillance programmes monitoring all forms of communications and digital information across all formats. Yesterday, they intercepted communications from the Palestinian Security Services regarding an Israeli national, David Rubin. Mr Rubin spent many years working for Mossad's Kidon unit—that's their assassination team—and according to Mossad's director, he was extremely proficient, as Mossad agents tend to be, until he started taking on some extracurricular freelance work and was kicked out.'

The Home Secretary continued, 'Now, the PSS keeps tabs on people like Mr Rubin, especially when they are suspected of the multiple murders of Palestinians or their allies. Rubin and his Palestinian girlfriend had a bit of a falling out. She thought he was fooling around with someone else, he wasn't spending as much time with her, and seemed distracted. So she started looking through his papers. She found a receipt from a bullion dealer in Jerusalem; the deal was for over four million shekels, about a million pounds. She confronted him about it, they had a blazing row, and he said he had no time for her now, as he had a big job on in England. She stormed out.'

'To cut a long story short, the husband of one of her girlfriends works for the Palestinian Police. He found out and contacted the Security Services, as well as the Israeli Police, who attempted to contact Rubin at the address she provided. He wasn't there. Cleared out, along with his money and his passport. The Israelis say that since he left Mossad, he is suspected of being involved in several mercenary ventures and unauthorised attacks on Palestinian targets. They are covering the ports and airports, but he may have already left the country. This man is resourceful, a killer of high-value targets, whom we suspect may have been paid a million pounds for an unspecified contract, possibly here in the UK. Interpol has his photo and his details. We have to work with our international colleagues to find this man, Director.'

'Thank you, Home Secretary. Well, there we are. Our task is relatively straightforward. One way or another, we have to find this man. We must presume that he is travelling under a different passport and may have changed his appearance. Interpol and Europol are on alert. If they catch him, they'll pick him up. Border Force has his details, but this man is highly professional, and we'll have to get lucky to pick him up at Passport Control. All the details we have on him are in the files in front of you. I'll discuss your individual assignments when I see you after this briefing. Is there anything else you wish to add, Home Secretary?'

He stood up and escorted the Home Secretary across the floor and out of the briefing room via the side door. Stanley rose from his seat and picked up the thin folder on the table next to him, which contained a photograph of Rubin, together with his biographical details and as much of his service history as Mossad felt appropriate to share, which wasn't a lot.

'That was interesting,' said Stanley.

'Yes, but I don't see why I had to be brought back. What's it got to do with me?' said Travers.

'The Director General told me to bring you in; your star is rising, Greg. When the head of MI5 asks for you, "why" isn't one of the questions you ask. Come on, let's get back to my office,' said Stanley.

A few minutes later, Stanley and Travers returned to his first-floor office.

'Sit down, Greg. The DG insisted on bringing you on board because he trusts your instincts. He's worried about this NSA news. There are several potential targets visiting the UK in the next few months, not to mention domestic targets—Royalty, Members of Parliament, and industrialists. It's a needle in a haystack, and we have to find it,' said Stanley.

'Sir, this is not a needle in a haystack, it's a needle in a field of haystacks. Under the circumstances, we'd have a better chance of tracing the money. The transfer of a million pounds worth of gold must be easier to trace than this guy. We know where the gold ended up; let's backtrack it. Follow the money. Someone has paid out a million pounds to a bullion dealer for a ton of gold that ended up in Jerusalem.'

'If the hit is to take place in the UK, the chances are that the originator is also in the UK,' continued Travers.

'That's a bit of an assumption, Greg.'

'Sir, we are trying to find your needle, and we need to find it quickly, so we have to cut some corners and take a leap of faith.'

'OK, what's your plan?'

'The UK, and London specifically, is the largest gold dealing hub in the world. There are around 150 or so bullion dealers in the country. We'll need to check them all. One of them might be the dealer that set up the transfer. It would also help if we knew the name of the dealer in Israel. Did the Israeli police find the gold receipt when they searched Rubin's house? Can you ask the Director?'

'Will that be all, sir?' added Travers.

'Why, have you got a date, Greg?' said Stanley, nodding towards the partially open door.

'I just thought I would catch up with Alicia, see how her day's gone.'

'Ah, yes, how are you two getting along?' asked Stanley.

'Just fine, thanks, sir,' responded Travers as he stood up and began to walk towards the door.

After leaving Stanley's office, Travers headed straight for the restaurant for some much-needed caffeine before returning to his desk. It was likely to be a long afternoon trawling through the names and details of all the UK's bullion dealers. The originator may not even be based in the UK. It was only a hunch, but he had to start somewhere. Maybe—just maybe—one of them would have a record of a recent million-pound gold transfer to Israel in favour of a man called David Rubin. Before that, he had an important phone call to make.

'Hi Alicia, it's Greg. How are you? Any news where you are?'

'Hi Greg, it's good to hear from you. Things are pretty quiet here. I've just signed for some equipment that Stanley sent, and it's arrived. I'm planning to go into Albatross House tomorrow,' said Downes.

'I wish you would wait until I get back down there, Alicia. I don't like the thought of you being on your own,' said Travers. 'Anyway, how are you going to get in there in the first place?' Travers continued.

'As you pointed out, the Foundation lets out space in the building for other charities. Olga Devereux's office suite is at the top of B Block. There is an unrelated charity organisation occupying the top of A Block. I have arranged a late afternoon appointment. As you are aware, the security services created dummy companies which they can use as cover for intelligence gathering. I'm posing as the representative of a potential donor. I am hoping that once I'm up there, I'll be able to slip away and stay out of sight until most people have gone home,' said Downes.

'And what then? How are you going to get from there into Devereux's office?' asked Travers.

'When I visited Albatross House, I noticed that the Foundation offices have fingerprint security access, but they had suspended ceilings over a metal framework. So, it will be a case of up and over. Then I'll lower myself down through Devereux's ceiling, locate her safe, open it, and eureka, photograph anything important,' said Downes.

'Just like that?'

'It's an office block, not a maximum-security prison, Greg,' said Downes, trying to reassure him.

'And assuming you can actually open the safe, how do you get out of the building?'

'I'll use my initiative, Greg. Anyway, I'll check in with you later. So, what's your flap about?' asked Downes.

'The NSA picked up some intelligence chatter about an Israeli ex-Mossad agent who's gone AWOL with a million pounds worth of gold in his pocket and a possible contract to hit someone over here. We had a meeting today with the Director General and the Home Secretary as well, so everyone is running around like headless chickens trying to catch this guy before he does something. Trouble is, no one knows where he is, what name he's using, or who his target is, and I've been hauled in to find him. God knows when I'll see you again. Anyway, I need to get on. Let me know how things go tomorrow. Good luck, Alicia.'

'Have you been pulled off the Constable case completely now?'

'Only while I'm looking for this Israeli. One of my colleagues is still going through the McKenzie and Hunt file. If anything crops up, I'll let you know,' said Travers.

'OK Greg, talk to you soon,' concluded Downes.

Alicia Downes returned to her room to prepare for her appointment at Albatross House. She gave the equipment she had received from an MI5 courier yesterday a final check and dressed in an appropriate charcoal-coloured business suit. Greg Travers had left his car in her keeping while he was otherwise engaged in London. She loved fast cars. The drive down from London had been exhilarating, so she was disappointed that the trip she was about to make wasn't much more than a mile. Carrying a small black leather case, she left the hotel and walked around to the car park. She deactivated the alarm, opened the large grey driver's door, which closed with a reassuringly solid clunk, and sat down in the comfortable leather seat, making a slight adjustment to the seating position before firing up the four-and-a-half-litre engine. As a self-confessed 'petrol head,' she adored the deep growling purr the engine produced, something that the new electric cars just couldn't replicate.

A few moments later, she was ready to go. Driving down to Shore Road before turning right and heading to Poole Town Centre. Avoiding the Foundation's own car park, she parked nearby and walked the short distance to Albatross House. Climbing up the stone steps leading to the entrance of the building, she was thankful for her previous visit with the local police. It took away much of the uncertainty she sometimes felt walking into a strange building for the first time when undercover. She stepped across to the reception desk and held out the business card she had selected for the visit.

'My name is Rebecca Lancaster, from Fleming Investments. I have an appointment with Purbeck Voices,' said Downes.

The receptionist handed back the card that Downes had presented and gestured towards the turnstile. At this time of the day, more people were leaving than arriving. Downes passed through the barrier and waited for the next lift to arrive. Within a few minutes, she stepped out of the lift on the 7th floor and walked towards A block. Unlike the other blocks, the entry doors were not protected by electromagnets, so she was able to pass freely into the office. Several storage rooms were located in the corridors that linked the blocks. While there was no direct access to B Block from the corridors, Downes was able to climb up to the ceiling in one of the storage rooms and easily remove one of the suspended ceiling panels.

After studying the blueprints that Travers had provided, she could see that behind the ceiling panels was a sturdy metal framework that should support her. She gingerly climbed onto the frame, pausing for a moment to ensure that the structure could bear her weight before she started to inch her way across the ceiling. Downes knew where Olga Devereux's office suite was in relation to her starting point, and it wouldn't take too long to reach it.

She edged her way across the metal structure, spreading her weight as best she could. One false step and she risked falling through the lightweight ceiling panels. Twenty minutes later, she arrived at what she hoped was her entry point, a small room adjoining Mrs. Devereux's suite. She slightly raised one of the ceiling panels and peered through the small gap for any signs of human activity. There were none. Downes didn't want to linger there any longer than necessary. The earlier she could get out, the greater the chances of bluffing her way out of the building as a late worker if she was challenged by security. She waited for several minutes, listening for any noise or indication that the office might be occupied. She then removed the suspended ceiling panel completely.

Believing the coast to be clear, she reached into her bag and produced a miniature high-tensile steel wire rope ladder. Attaching one end of the rope ladder to the metal ceiling frame, she gently lowered the ladder downward toward the floor. Casting one last look around as far as she could see, Downes then placed her foot on the first rung of the wire ladder, praying that the ceiling structure would bear the concentrated weight as she lowered herself down the swaying ladder until she reached the floor. She listened intently for any sounds from the rooms beyond. The only discernible noise was the tick-tick of an ornamental clock. If only her heart rate was as slow and regular as those metronomic ticks. She peered around the corner into the main office suite. Other than the ticking clock, there was no evidence of any recent activity.

She moved swiftly across the plush carpeted floor toward the large oil painting of Olga Devereux's parents that Downes had seen previously. If her instincts were right, behind it would be Devereux's safe, hopefully containing all the evidence the police would need to move in and shut her operation down. She stood facing the richly detailed portrait before moving forward to examine the frame for any tell-tale indications of an alarm. Finding no wires or pressure pads, she held the frame, noticing two small brass hinges on the left-hand side of the frame. She pulled the right side towards her to reveal what she had hoped to find: Olga Devereux's safe.

As she suspected, it was not a simple tumbler combination safe; for a woman of her talents, that would have been child's play. It was a biometric safe, and she was going to have to find Olga's fingerprints to scan. The first and most obvious place was the safe scanner itself. Downes reached into her pocket for her mobile phone and scanned the pad. The scan was negative; either the pad had been wiped since it was last used, or the latent fingerprint was smudged and unreadable. She was going to have to work a little harder to find her fingerprint. She looked around for a likely place; flat surfaces were best—metal or glass. As her eyes wandered around the opulent office, she caught sight of Olga Devereux's landline telephone sitting on her desk, partially hidden by a wooden framed photograph of a man. Provided the cleaners hadn't been in already, that was one place you were guaranteed to find fingerprints, and they could really only be Olga Devereux's. If not, possibly her eldest son, Hector, or Chief of Staff Rackman, and they were the only ones with access to the safe anyway.

Downes took a miniature MOF Crystal aerosol and sprayed the handset of the phone. She waited until the latent prints began to reveal themselves, then scanned the print using her phone. It was a good, clear fingerprint. Returning to the safe, she held the image of the fingerprint on her phone against the safe's scanner. There was an immediate click, and a small red LED light close to the fingerprint scanner turned green. She looked around once more toward the office door before taking hold of the chrome-finished handle of the safe and pulling it down, opening the door.

Inside were several folders, a small black notebook, a bottle of small green caplets, several syringes, and what appeared to be a selection of drugs, along with the obligatory wads of cash. Downes picked up the top folder and opened it. Inside were detailed records of all the Foundation's charitable skeletons in cupboards around the world, worth hundreds of millions of pounds in illegally extracted mineral and precious metal deposits. Downes photographed page after page of damning evidence. It was almost beyond belief.

Underneath the top folder was a single foolscap envelope, containing details of a large CHAPS payment to Midas Gold Solutions in London and a separate note of a man's name and bank account details in the Middle East. Downes recalled her last conversation with Travers and his urgent new task to trace an Israeli, which involved a large quantity of gold. She quickly grabbed her phone and dialled his number, but there was no reply. The next folder contained an old photograph of a man in a German military SS uniform. It also contained extensive newspaper cuttings and biographical information. As she thumbed through the papers, she heard voices.

Anxiously, she turned her head toward the wooden door. Were they coming in or just passing? If they were coming in, she had only a matter of seconds. She replaced the folder she had been looking at, shut the safe door, and locked it. She had just enough time to dart back into the adjoining room, where her ladder still hung, as two people entered the office suite. As swiftly as she dared, Downes climbed back up the ladder and through the small opening, replacing the ceiling panel behind her. Not wishing to push her luck, she decided not to wait and see who it was or wait until they had left to re-enter the office. She crawled back across the ceiling frame, back to A Block the way she had come.

Downes tried to call Travers again but was unable to get through. Fearing that she might be discovered, she sent a text to Travers containing a picture of the German officer she had found in Devereux's safe; perhaps he could identify him and his significance. She arrived at the spot over the A Block storage room she had used earlier. Removing the ceiling panel, she descended back into the room and then replaced the panel. All that was needed now was to get out.

On leaving the storage room, Downes checked the immediate vicinity. All was quiet as she walked toward the exit door of the 7A Block. If she met anyone, she would just brazen it out. Half the skill in working undercover was confidence. 'Bullshit baffles brains,' was her mantra. She quickly made her way out of the block and went down the main stairs toward the foyer. She was almost there. As she turned the corner, she waved casually at the security man at the reception desk to let her out. A second man suddenly appeared from inside the small glass-fronted control room behind the reception desk. Then, behind him, also emerging from the security room, were Olga Devereux and Richard Rackman.

'Good evening, Miss Lancaster, or is it still Officer Downes?' said Devereux, turning to the two security guards.

'Would you escort this young lady to my office, please, and keep her company until I arrive?'

The burly guards stood on either side of Downes as they led her to the lifts and then up to the top of B Block. A few minutes later, she was walking back into the office she had so recently left. She tried to collect her thoughts. How had they got on to her? Had she slipped up somewhere? Had someone recognised her? Five minutes later, Olga Devereux and two other men walked through the doorway and came toward her. One of the security detail passed Downes' phone to Mrs. Devereux as they handed her over.

Devereux dismissed the regular security men. The two new men resembled hoodlums from a 60s Cold War B movie—unsmiling, unfriendly, and exuding menace.

'Well now,' said Devereux, 'where shall we begin? What are you really doing here?'

'Collecting for the Red Cross?' said Downes sarcastically, still smarting from having been caught at the last moment.

'Try again, Miss Downes,' said Devereux, who then tossed Downes' phone to one of the men.

'Here, I want to know what's on it,' she said curtly.

'Now then, Miss Downes, where are my manners? Would you care for a drink? I think we should have a drink and discuss this like civilised people,' said a smiling Devereux.

'No, thank you.'

'Oh, but I insist,' said Devereux as she motioned to the two men, who grabbed Downes and dragged her over to the white leather sofa, forcing her to sit down. She resisted as best she could, but she was no match for the two burly men, who seemed to enjoy overpowering her.

'Now that you are sitting comfortably, I'll ask you again, Miss Downes,' continued Devereux. 'Nothing to say? Well, perhaps a drink will help you relax and improve your memory. Vodka, gin, brandy, whisky, or perhaps a glass of wine?'

Devereux walked across to her safe, opened it, and removed a small bottle of tablets. She returned with a small green capsule and a glass tumbler, which she proceeded to fill with white wine.

'Miss Downes, you have posed as a police officer, you have broken into my office, and doubtless tried to open my safe. I want to know why?' demanded Devereux, who sat on the sofa opposite.

'I'm a private investigator, working for a magazine investigating corruption in large charity organisations,' said Downes, not wishing to implicate the security services.

Olga Devereux looked both dissatisfied and unconvinced by her response. She sat back in her seat and glanced up at one of the men, who stepped forward in front of Downes. Downes knew what was coming next and braced herself for the inevitable pain. The anticipated slap never came; what she got was worse, much worse. A large fist crashed into her face, throwing her across the sofa and almost onto the floor, followed by the most searing pain. The men hauled her back into the centre of the sofa. She could feel blood streaming from what she assumed was her broken nose.

'Oh dear, I can see that this will be a long and painful night, especially for you. Now, shall we try again?' said Devereux.

'Fuck you!' spat out Downes. The situation was not going to end well, and there was now nothing to be gained by holding back.

Again, the man leaned across and slapped her viciously across her cheek. Blood was now flowing freely down her face.

Devereux stood up and offered her handkerchief to Downes, who wiped her face with it before disdainfully tossing the crimson-stained hankie back to its owner.

'We will find out eventually, one way or another. Why not be reasonable? These gentlemen learned their trade in the FSB. I'm afraid they are not very subtle, but they get results,' said Devereux, who then picked up the tumbler of wine and dropped the green capsule into it. Soon, it began to dissolve, giving the wine a slight bluish tint.

'I prefer something a little more refined. I'm sure you know what this is – Flunitrazepam, otherwise known as Rohypnol. In small amounts, it can make you feel very good; in larger doses, it can cause confusion, incapacitation, and even death. But of course, you already know that, don't you, Miss Downes… last chance!'

Devereux gestured to the two men, who took hold of Downes's arms and held her down. Devereux stepped across from her sofa, holding the glass.

'Very well, time for your libation, Miss Downes,' said Devereux.

Downes clamped her mouth shut, prompting one of the men to grip her mouth with both hands in an attempt to prize her jaws apart. As her resistance began to weaken, one of the men's fingers entered the inside of her lips and started roughly pulling her cheek back. If she was going down, she was going down swinging, and with every ounce of strength she could muster, she slammed her jaw hard down on the invading finger. Blood spewed from the wound as the man cried out, frantically trying to extricate his blood-soaked finger from Downes's mouth. The enraged man grabbed her by the throat. Devereux gripped Downes's bloody and disfigured nose and waited for a few moments until Downes's lungs desperately cried out for air. The moment she opened her mouth, Devereux poured the full glass of drugged wine into her mouth and then held her mouth closed to prevent Downes from spitting it out.

'That's better. Now we'll just wait for a while; ten to twenty minutes should do it,' said Devereux, looking up at the two men. 'She'll be much more cooperative by then.'

As the minutes passed, Alicia started to feel the tension in her body disappear. She began to lose sensation before drifting in and out of consciousness. Devereux stood up from the opposite sofa, moving to sit next to her increasingly vulnerable captive. Taking hold of her hand, Devereux spoke to her softly and reassuringly as she sought to extract the answers she needed, while the redoubtable but now helpless MI5 officer sat back. Devereux had no scruples about taking advantage of someone when it suited her. Reaching across, she unbuttoned Downes's blouse and fondled her left breast, tweaking her nipple between her fingers as the now incapacitated woman's blood-spattered arms hung limply by her side, now incapable of offering any resistance. Despite the bloody beating she had endured, Alicia Downes had a fine figure, which had not escaped Devereux's voracious and lascivious nature. Olga was going to get her pound of flesh one way or the other. As the defenceless woman lay across the sofa, Devereux dismissed her minders as she leaned across and began to undo Downes's trousers. It would be a long night, after all.

Chapter 20

With the forensic examination of Travers' house in Wimbledon Village completed and signed off by the Met Police, Charles Stanley agreed to Travers' request to return home. As much as he was happy to be allowed back, it just didn't feel the same anymore. Notwithstanding the gruesome murder of a policeman that had taken place in his garden, his home had been violated; it didn't feel like his anymore. His treasured sanctuary, which he had shared with his wife, Cassandra, had been desecrated. He checked his mobile phone again. He had received two text messages from Alicia. The first was yesterday evening, with a single black-and-white photograph of a man in uniform. From the uniform insignia, Travers could immediately see that it was a German SS officer from the Second World War. The second text, sent several hours later, said that she had drawn a blank with Olga Devereux's safe and was following up on a new lead. She would contact him in a few days.

Travers arrived at Thames House. Officially, he was still required to continue his search for David Rubin, whose whereabouts were the top priority. However, he was more concerned that he was unable to speak or make direct contact with Alicia. He took the photograph of the German officer, which he had printed off at home, and went to Stanley's office.

'Good morning, sir.'

'Morning, Greg. Any news?'

'Have you heard from Alicia since yesterday, sir?' enquired Travers.

'No, I haven't. Why? Has something come up?'

'She sent me two text messages last night. One was an old photo of a German SS officer—no name, just the picture—and later, a really odd one saying that she had drawn a blank with Devereux's safe, that she was following up another lead, and would be in touch,' said Travers.

Stanley studied the photograph for a few seconds. He didn't recognise the officer. It was just another of the thousands of military photographs from the period in circulation.

'She obviously thinks this German is important. You'd better find out who he is. Contact the German Federal Archive—I think the Military Archive is in Freiburg. You could also try the Centre for Research Libraries in Chicago; the Americans seized masses of German military records after the war,' added Stanley.

'Yes, sir. Sir, I'd like to go back to Poole, as Alicia has not picked up my calls or contacted either of us. I've had these two odd messages. I just don't buy that Devereux's safe was clean. Everything points to her. I think Alicia's in trouble, sir.'

'No, I'm sorry, Greg. Your current job takes precedence. Alicia Downes is a professional and very experienced officer—she can look after herself.'

Reluctantly, Travers had to acquiesce, at least for the time being. Picking up the photograph from Stanley's desk, he left his office and returned to his desk. Before he re-joined his colleagues hunting for David Rubin, he sent off the photograph of the German SS officer, hoping that someone would quickly identify him. If Alicia found this picture while searching Devereux's office and thought it important enough to send to him without any further contact, then that in itself was a good enough reason for him to pursue it.

Travers spent the morning at his desk, pouring over UK-registered bullion dealer details. With the urgency of locating Rubin, the Home Secretary had ordered the Metropolitan Police to assist with the vetting process. If Travers' hunch was right, one of these companies' records would reveal the all-important transaction. However, if the transfer was completed by an overseas dealer or had been broken down into less significant or irregular amounts to avoid detection, they would be back to square one, and what was already an almost impossible job would become a completely impossible one. In between his phone calls, Travers continued to check his mobile in the hope that Alicia had made contact, but to his dismay, she hadn't. With every passing hour, he became more and more concerned. The only clue he had was that photograph.

Mid-afternoon brought a glimmer of light into the gloom-laden search when Travers' colleague, Nicky Andrew, made a discovery.

'Greg, I've just got off the phone with Midas Gold Solutions. They had five payments totalling a million pounds, spread over five days, in favour of the same dealer in Jerusalem,' said Nicky.

'Who made the payments?' asked Travers.

'Different brokers using different accounts.'

'Is there a connection?' enquired Travers.

'One of the brokers has an account with McKenzie and Hunt,' said Andrew.

Travers' eyes lit up. It was hardly conclusive, but it was quite a coincidence that one of the brokers had an account with the company they were investigating for suspected money laundering.

'Well done, Nicky. You know those accounts we found at McKenzie and Hunt? Focus on them. See if you can find any entries that link to any of those brokers, Midas Gold Solutions, or the dealer in Israel. I'll update Stanley.'

Travers had been deep in thought when his mobile phone rang. The sudden break in his concentration was jarring, and he scrambled for the handset hidden under various papers lying on his desk. He hoped it was Alicia. It wasn't.

'Guten Tag, es ist Reinhard aus der Military Archive, Freiburg.'

'Guten Tag, Reinhard. Sprechen Sie Englisch?' said Travers.

Travers hoped that his schoolboy German would be good enough to get over the first hurdle.

'Ja, Natürlich,' replied the German.

'Brilliant. Good afternoon, Reinhard. Thanks for calling back. I hope you have some good news for me,' continued Travers.

'We have identified your photograph: Standartenführer Wolfgang Dietrich, SS Colonel of the 2nd Bavarian Panzers.'

'Do you have his service record?' asked Travers.

'Yes, I'm emailing it to you now.'

'Was he ever indicted for war crimes after the surrender?'

'No, he disappeared,' said the German. 'He fled to Argentina, where there was a large German community. He was relatively safe there despite attempts by the Israelis to snatch him. He remarried, had several children, and was extremely wealthy. The Wiesenthal Centre says his wealth was largely accumulated during the war. He was suspected of multiple counts of crimes against humanity, but he was never brought to trial or prosecuted,' continued Reinhard.

'I presume he is dead now?' asked Travers.

'Ja, he died in the mid-seventies and was buried near Buenos Aires. His sons came back to Germany after he died, though, and of course, his grandson is very prominent in German politics.'

Travers stared down at the image of Colonel Dietrich standing in front of the heavily armoured Panzer Mark VI tank. But what was the connection with Devereux?

'What are their names?' asked Travers.

'Manfred and Richard Graf,' said Reinhard.

'Graf?' questioned a puzzled Travers.

'Yes, when Dietrich remarried after the war, he took his wife's name to add another layer of concealment. It was only when he died that the truth came out,' added Reinhard.

'So, his grandson is … Otto Graf?'

'Ja, ja, he is very popular, especially with younger generation. He is dynamic, full of energy, and wants Germany to be the dominant power in Europe. He is tipped to be the next Chancellor,' said Reinhard.

'Reinhard, that's been really helpful. I appreciate it. Vielen Dank.'

Travers put his phone down, sat back in his chair, and placed his hands behind his head, thinking for a moment. The plot had just grown considerably thicker and taken a potentially sinister twist. He leaned forward and called up his inbox to find that Reinhard's email had arrived containing all the available information about Oberst Wolfgang Dietrich and his children. This was information that needed to be kicked upstairs. Travers printed off the contents of the email, then picked up his phone and dialled Stanley's number. The conversation was brief and to the point. With the call ended, Travers collected his papers and headed straight for Stanley's office.

'Well, what have you got, Greg?' asked Stanley, whose appetite had been tweaked by Travers' teasing news over the phone.

'Two things, sir. Firstly, as far as the search for David Rubin is concerned, we believe one of the brokers involved in the purchase of the gold used an account held at McKenzie and Hunt. Nicky Andrew is searching the accounts we identified for any other links to either the brokers, the dealers, or Rubin. If we can connect Rubin to the accounts associated with the Albatross Foundation, we'll really be in business,' said Travers.

Stanley smiled with satisfaction. This was an unexpected and welcome development. He looked up approvingly at Travers.

'Brilliant! Well done, Greg. Do you need any additional support with this?' Without waiting for an answer, he continued: 'And what was the second?'

'We've got a line on our unknown German officer. He was an SS Colonel, Wolfgang Dietrich. I've not been through his full biography yet, but it looks like Oberst Dietrich was a committed party man—a proper dyed-in-the-wool Nazi. Suspected of numerous atrocities, including mass murder, he got out of Germany with his pockets bulging with loot, and ended up in Argentina, where he died in the '70s,' concluded Travers.

'What's the connection with Devereux then?' quizzed Stanley.

'I don't know, sir, but Dietrich's grandson is a very prominent German politician, and the family are rich—and I don't just mean well-off, I mean absolutely loaded,' said Travers.

'OK, Greg, keep digging. See if you can find a link between Devereux and Rubin. I'd better let the Director know about the new developments. I'm sure the Home Secretary is bending his ear every day, wanting to know what we are doing and if we have found Rubin yet,' said Stanley.

A few hours later, Travers was home after an intensive day. A good meal, a hot bath, and a good night's sleep, and he would be ready to rejoin the fray in the morning. Despite feeling exhausted, it had been a good day. More pieces of the puzzle were beginning to appear. He just needed to work out what the big picture was and how they all fitted together. Still, at the back of his mind was Alicia—what had happened to her.

He had just started a large vodka and lemonade when his phone rang. It was the Poole Police Station. They reported that his car had overstayed its welcome where Alicia had parked it, and as a result, it had been towed away and was currently in the Police pound awaiting collection. This was desperately concerning news. So much for Alicia following up a lead somewhere else. It looked like she had never left Poole. So who, then, had sent the message? He immediately contacted Stanley to appraise him of the information and once again asked if he could return to Poole. This time, Stanley could not refuse, provided he still coordinated the team's search for Rubin. That was good enough for Travers. Within ten minutes, he was heading southwest in the company car he had been assigned. In two hours, he would be back in Poole.

He stopped off to collect his car from the Police pound before returning to the Harbour Heights in Sandbanks, where his room had been held. He walked across to the reception desk and asked the lady on duty if there were any messages left for him. He didn't anticipate there being any, after all, Alicia would have expected to make a report in person on her return. What he didn't expect to hear was that, according to the hotel manager, Alicia had contacted them, checked out, and requested that her belongings be placed in storage until they could be picked up.

'She's checked out? Are you sure?' asked Travers.

'Yes, sir. She said something very urgent had cropped up, and she had to check out. She asked us to hold her belongings, but she would arrange for someone to pick them up,' said the receptionist.

'Did she check out in person?' asked Travers.

'No, sir. She rang up and spoke to my colleague. She said someone would be round to pick up her bags.'

'So, no one has seen Miss Downes in person?

'No, sir, not as far as I know,' continued the receptionist.

'Was there any mention of the hotel bill? Did they offer to settle it?' asked Travers.

'I'm sorry, sir, I can't discuss it any further, confidentiality, you understand,' said the receptionist.

'You have CCTV covering both the reception area and the car park, don't you?' asked Travers.

'Yes, sir,' said the now irritated receptionist.

'Are your recordings kept for 31 days?'

'Yes, I believe so.'

Travers pulled out his mobile phone and quickly found the local Police Station phone number.

'Detective Inspector Roberts, please, urgent,' said Travers.

A few moments later, the call was being transferred, and the next voice he heard was a man's.

'DI Roberts, how can I help you?'

'Detective Inspector, this is Greg Travers, MI5. I am sorry to bother you so late, but I am a colleague of Alicia Downes, who accompanied you on a visit to Albatross House a few days ago to talk to Olga Devereux,' explained Travers.

'Yes, I remember her. What can I do for you?' said Roberts.

'I need your help, Inspector. Miss Downes has gone missing. We've had Mrs Devereux and the Albatross Foundation under investigation for some time. Two days ago, she went into the building to obtain evidence, and we have not heard from her since. We were staying at the Harbour Heights Hotel in Sandbanks. The hotel says she checked out this morning after we lost contact with her. Someone has been in, and collected her luggage. They have CCTV here, and it's possible that if we can isolate the timeframe, we might be able to spot the person who paid the bill and, if we're lucky, identify the car they were driving,' said Travers.

'Ok, Mr Travers, stay there, I'll come over and we'll see what we can do.'

Travers turned to the receptionist, who had just ended a phone call.

'Thank you for your help. I didn't mean to badger you. I'll be in the bar. When the police arrive, could you point them in my direction, please?' said Travers, then walked the short distance through the lobby to the bar and ordered a vodka and lemonade.

About thirty minutes later, Travers, who was sitting at the bar, noticed the receptionist gesturing to a man and woman who had just come in and pointing towards him. Travers slid off his bar stool in preparation to greet who he assumed were from the local constabulary. The plainclothes couple walked towards him. The man, whom Travers presumed was DI Roberts, was a large, burly man, slightly balding, probably in his late 40s. The woman was younger, possibly in her early 30s, slim, with shoulder-length brunette hair, and smartly dressed.

They walked up to the bar and introduced themselves as DI Roberts and Detective Harris. They walked to a quiet table where Travers recounted the recent events in as much detail as he felt was reasonable under the circumstances, so the officers would understand what was required.

They returned to the front desk, where the receptionist was busy attending to another guest. DI Roberts introduced himself and asked to see the hotel night manager. The receptionist got up from her seat and knocked on the door of the office behind the reception area.

A tall and immaculately dressed man emerged and politely greeted the police officers, who explained the information they needed. The manager flicked through a notepad on his desk. His daytime counterpart had jotted down the details of the occurrence. He noted that a man had come to the desk explaining that he had been asked by Downes to retrieve her luggage. He had also tried to settle Downes' hotel bill, apparently unaware that she had already arranged for it to be covered centrally. Fortunately, the note also included the exact time of the incident. With a time frame secured, the police officers followed the manager into his small office, where he logged on to his computer to locate the relevant CCTV timeframe showing the arrival—and with any luck, the departure—of the person Travers hoped would provide a tangible lead in his search for Alicia.

The two police officers and Travers watched intently, as the manager skipped through the coverage until it reached the precise point he had been searching for. The CCTV footage revealed a clear image of a well-built man in his thirties, tall, white, wearing a white shirt, dark jacket, and a pair of ripped jeans. Roberts froze the recording at the clearest frame of the man and copied the picture. The rest of the footage would be crucial. The man picked up Downes' two suitcases and walked out of the hotel foyer and into the car park.

'Right, sir, what we need now is the front car park CCTV for the same time,' said Roberts.

The CCTV camera showed the man exiting the hotel lobby and walking towards a car, a black Mercedes. It wasn't until the car started moving and the angle changed that the camera was able to pick up the registration. Roberts once again freeze-framed the car showing the plate and turned to his colleague.

'Harris, get onto the DVLA. I want the car, the owner, and their address, and I want it now.' Then turning to the hotel manager. 'Sir, we'll need copies of that footage please as part of our investigation.

With that, the two police officers and Travers left the reception area and walked out into the car park. Detective Harris quickly finished her call.

'Sir, the car is a rental from Exclusive Car Rentals,' said Harris.

'Shit, it would be; all right, call them up and find out who hired it, and get copies of the documents they provided,' said Roberts.

'Mr. Travers, I presume you are remaining here for the time being?' enquired Roberts.

'Yes, Inspector, until I know what's happened to Miss Downes or I am recalled to London. Will you keep me updated about this? It's very important.'

'Yes, Mr. Travers. If we track this character down, I'll call you personally,' said Roberts.

Travers returned to the hotel and up to his room. As he stood by the window, he looked out across the harbour. He felt alone. He missed the fact that Alicia was no longer next door. He knew he had to dismiss any sentimental thoughts and focus on the investigation.

Firstly, he needed to update Stanley on the search for Alicia. She was still missing, possibly already dead, but at least now he had a lead, albeit tenuous. He just hoped the police could come up with something. He also needed to check in with his team to see how the search for David Rubin was going. Stanley said that so far, neither Interpol nor Europol had been able to trace Rubin. For all they knew, he might already be in the UK or still traveling across Europe under an assumed identity. Stanley also shared his concerns for Alicia Downes and said he would speak to Dorset's Chief Constable to emphasize the seriousness of the situation and ensure it was given the necessary priority. Travers promised to advise him of any developments.

The afternoon brought more positive news from his team. The analysis of McKenzie and Hunt's accounts, had confirmed that there was indeed a linkage between several of the brokers involved in the payment for the gold shipment to Rubin and the Albatross Foundation. Just as they say that all roads lead to Rome, all the evidence was leading to the Albatross Foundation and Olga Devereux. He just needed proof. At this point, he recalled the search of journalist Olivia Hunter's house in Corfe. Hunter had been investigating the Albatross Foundation and had been communicating with one of its staff. She had obviously come up with something significant, as both she and her contact had been killed. While nothing had been discovered in her house, Hunter's publisher had furnished him with the name and address of the self-storage company called Aladdin's, used by the journalist. So, with the police trying to track down the man at the hotel, Travers determined to pursue the only other active local lead.

The company was on the outskirts of town and resembled nothing more than a medium-sized warehouse that had seen better days. Leaving his car in the weed infested car park, Travers walked into a small reception room, where a young woman sat behind the desk, listening to a radio. Travers stood at the desk, while the woman, clearly oblivious to his presence, continued to listen to the radio while filing her nails. Travers cleared his throat, which produced the desired effect. The girl put down her file and walked across to the counter.

'Good afternoon, my name is Travers, Greg Travers.' producing his MI5 identification.

'Yes, sir, how can I help you?' she said enthusiastically.

The woman was either impressed with Travers' credentials or embarrassed at being caught doing her nails and was now trying belatedly to make a good impression. Travers wasn't sure which.

'I understand you have an account for a Miss Olivia Hunter?' he asked.

The woman turned to her desktop computer and typed in Olivia Hunter's name.

'Yes, sir, she does.'

'Can you tell me the last time she left something here?' Travers asked.

The woman looked down at her computer screen.

'About two weeks ago, sir,' she said.

'Do you have a record of what it was?' asked Travers.

The woman checked the entry in her log.

'Err... it was a box file.'

'Is it still here?' asked Travers.

'Yes, sir,' she said.

'Would you get it, please?' said Travers.

The woman disappeared for several minutes before returning with a large pink box file, which she placed on the desk. Travers opened the lid of the box, which contained several reporter's notepads, an A4 pad, some photographs, and a few newspaper cuttings.

'I'll need to take this box.'

'I'm sorry, but this belongs to Miss Hunter. I would need her authority,' she replied.

'Then you'd better phone a medium,' said Travers. 'Miss Hunter has been murdered, and this box may contain information that will help catch her killer.'

'Well, you'll have to sign for it.'

'If you get any trouble from your manager, refer them to DI Roberts with the Poole Police,' Travers said. He thanked the girl for her assistance, put the box under his arm, and walked out to his car.

Within 30 minutes, Travers had arrived back at his hotel. For a few moments, he sat in his car, looking at the bright pink box file sitting on the passenger seat, wondering what vital secrets it might contain. Travers reached across, picked up the box, left his car, and walked through the foyer and up the stairs to his room. He opened the box and removed the first notepad, flipping through the pages, then the second, and the third. After skimming through the other pages, he flung it onto the bed and picked up the second small notebook. It was the same.

Travers swore softly under his breath. 'Bloody hell, shorthand,' he muttered. 'It might as well be Chinese.' In these days of advanced digital technology, who still used Pitman's shorthand? He thumbed through the contents of the box. There were several copies of extracts from foreign newspapers, many of which seemed to be from African and Asian sources. While he couldn't understand the text, Travers was able to pick out the names *Albatross* and *Devereux* in many of them. There were also photographs of what appeared to be either drilling rigs or mining excavations, with place names written on the back.

Travers' phone rang. It was the police. They had arrested the man who had attempted to pay Alicia Downes's hotel bill and picked up her luggage.

'He claims he's just a courier and that he knows nothing about her, but that he was instructed by a woman to go there, pay the bill, and pick up the bags,' said Inspector Roberts.

'Where did he take the bags?' asked Travers.

'Nowhere. They were still in his car. He says the woman told him that someone would pick them up from him,' said Roberts.

'Do you believe him, Inspector?' asked Travers.

'We're still questioning him, Mr. Travers. At the moment, he's insisting that's all he knows,' said the inspector.

'What about his background check? Where is he from, and does he have any connection with the Albatross organisation?' asked Travers.

'We're still checking. We'll get back to you when we have more information on this guy,' said Roberts.

'Okay, thanks, Inspector Roberts.'

It had been a frustrating day for Greg Travers. Still no news of Alicia Downes. Yet two glimmers of hope had appeared: the arrest of the man at the hotel and the discovery of investigative journalist Olivia Hunter's vital notes. Though the man insisted he knew nothing and had done nothing wrong, Hunter's notes were all in shorthand and would need to be transcribed before they revealed what she had discovered. Travers called Stanley to bring him up to speed on today's developments. Stanley's response was swift. Travers was to report back to London immediately, with the box file, where they had the resources to uncover its secrets discreetly and quickly.

Chapter 21

Travers had barely had time to sit down, and certainly not enough time to boot up his computer, before his phone rang. If there was one thing he disliked, it was being rushed before he had properly woken up. He stretched out his arm and picked up the receiver of the black landline phone that sat on his desk. It was his boss, Charles Stanley.

'Good morning, Greg, good to see you're in at last!' said Stanley, his tone dripping with sarcasm.

'At last, sir? It's only just 8 o'clock,' said Travers, still groggy.

'Consider yourself lucky. I had a call from the Director at 6:00 am this morning and a meeting with him and the Home Secretary at 7:00,' Stanley replied.

'Blimey, what's happened, sir?' Travers asked.

'I gave the Director a progress report last night after we spoke. He must have updated the Home Secretary. Now all hell's broken loose. Your German Colonel's grandson, Otto Graf, is visiting the UK this week,' Stanley said.

'I hadn't heard that, sir,' said Travers, surprised.

Stanley continued, 'It's not an official visit. The PM is trying to keep it off the radar as much as possible. They've been speaking over the phone in recent months on various policy issues and have been getting quite chummy. The PM is hedging his bets. If Graf is elected as the next German Chancellor, as many people think likely, it could be extremely beneficial, especially for the UK, considering our relationship with the EU. With David Rubin heading our way, and a possible connection with this woman Devereux, the Prime Minister is in a terrible flap. The last thing we need is a political assassination on UK soil. It would be an unmitigated disaster.'

'Do we have a timetable for this unofficial visit, sir?' Travers asked.

'He's flying in tomorrow morning and meeting the PM for lunch. After that, he has a meeting with the Chairman of the CBI and the Business Secretary. There's a dinner in the evening, and the next day, he's meeting up with his parents in Portsmouth,' Stanley said.

'Portsmouth? What are his parents doing there, coincidence?' Travers asked.

'His parents have been swanning around in the Med for the last month on the *Anni-Frid*, celebrating their wedding anniversary.'

'The *Anni-Frid*?' Travers repeated.

'It's their boat, Greg, named after Otto's grandmother. When I say boat, I use the term loosely. It's actually a £15 million superyacht. They're docking tonight, entertaining some friends in the evening, and as I understand it, Otto Graf is joining them. Then they're sailing down the south coast before heading back to the Fatherland,' Stanley explained.

'So, he's only here for two days. Has he been told about the threat, sir?' Travers asked.

'Yes, the Home Secretary has spoken to him on the phone and advised him to postpone his trip for a while or at least until we've cleared this up,' Stanley said.

'Presumably, if he's still coming, he's ignoring the threat,' Travers remarked.

'That's right, Greg. So, it's up to the Police and us to ensure nothing happens to him on our watch.'

'Sir, we still have no idea where this man Rubin is. We don't even know if he's in the UK,' Travers said, frustration creeping into his voice.

'Greg, for the next forty-eight hours, we must assume he is and that he's going to attempt to kill Graf, probably in London or Portsmouth,' Stanley said firmly.

'Have you had any luck getting those notebooks transcribed?' Travers asked. 'We need all the information we can get.'

'I've got someone working on them now. As soon as they're ready, I'll give you a call,' added Stanley.

'Okay, sir. If it's alright with you, I'd like to return to Poole. I just feel that's the epicentre of what's going on, and that's where we're going to find the answers,' said Travers.

'All right, Greg. Stay in touch,' said Stanley.

Less than ten minutes later, Stanley rang Travers again, and the news wasn't good.

'Greg, the notebooks are encrypted.'

'Coded? You're kidding! Who encrypts shorthand?' said an exasperated Travers.

'Someone who has something very important to keep away from prying eyes, Greg. The books are going to have to go to Cryptography. Hopefully, they can sort it out,' Stanley said. 'In the meantime, get back to Poole and keep an eye on things.'

Chapter 22

Olga Devereux sat on her veranda on Parkson Island, enjoying a chilled glass of Bollinger as she chatted casually with her house guest. Despite the drama of the last few days, things were going well. The unwelcome, though not unexpected, attention of the police over the death of Monica Stein had been dealt with satisfactorily, at least for the present. However, the discovery of the intruder, Alicia Downes, in her office was altogether different. How she got access was largely academic; what troubled Devereux was who she was and whether she had found anything incriminating and communicated it to someone on the outside before she was apprehended.

The disposal of Monica was unfortunate but necessary. Miss Downes, on the other hand, presented a different problem. She was known to the authorities and would therefore be missed. Her drug-infused interrogation eventually revealed her identity and the reason for the break-in. Despite the fact that she was undoubtedly a serious threat to the Foundation's clandestine operations, Devereux greatly admired her ability and bravery. As one strong, resourceful woman to another, Devereux couldn't help but respect her courage under fire. It had taken a lot to break her. But it had to be done—there was too much at stake to allow sentiment to cloud her judgment.

Devereux turned towards the door as she heard footsteps approaching. It was her son, Hector.

'Hello, Mother,' Hector said as he breezed through the door onto the veranda, kissed her on the cheek, then stopped and stared at the figure sitting in the chair opposite.

'Hello, Hector. I don't believe you know my guest. May I introduce David Rubin?'

'David, this is my eldest son, Hector,' she added, gesturing toward her son.

Hector stepped across and offered his hand to Rubin, who shook it cordially.

'Mr. Rubin, how do you do?' 'You know that the world and his wife are looking for you?'

'That's why I invited him here. Thanks to our man in Jersey, no one knows he's in the country,' said Devereux.

'What are you going to do about Downes, Mother? You can't let her go. You should kill her and have done with it,' said Hector.

'All in good time, Hector. I agree we can't let her go, but she might be of use should the authorities start poking their noses around again,' Devereux replied calmly.

'Where is she?' asked Hector.

'The old cottage at Durdle Door. If she becomes too much trouble, or it becomes necessary, you can throw her off the cliff,' said Devereux without an ounce of emotion.

David Rubin had been listening intently to the conversation. His journey from Israel across Europe to England had been fraught with danger, with his face plastered across every newspaper, billboard, and television news headline. It was alarming to hear that the family harbouring him had kidnapped and tortured a member of the British intelligence community. There were bound to be serious repercussions.

'Mrs. Devereux, are you sure you have matters under control?' Rubin asked. 'If they know their operative is missing, they won't let it go. They'll come looking for her, and sooner or later, they'll come here.'

'Mr. Rubin, I have homes all over the world,' Devereux replied coolly. 'I enjoy the privacy this island offers, but if it becomes too popular, I'll simply move, and the police will find nothing here but charred ruins. Anyway, once your work is done, I'll toast your success and take a holiday somewhere far away. Don't worry, in a few days, it will all be over.'

With that, Devereux got up and left Rubin to ponder the situation he found himself in. Hector followed his mother into the house. She paused, sensing that he still had something on his mind.

'Well, out with it, Hector,' she said.

'I'm sorry, Mother, but this is madness. That man is public enemy number one. His face is everywhere, and he's right. Sooner or later, the authorities are going to come here looking for Downes.'

'Get a grip, Hector. If the police do come here, they won't find her, and they certainly won't find Rubin. He'll be long gone. When he's completed his contract, Phoenix will arrange for his safe passage back to the Middle East or South America, well beyond the reach of British jurisdiction.'

'What's the deal with Otto Graf, then?' Hector asked.

'Our German friends have provided Graf's itinerary, which I've passed on to Rubin. He knows his business. The exact details I've left up to him. In the meantime, we'll hold on to Miss Downes until Rubin has finished his job and is safely out of the country. After that, she's expendable, and you can take care of her. We don't want to be tripped up by any loose ends.'

Chapter 23

Travers was anxious to pursue every possible lead, and returning to Poole as soon as possible was going to be key, both in continuing the search for Alicia and in the pursuit of David Rubin. The only active line of enquiry was the man Detective Roberts had picked up yesterday. So far, he was pleading his innocence, but that was yesterday. Travers knew they could only hold him for twenty-four hours without charge. Travers wanted an update before the police released him.

'Good morning, Detective Inspector Roberts, please,' said Travers. A moment later, Roberts answered the phone.

'Roberts speaking. How can I help?'

'Inspector, it's Greg Travers here. Have you any further news for me?'

'Yes, sir. I was about to call you. We've had a breakthrough of sorts. We managed to persuade him that with Miss Downes missing and possibly dead, he was now an accessory after the fact, and if she was dead, he could be charged with murder. If he co-operated, we might drop the murder charge and leave it at possession of stolen property. The thought of doing twenty years didn't appeal to him one bit,' said Roberts.

'What did he have to say?' Travers asked.

'He works as a security guard for the Albatross Foundation. He still says he doesn't know who spoke to him, apart from the fact that it was definitely a woman. An envelope was given to him with instructions. All he had to do was collect Downes' bags and pay her bill,' Roberts explained.

'Inspector, we need to push this. The man said that someone would collect the bags from him, right? Then tell him that if he wants to stay out of jail, he'd better start cooperating and should tell his contact that he has Downes' bags and ask that they be picked up, as per the agreed arrangement. Stick a wire on him and see where he goes, and more importantly, who picks the bags up,' suggested Travers.

'Okay, it's worth a try,' said Roberts.

Three hours later, Travers was back at the Harbour Heights. Having left his bag on the floor beside the bed, Travers left his room. As he shut the door, he hesitated momentarily, looked at the door next to his, and thought, *Where are you, Alicia?* He refused to admit, even in the privacy of his own thoughts, that she wasn't still alive somewhere.

Having stopped first at the bar for a large vodka and lemonade, Travers wandered through the double doors leading to the patio and then walked across the crowded sun terrace to a more secluded area. He stepped forward, leaned on the glass-fronted balustrade, and looked out over the harbour. The blue water was still teeming with kite surfers and boats of all sizes.

The relaxing ambience was completely at odds with the state of his mind and the two questions preoccupying his thoughts—the two people he was desperate to find, for two very different reasons, but linked by a single person. The answer had to be here. Olga Devereux was the key. She was the one pulling the strings. She was the puppet master.

Travers put his glass down on a nearby table and reached into his black leather wallet, producing the business card given to him by the writer Ryan Jones, whom he had met at the Compton Acres event. Travers remembered Jones talking about his interview with Devereux a few weeks ago and how her parents had escaped from Germany during the war. Perhaps she had said something to him—something that might provide a clue to her motivations and state of mind. Jones had said that he lived locally. Travers just hoped he would pick up his phone.

'Hello?' said the voice on the phone.

'Hello, Ryan? This is Greg Travers, we met at Olga Devereux's charity bash the other day.'

'Oh yes, I remember, how are you?' replied Jones.

'Fine, thanks. Have you got a few minutes?' asked Travers.

'Sure, how can I help you, Greg?'

'It's about Olga Devereux. You mentioned something about her family getting out of Germany during the war and fleeing to the UK. I'm interested to know a bit more. Did she go into any details?'

'Well, this was all well before she was born, of course. The Germans came to the village where her grandparents lived. There was quite a large Jewish community there. She said the Germans just marched into people's houses and dragged them out. Most were put onto trucks, but any that resisted were shot on the spot. Olga's grandfather was one. When his wife refused to leave him, they shot her too and left them by the roadside. Their teenage daughter, Olga's mother, was raped by the German commander within sight of her dead parents,' explained Jones.

'Jesus! That explains a lot,'... 'Does she know who was responsible?'

'Her mother said it was an SS unit, but she didn't know the name. She did recognise the insignia of the man who raped her—he was a Colonel. She had nightmares for years. Olga said her mother never got over it. She told me that she never wanted to be as helpless or powerless as her mother had been, and that has been her driving force all her life,' said Jones.

'Thanks, Ryan, that's really helpful. When is your interview coming out? I have a feeling it's going to sell well,' commented Travers.

'Next month, I believe.'

'Well, I'll look forward to reading it. Thanks again, Ryan.'

The information Ryan Jones provided confirmed Travers' worst fears. There was now no doubt in his mind that Devereux, having obviously discovered the identity of the man who raped her mother, planned to exact her revenge on his grandson, Otto Graf. Travers immediately alerted Stanley, confirming that in his opinion the threat against Graf had been validated. But what about Rubin? There was still no evidence suggesting he was even in the country.

'Well, Greg, the Met and the anti-terrorist units will be on full alert tomorrow, but it's pretty hard to stop a determined assassin who is intent on killing someone who is equally determined not to be cowered by threats,' said Stanley.

'Sir, I'd like to play a hunch,' said Travers.

'Okay, I'm listening.' Stanley, who knew Travers well enough by now to trust his instincts.

'Devereux knows that Graf is the grandson of the SS Colonel who murdered her grandparents, and she has lined up this guy Rubin to take him out. But suppose she also knows that Graf's parents will be here too? She could literally kill two birds with one stone—son and grandson.'

'You're suggesting the target is Portsmouth, Greg?'

'That would be my guess, sir,' Travers replied.

'Alright, Greg, I'll send your theory upstairs. What's the news from Poole? Any developments?'

'No, not really. The man who took Alicia's bags is starting to crack at the thought of prison time on a murder charge. DI Roberts is trying to cut a deal with him—drop the murder charge if he cooperates and leads us to his contact,' said Travers.

'Greg, Otto Graf is arriving tomorrow. We don't have time to sit down with beer and sandwiches and negotiate until he decides to favour us with a decision. Get down there and start waving a big stick under his nose. Either he cooperates now, or it's a murder charge and a minimum of twenty years. He can take it or leave it,' said Stanley.

'Yes, sir,' said Travers.

Stanley had left no doubt in Travers' mind that it was time to take the gloves off and roll the dice. Travers would like nothing better than to march into Olga Devereux's office, present his MI5 credentials, and confront her, but without actual evidence, it would be asking for trouble. The bag carrier, on the other hand, was another matter. He had already been caught in possession of stolen property, was sitting in a police cell, and was beginning to buckle under pressure. He was ready to crack. Travers was going to provide the final straw. He picked up his mobile phone and spoke briefly to DI Roberts before grabbing his jacket, leaving his hotel room, and heading to the car park, then the police station.'

Travers and DI Roberts walked into the interview room, where they were met by the suspect, Alan Houseman, and his solicitor. Roberts switched on the audio recorder, and after introducing himself, turned to Houseman.

'Mr. Houseman, you attended the Harbour Heights Hotel yesterday and retrieved the baggage belonging to resident Alicia

Downes. Miss Downes has disappeared, and her bags are in your boot. Now, we can stick with theft, possession of stolen property, or if you like, we can add abduction and possibly murder to the list. The choice is yours,' said Roberts.

'Mr. Houseman, we've spoken to our superiors, and we have the authority to make these charges go away. You could walk out of here a free man,' said Travers. 'All you have to do is help us. You are just a pawn in someone else's game, so do yourself a massive favour.'

'What do you want?' asked Houseman.

'All we want you to do is what you were going to do anyway. Contact the person who gave you the instructions and simply say you have the bags and request their instructions. And remember, we'll be listening. Play it straight, and you might just walk out of here. Screw up, and you'll go to jail. And if she's been kidnapped or murdered, you'll be going to jail for a very long time,' said Travers.

Houseman looked fleetingly at his solicitor before reluctantly nodding in agreement at Travers and Roberts' request.

'Okay, I'll do what you want,' said Houseman reluctantly.

'What are your instructions?' asked Roberts.

'Once I have collected the woman's bags, I call a number. I'll be told where to deliver them,' Houseman replied.

Roberts pointed to the phone on the table. 'Call it,' said Roberts firmly.

The phone rang half a dozen times before a woman answered. The conversation was brief.

'Well?' said Travers.

'It was a foreign-sounding woman. I'm to meet her in two hours at the layby on the westbound road out of town.'

Travers turned to Detective Roberts. 'Do you know it?'

'Yes, it's sometimes used by lorry drivers as a stopover. It's about a mile out of town,' said Roberts.

'And what then?' asked Travers.

'That's all I know—meet her, hand over the bags, and leave,' said Houseman.

'Was it the same woman you spoke to before? Did she give her name?' asked Roberts.

'No, I've never met her. I don't know her name,' said Houseman.

Travers sighed and rubbed his face with his hands as he thought through the possibilities.

'So you don't think she knows you personally?' asked Travers.

'Detective Roberts, unless we get some answers soon, there could be a major political assassination within the next 48 hours. The last time I got involved in fieldwork, I got properly screwed, but we are out of options. I'm going to take Houseman's place and make that rendezvous. Can you put a tracker on the car and the bags?' Travers asked. 'We can either grab the woman or track the car.'

'That's pretty risky. We don't know who else might be there. It's an isolated spot if things go south,' said Roberts.

'Like I said, we're out of options. Just sort out the bugs. If she really doesn't know Houseman by sight, there shouldn't be a problem. I'll just hand over the luggage and let her go. Then it's up to you to track her. If there's a problem, we'll just have to try and grab her and hope she talks.'

After giving the matter some thought, Roberts decided to turn down Travers' idea. It was his beat and ultimately his call. He had considered going himself, but if there were locals involved, he might be recognized. Houseman would have to take the bags.

Travers returned to his hotel to freshen up. After showering, he lay on the bed with a freshly poured glass of vodka on his bedside table, contemplating what the next few hours might bring. In theory, it was a simple exercise, but even straightforward assignments could sometimes come crashing down. However, beyond the impending threat of an international incident, Alicia was still missing, and the woman who arranged the pickup probably knew where she was—or at least whether she was still alive. Travers updated Stanley before dressing and heading off to the Police Station, where DI Roberts briefed him. Alicia's two suitcases had small trackers inserted into the lining, and a magnetic tracker had been hidden behind the exhaust pipe of Houseman's car. Houseman himself was wearing a microphone, and Roberts' team would have him under constant surveillance the entire time the transfer took place.

Twenty minutes before the agreed time, Houseman left the police car park and drove the short distance out of town. Finding the layby, he pulled over and waited. It was deserted, with only the occasional car passing along the road to break the mounting tension. A few minutes after seven, a black Range Rover, coming towards him on the opposite side of the road, indicated right, crossed the road, and pulled into the layby. The large vehicle drove slowly towards his car, stopping a few feet in front of him. He was reminded by Detective Roberts that they were listening and to follow the instructions to the letter. There was no movement from the recently arrived vehicle, although Houseman could see at least two people inside. The driver was a woman, beside her, a man.

Houseman opened his door, got out, stood beside his car, and waited for a response. Three doors of the Range Rover opened simultaneously. A young dark-haired woman and two tall men got out and stood in front of their car. The two well-built men created an intimidating and ominous presence.

'Mr. Houseman?' the woman asked.

'Yes.'

'Have you got them?'

'Yes, they're in the boot.'

The woman gestured to the two men, who stepped forward toward Houseman's car. He walked back to the rear of his car, opened the boot, retrieved the two cases, and placed them on the ground in front of the approaching men. One of the men picked up the cases, glared at him, then turned toward the Range Rover, effortlessly tossing the large cases into the back of the car. The woman, accompanied by the other man, walked towards Houseman until she stood a few feet in front of him, looking at him intently for several seconds. She reached into her large handbag and pulled out an envelope, which she handed to him.

'Thank you, Mr. Houseman. That's a little bonus for you.' He opened the unsealed envelope and thumbed through the wedge of notes.

'That's all. You can go now,' she said.

Houseman returned to his car, placing the envelope in his jacket pocket. Travers and Roberts, waiting in their car a few hundred yards away, looked at each other, relieved at how smoothly the operation seemed to have gone. All they needed to do now was follow the Range Rover and hope the tracker did its job.

As Houseman started his engine and prepared to drive off, he noticed the woman from the Range Rover, who had paused by her door, had turned and was now walking back towards him. As she approached, he wound down his window. Once more, she reached into her handbag.

'Mr. Houseman, there's just one more thing.'

Travers and Roberts, who had been listening as the scene unfolded, quickly reached for their binoculars again. At that moment, they heard the dull thud of a suppressed gunshot. Looking through their field glasses, they could see Houseman slumped over his steering wheel, blood running down his face from a small wound to his right temple. The woman waited a moment before firing a second shot into the back of Houseman's head. She then retrieved the envelope containing the money from his jacket pocket before quickly returning to the Range Rover, which sped off into the night.

'Christ! They've shot him,' exclaimed Roberts.

Chapter 24

Otto Graf's arrival at a rather cloudy London Stansted Airport had gone largely unnoticed. Nothing seemed out of the ordinary, except for a slightly higher-than-usual number of armed policemen patrolling the airport. Graf was met by two plainclothes detectives and a member of the Foreign Office, who whisked him through customs and passport control and straight to the German Embassy in Belgrave Square, where he would be staying overnight. The meeting with the Prime Minister was due to take place at midday at Downing Street. On the advice of the Home Secretary, it was decided that the most sensible option under the circumstances was to avoid the usual Whitehall approach and enter via Horse Guards, using the rear entrance. This would avoid the publicity that always accompanies official visitors as they approach Number 10's famous black door, along with the barrage of reporters and cameramen stationed there, ready to ask awkward questions.

Charles Stanley was satisfied that Graf's arrival had passed without incident. The Director General had assigned him the unenviable task of safeguarding their visitor for the duration of his stay, with the knowledge that a verifiable threat to Graf's life had already been established. Given the connection to the Constable case, Stanley had requested that DCI John Deery lead the Met team to provide police cover while Graf was in the capital. There had still been no confirmed report of David Rubin entering the country. If he was already here, how could they stop him? Stanley put down his mug of freshly made tea and picked up his phone to confer with his counterpart.

'John? It's Stanley here. How's everything on your end?'

'Good morning, Charles. So far so good. I spoke to the Embassy a short time ago. Mr. Graf will be leaving them at around 11:40. We'll pick him up at the entrance and escort him to the back of Downing Street. For ease of security, he's going to hold his afternoon meetings in the Cabinet Office. When he's finished, the Embassy car will return him to Belgrave Square under police escort. Tonight's dinner has also been moved to the Embassy, with additional officers on duty. All the staff have been re-vetted, and guests will be checked as they enter. The Ambassador has agreed to have two of my men stay at the embassy during the dinner,' Deery reported.

'Is the Embassy providing the catering, John?' asked Stanley.

'Yes, and I'll be there myself to oversee everything,' said the Chief Inspector.

'Alright, John. I don't think we've overlooked anything. At least Graf won't be leaving the Embassy until tomorrow. We just need to make sure nothing happens tonight.'

'I just wish we had some idea where this guy Rubin is. If we're careful today, we can minimize the risk and be fine. Tomorrow, though, when Graf travels to the coast, it'll be open season,' said Deery.

Following the cold-blooded murder of Houseman in Poole, the police had successfully tracked the Range Rover to Durdle Door on the Dorset coast. The car had pulled up outside an old stone-clad cottage not far from the cliffs and the famous limestone arch. Roberts and Travers had been able to observe the house from a rocky outcrop about two hundred yards away. Travers had wanted to storm the house immediately, but Roberts had wisely counselled waiting to see who was inside, especially as darkness was falling.

Roberts had called for backup, and within an hour, the stakeout team had arrived and set up their night vision cameras and long-range audio surveillance equipment. When the suitcases were unloaded, the woman and two men entered the cottage, where they remained for a short time. About an hour later, they left. This time, the police would pick them up. Since then, everything had been quiet. With the stakeout team in position, Travers and Roberts returned to their car to prepare for a long night of vigilance.

When dawn broke, they returned to the cover of the undulating rocks overlooking the cottage. Travers turned to the officer monitoring the audio communications from the house.

'Pick up anything?' he asked.

'Not much. There's been one phone call, and what little chat there has been is pretty innocuous—no raised voices or shouting. The main thing I picked up was a conversation where they were waiting for instructions about a package. It was a woman's voice. She was telling someone else to hold on to the package for a day or two, then mentioned dropping it off. I'm afraid we're at the edge of our maximum range. We can't get any closer without risking our position,' the officer reported.

'Okay, thanks,' said Travers, who then contacted Stanley to update him on the latest and get a sense of how long to keep monitoring before moving in.

'Good morning, sir.'

'Morning, Greg,' said Stanley. 'What's the situation?'

'I'm with DI Roberts and his team at Durdle Door on the coast. We've got eyes on a cottage here. We bugged Alicia's bags, and when Houseman's contact picked them up, we were able to follow them. Sir, I'm pretty sure she's being held at this cottage. Otherwise, why go through all the trouble of carting the bags all the way out here? They could have just discarded them in Poole. They must need them for some reason,' said Travers.

'Agreed. What's your plan?' asked Stanley.

'At the moment, it's watch and wait, sir. DI Roberts has the place under surveillance, but we haven't been able to positively confirm that Alicia is there or how many people are inside. Until we can, he's reluctant to move in,' said Travers.

'Greg, we're looking after Herr Graf here today, along with DCI Deery and his team. Tomorrow, Graf is going to Portsmouth to meet his parents. The Met's got things well covered here, but tomorrow is what worries me. I'm traveling down to Portsmouth to help coordinate with the locals. I think you're right—if anything is going to happen, it will be tomorrow. Stay on your toes, Greg. As soon as you're able to confirm Miss Downes is in that cottage, go in and get her. The situation there might change suddenly depending on what happens over the next 48 hours.'

'Yes, sir. We'll be ready,' added Travers.

The visit to the Prime Minister at 10 Downing Street went as smoothly as Deery could have hoped. Entering the iconic building through the back door, Graf had managed to completely bypass the press pack, experiencing a level of anonymity enjoyed by few visitors who usually walk through the famous black gloss-finished steel front door. While Graf was inside Downing Street, he was confident that the German politician was safe. He wouldn't have to leave the building until he had completed his two subsequent meetings.

The Chief Inspector made himself comfortable in one of the Cabinet Office rooms. After getting a cup of tea from the kitchen, he glanced through a magazine rack and, after some deliberation, picked up today's *Times* newspaper. He took a seat by the window and began thumbing through the pages until he found the crossword. Ordinarily, his taste ran more toward the red-top tabloids, but he had an hour to kill, and perhaps the *Times* crossword would provide more of a challenge and distract him from the pressing matter of preventing an invisible man from turning one of Germany's most prominent politicians into a corpse on British soil.

At 3:30 pm, the door to his room opened.

'Excuse me, the chauffeur with the Embassy car has arrived to pick up Mr. Graf.'

'Okay, Mr. Graf hasn't finished his last meeting yet. Would you ask him to wait by his car? I don't want it left unattended,' Deery replied, immediately notifying his own men to get ready to escort their charge back to the Embassy.

With Graf now safely back at the relative security of the German Embassy, the Inspector and his team returned to the Victoria Embankment. Uniformed officers would remain on duty at the Embassy until Graf left for Portsmouth the following day, while plainclothes officers circulated inside the Embassy during Graf's dinner engagement that evening.

Three hours later, Deery and his team were back at the Embassy. Preparations were in full swing, although it wasn't a formal Embassy dinner. The caterers were setting up under the watchful gaze of one of the Inspector's men. Deery caught the eye of the Ambassador as he walked through the dining room and made his way toward him.

'Mr. Ambassador, good evening, sir,' said Deery, shaking the Ambassador's hand with a nod of respect.

'Detective Chief Inspector,' the diplomat acknowledged benevolently.

'I'd like to thank you once again for your cooperation. We'll try not to get in your way this evening,' said the Chief Inspector.

'This is a private dinner, Chief Inspector. I shall not be present,' the Ambassador replied.

'Mr. Graf was kind enough to provide a guest list, which we have cross-checked as far as we can. Are you familiar with the list, sir?' asked the detective.

'Otto Graf is both a prominent politician and part of a very successful German family. They have business interests and many contacts in this country, and the guest list reflects that. Some of the guests are personal friends of Otto, and others are influential business leaders with connections to the Graf family,' said the Ambassador.

'I see. Well, thank you, Ambassador. We will keep an eye on things until the guests have left the Embassy grounds tonight.'

With that, the Ambassador wished Deery well and left the room. The detective wandered around the long mahogany dining table, which was surrounded by richly decorated red walls punctuated by large oil paintings. As he admired a large tapestry hanging opposite the fireplace, Otto Graf appeared around the corner of the open-ended room.

'Chief Inspector Deery, the Ambassador told me that you were here.'

'Good evening, Herr Graf. I was just admiring the room,' he replied, taking in the elegance of the space.

'Yes, it's beautiful,' Graf said, looking around appreciatively.

'Your guests are due to arrive shortly, sir. We'll check them in at the front door. We certainly don't want any unauthorized gatecrashers, do we? I have men keeping an eye on things in the kitchen as well. I presume you know all your guests by sight, sir?' Deery asked.

'Yes, of course, Chief Inspector,' Graf replied.

'Well, that's one thing settled. Enjoy your dinner, sir. We'll be as unobtrusive as possible,' said Deery, as the pair parted company.

Within an hour, the dinner was in full swing. All the guests had arrived and been accounted for—an eclectic mix of individuals reflecting the broad range of political, business, and social interests that Graf enjoyed. The nearby Royal Brompton Hospital had been put on alert in case of an emergency.

The Inspector walked through the hall to the kitchen, which was bustling with activity, with chefs and waiters either preparing food or conveying it to the dining room. He stopped beside one of his colleagues who had been monitoring the proceedings closely.

'Fred,' Deery said as he stood next to his fellow detective at the doorway.

'Boss,' Fred greeted him with a casual nod.

'How's everything going?'

'I haven't seen anyone pouring rat poison into the gravy, but sir, how are we supposed to know what they're putting in? It could be white pepper or just as easily be arsenic. I wouldn't know the difference until the ambulance turned up,' said the policeman.

'Just keep your eye out for anyone looking shifty or nervous,' Deery replied, before casually walking out of the kitchen and across the hall to check in with his men patrolling the grounds. He made a final round of the Embassy before returning inside.

With the main and dessert courses completed, it was time for 'cigars and brandy.' Deery watched as six waiters carrying silver trays brought a variety of drinks for the now-satisfied diners. He observed each waiter carefully as they approached the guests, looking for any sign that one of them might have more on their mind than just serving a drink. His attention was drawn to one waiter, who appeared slightly uneasy—more so than the others—and was avoiding eye contact with the increasingly watchful Chief Inspector.

Deery's gaze followed the waiter as he moved toward the table, distributing drinks to each guest. He tensed when the waiter reached Otto Graf, handing him a glass of Amaretto with black peppercorns floating on the surface. The Chief Inspector's instincts kicked in, and he walked towards Graf, trying to appear nonchalant so as not to arouse any concern among the guests.

The waiter, tall and lean, clearly fit with a Mediterranean complexion, handed the glass to Graf. Deery's eyes never left him as he carefully made his way to Graf's side. As Graf prepared to raise his glass for a toast, the Chief Inspector caught his eye and subtly shook his head.

Graf paused, slightly confused. The Chief Inspector moved quickly, taking the glass from Graf's hand.

'Just a moment, sir,' he said. 'I think you have a dirty glass there. Allow me to get you a fresh one.'

If the detective's intervention alarmed Graf, he didn't show it. He leaned back casually and allowed Deery to take the small shot glass. A few moments later, he returned with a fresh glass of the liquor, and Graf stood to propose a toast to the assembled gathering.

Shortly after midnight, the evening drew to a close, and the guests began to leave. The detective's team accounted for all the catering staff as they packed up. He exchanged a few words with the relieved host before rejoining his men. After a final sweep of the building and grounds, they left. It had been a tense few hours, and Deery couldn't help but feel a sense of relief that it was finally over.

Back in his office, The Detective Chief Inspector called Charles Stanley as promised.

'Charles, it's John Deery.'

'Good evening, John. How did the evening go? No dramas, I hope?' Stanley asked.

'Just one. We had a bit of a moment late on with one of the waiters, but it turned out to be a false alarm. He was Turkish, not Israeli, and had worked for the embassy for several years. When are you heading down to Portsmouth?'

'Early tomorrow morning. We'll meet Graf and his party when his private jet arrives at Southampton Airport. I understand he has a limo waiting to take him directly to King Alfred's Wharf in Portsmouth, where the Graf yacht is moored. As far as I know, he'll be staying on board until they cast off. The local police have been keeping a close eye on the yacht since it docked, and they've spoken with Graf senior, making him aware of the threat. The RN Bravo Squadron at Horsea Island has made a sweep around the *Anni-Frid* and found nothing. They'll do another sweep before she leaves harbour just in case.'

'Alright, John. We'll make sure Graf gets to Stansted in one piece tomorrow and send him on his way. Good luck, and let me know if you need anything,' said Deery.

'Thanks, John. Good night,' Stanley replied.

Chapter 25

By 7:00 AM the following morning, Charles Stanley and his small team were well on their way down the M3 to the South Coast. The Transport Police had already been briefed at Southampton Airport, and Stanley wanted to ensure every precaution was in place before Graf's aircraft arrived. By 9:30 AM, Stanley was on the ground in the terminal building, discussing the arrival with the UK Border Force and the Tactical Firearms Unit that had been assigned for support.

Stanley's phone rang—it was Detective Chief Inspector Deery.

'Good morning, Charles. I thought you'd want to know that "Elvis has left the building." His plane took off from Stansted five minutes ago. He should be with you in about 35.'

'Right, thanks for the update. We're all set here. I just wish we had some news about Rubin—at least if we knew he was here, we could be sure of something,' said Stanley.

'Welcome to the club,' the Inspector replied with a chuckle. 'I had that same feeling last night and almost made a complete arse of myself.'

'It's going to be a long day. I'll call you later,' said Stanley.

Right on time, the white twin-engine Gulfstream G650 came into view, touching down smoothly on the single runway. A marshal directed the plane to a stand not far from the terminal. As it came to a stop, the black limousine and two police Range Rovers, under the command of Inspector Williams, drove out and parked in front of the plane. Police binoculars scoured the adjacent buildings and grounds for any signs of potential threat.

The plane's door swung open. Charles Stanley leapt from the passenger seat of the leading police car and sprinted up the stairway before anyone appeared in the doorway to offer themselves as a target. At the top of the stairs, Stanley raised his radio to his lips, scanning the expanse of the airfield. It had been many years since he'd left the demands of fieldwork for the responsibilities of desk duty, and the familiar tension of the situation instantly took him back.

As he surveyed the area, his eyes caught a glint of light—possibly a reflection. But was it someone's sunglasses, or the end of a telescopic sight attached to a rifle? Either way, he or Graf would be sitting targets for a trained sniper with a high-powered rifle. 'All clear,' came the reassuring word from the ground surveillance team.

Stanley stepped into the plane, greeted by Otto Graf, who stood waiting. The two men descended the stairs together and made their way to the waiting car, followed by Graf's entourage. Graf shifted uneasily in his seat.

'Are you alright, sir?' Stanley asked, noticing his discomfort.

'Yes, thank you, Mr. Stanley. Your associate in London, Detective Chief Inspector Deery, is a very cautious man. He made me wear a bulletproof vest under my suit. It's rather... constricting,' Graf replied, fidgeting with the fabric.

'I understand you're heading straight to your father's yacht in Portsmouth, sir?' Stanley asked, trying to shift the conversation.

'Yes, well, actually it's moored in Gosport, Mr. Stanley, just a few hundred metres across the harbour.'

With all the passengers accounted for, the limousine, sandwiched between the two Range Rovers, pulled out of the airport for the 60-minute drive along the M27, before branching off toward Gosport. A police helicopter buzzed overhead, providing added reassurance.

As the convoy approached Gosport Marina, Stanley caught his first sight of the *Anni-Frid*, a colossal yacht that dwarfed the others in the harbour. The cars pulled up alongside the giant vessel. As the car doors opened, several people on board came up on deck to greet them, walking toward the gangplank.

Graf paused before stepping onto the plank and turned toward Stanley.

'Mr. Stanley, may I thank you and your team for your dedication. I am very grateful,' Graf said, his voice sincere.

'All in a day's work, Herr Graf. We're happy to be of service. May I recommend that you stay aboard until your departure, sir?' recommended Stanley.

'Very well, if it will make you happy, Mr. Stanley,' Graf said. 'We have a dinner on board tonight with some friends, and tomorrow morning we cast off. I believe we're sailing down to Land's End before returning to Germany.'

'I see,' Stanley replied. 'We'll have our men in place until you set sail, just to be on the safe side. And the Royal Navy will conduct a second sweep of the yacht tonight to ensure no one's left any... unwanted parting gifts. May I wish you a safe trip home, Herr Graf. Perhaps we'll meet again in the not-too-distant future.'

'Thank you, Mr. Stanley. That is very kind,' Graf said, nodding gratefully.

With that, Graf turned and boarded the *Anni-Frid*, where he was warmly greeted by his father and mother.

Leaving two uniformed officers stationed at the jetty, Stanley and Inspector Williams returned to one of the Range Rovers. As they approached, a junior officer waved them over, his hand signalling an urgent incoming radio message. Stanley stood by the open passenger door, stretched across the seat, and grabbed the receiver.

'Stanley'

'Good morning, sir. This is Commander Beatty, Defence Intelligence, MOD. Facial recognition has flagged up a subject of interest near one of our bases. We contacted your HQ, which patched me through to you. I understand you have an ongoing operation?'

'Good morning, Commander. Who is the 'person of interest'?' Stanley asked, his tone now more focused.

'David Rubin,' Beatty replied flatly.

'Rubin? Are you sure? Quite sure?' Stanley asked, his voice tightening with disbelief.

'Yes, sir. Well, according to our program, there is an 80% probability,' Beatty said. 'I've sent you the photo.'

Stanley immediately reached into his pocket for his mobile phone, quickly calling up the image.

'Commander, is that the best image you have? It could be my mother-in-law!' Stanley muttered, inspecting the blurry, grainy photo.

'We managed to pick him up on local CCTV for a while but lost him in the crowds. We're trying to re-acquire him,' Beatty explained.

'Alright, Commander, well done. Where did you pick him up?' Stanley asked, his mind racing.

'Queen Street, Portsmouth,' Beatty replied.

'Portsmouth?!' Stanley repeated, his pulse quickening. 'Bloody hell. Where was he heading when you lost contact?'

'West, along Queen Street, toward the harbour and HMS *Warrior*,' Beatty added.

'Thank you, Commander. If you re-establish contact, please let me know immediately,' Stanley said, his mind already shifting into high gear.

Stanley gathered his team, the urgency of the situation pressing down on him. He crossed to the uniformed officers by the *Anni-Frid*.

'No one gets off that yacht until I return, understand? Any issues, refer them to me,' Stanley barked, his voice sharp.

'Rubin's been spotted in Portsmouth, heading toward the Harbour front. It'll take too long to drive around. Requisition a boat, Inspector—we've got to get over there now. Tell your men on the Portsmouth side to stay sharp. Defence Intelligence has sent us a new image of him—it's not great, but it's all we have. We need to grab him, now,' Stanley ordered.

Within minutes, they were crossing the channel on the commandeered RIB. The boat's engine roared as they made their way to Gunwharf Quays Marina. Stanley and his team quickly disembarked, hugging the shoreline and heading north toward Rubin's last known location.

The babysitting of Otto Graf had been going smoothly, but now a cold knot of anxiety twisted in Stanley's gut. Everything they had worked for—every precaution, every plan—would be worthless if Rubin succeeded in fulfilling his contract and caused an international incident.

A crackle came through the Police Inspector's radio. A colleague had spotted Rubin. He was approaching the Spinnaker Tower from the north.

Stanley's pace quickened, his heart pounding as they reached the northern end of the promenade. The 560-foot observation platform loomed ahead of them. The reporting sergeant dashed toward Williams as soon as he spotted him.

'Where is he? Where did he go?' demanded Williams, his voice tight with frustration.

'He was heading this way, sir. As soon as I saw him, I grabbed my radio. But when I looked up, he had vanished,' the sergeant reported, his eyes wide.

'Did he see you?' Williams pressed, his gaze scanning the crowd.

'No, sir. I don't think so,' the sergeant replied, shaking his head.

Stanley ordered his men to spread out around the tower area, hoping for another sighting of Rubin. It seemed like an impossible task. Both the Spinnaker Tower and Gunwharf Marina were packed with tourists. It would be a miracle to spot him.

Standing by the railings, Stanley looked out toward Gosport, spotting the *Anni-Frid* in the distance. He could see figures walking on the deck, confirming that Graf and his party were still aboard. Stanley's thoughts were interrupted by a tourist sitting nearby, watching the passing ships with a pair of binoculars.

'Excuse me, sir, may I borrow those for a moment?' Stanley asked, his tone polite but urgent.

The man handed him the binoculars. Stanley scanned the yacht from his position, the *Anni-Frid* coming into sharper focus through the lenses. He then returned the glasses to the tourist.

'Thank you,' said Stanley.

'If you want a proper look, you should go up there,' said Williams, gesturing toward the top of the Spinnaker Tower.

'A perfectly spectacular view for miles in every direction, whatever the weather'

'How far would you say it is to King Alfred Wharf from here, Inspector?' Stanley asked, his mind already working through the possibilities.

'Not far—about 600 yards or so,' Williams said, considering the distance.

'Well within the range of a half-decent sniper with a good field of view,' said Stanley, his eyes fixed on the tower.

'Up there?' Williams asked, his brow furrowing in confusion.

'Why not?' Stanley replied. 'Come on.'

Inside the Spinnaker Tower, Stanley and Inspector Williams jostled their way across the bustling ground floor. They approached a steward, who quickly called over the floor manager, Miss Cahill.

Stanley and Williams flashed their identification, hurriedly explaining the situation to her in succinct terms.

'The three viewing platforms are all glass-enclosed, Inspector,' Miss Cahill said, gesturing toward the elevator.

'How high are they?' Stanley asked, his focus sharp.

'The lowest is 100 metres, and the highest is 110 metres. There's a high-speed lift, or if you're up for it, 560 steps,' said Miss Cahill, with a just a suspicion of sarcasm in her voice as she looked at Stanley's beefy frame.

Stanley nodded. 'I think we'll take the lift. What's above the top viewing platform?'

'Just the 27-metre spire,' Cahill replied.

'Is there access to the area above the top platform and the spire?' Stanley asked, his voice reflecting an increased urgency.

'Only a maintenance hatch above the top platform,' she explained.

'We'd better have a look,' Stanley said, turning to Williams. 'Inspector, I'm going to check that top floor and maintenance access point. You have a look at the other two viewing platforms. Have your men stand by the ground-level entrances. If Rubin's here, we might flush him out and he'll make a run for it.'

'Thank you, Miss Cahill. Oh, one more thing—have you had any maintenance men around here this afternoon?' Stanley asked, his eyes narrowing with suspicion.

'We did have one earlier. He was working on the spire, but I haven't seen him since this morning. I assume he's gone now,' she replied, her tone casual.

Stanley exchanged a look with Williams, then the pair turned toward the lift. Stepping inside, the lift doors closed and it quickly began its ascent. Shortly, the doors slid open at the lowest platform. Inspector Williams wished Stanley good luck before stepping out and disappearing from sight.

Seconds later, Stanley's lift ascended to the topmost viewing platform. As the doors opened, Stanley scanned the area, noting the groups of tourists wandering around, gazing at the panoramic views through the reinforced glass. His eyes drifted upward to the ceiling, where he spotted the access hatch in the corner, complete with a steel ladder affixed to the wall.

Stanley climbed the ladder, each rung creaking under his weight, until he reached the top. The padlocks on the hatch were gone.

With a quick push, Stanley opened the hatch and crawled onto the roof. He paused, eyeing the small safety railing that ran around the edge. Even with it in place, Stanley resisted the urge to venture too close to the sheer drop of over 300 feet.

He walked across the roof toward a large storage cupboard and pried it open. Inside were nylon ropes, harnesses, and various safety tools. Moving to the next cupboard, Stanley opened the door and froze. A body, near-naked, covered in blood, was crammed inside, lifeless. As Stanley pulled the door open fully, the body fell to the floor at his feet, still warm. Blood pooled beneath it, seeping from multiple stab wounds. It must have been the maintenance man.

Heart pounding, Stanley reached for his radio, his fingers trembling. But before he could make the call, a violent blow to his back sent him reeling. A powerful hand clamped over his nose and mouth, suffocating him. The radio slipped from his grasp and clattered to the floor.

He reached around to grab his assailant's suffocating hand, whilst at the same time slamming his right elbow with all his might into the side of his opponent and wheeling around to the left in an attempt to throw the powerful man off balance. The radio crackled into life— Inspector Williams was reporting that the lower platforms were clear.

But Stanley couldn't reach the radio. He could feel the assailant's grip tightening, pulling his arm behind his back. He fleetingly saw the flashing glint of stainless steel as Rubin plunged his knife up to the hilt between Stanley's ribs. He gasped as Rubin withdrew the six-inch blade and blood immediately began to pour from the wound.

The commotion had now been heard by those in the viewing gallery below. Stanley could hear the screams of the panicking tourists followed by hurried footsteps and raised voices. Then across the floor, climbing up through the open hatch he saw Inspector Williams followed by an armed policeman. Without hesitation Rubin drew his knife across Stanley's throat, blood poured across the floor from the laceration, killing him within seconds. Rubin stood up and looked towards his rifle nearby. Before he could reach it, two shots rang out as the firearms officer shot Rubin twice in the centre of his chest. He dropped the blood-soaked knife and staggered back towards the edge of the roof before toppling over the low rail and plunging to the ground, arriving with a sickening thud to the horror of all those below..

Inspector Williams stood over Stanley's blood-soaked body, the silence of the moment thick with horror and disbelief. His hand remained on Stanley's shoulder, but it was clear—his comrade in arms was dead.

Chapter 26

Alicia Downes slowly began to stir, the haze of the drug-induced unconsciousness slowly lifting, but the world remained a blur. Every movement sent searing pain coursing through her body—almost everything hurt, and what didn't, ached. She could barely focus her eyes, but she forced herself to take in her surroundings. There were no windows, no natural light—just a small storage room with a camp bed and a single ceiling light hanging above her.

Downes looked down at her bloodied hands and bruised fingers, both trembling and raw. Two fingernails were missing, torn off with brutal force. She didn't know how she got here, but the memory of the ferocious beatings she had endured was vivid. Her secondment to MI6 had included interrogation resistance training—confrontation, sensory deprivation—but nothing had prepared her for the savagery of Olga Devereux's methods.

Every inch of her body was bruised, battered, and broken, she couldn't even tell if she had any fractures. She was too weak to even sit up.

Then, the sound of a heavy bolt being drawn back from the door made her flinch. Alicia instinctively braced herself, knowing that escape, if it ever came, would be a miracle. The small wooden door creaked open, and Hector Devereux entered, holding a tray with a sandwich and a hot drink. Even through the haze of her blurred vision, Alicia recognised him immediately. He was Olga's eldest son and the one overseeing her interrogation.

'Here, some food for you,' Hector said, his tone cold and arrogant.

'Where am I?' Alicia croaked, still trying to clear the fog from her head.

'Somewhere safe, where no one will find you,' Hector replied menacingly.

As Hector spoke, Alicia heard the faint sound of a phone ringing from behind him. Hector turned away, stepping out of the room, and closed the door behind him with a loud click, followed by the unmistakable sound of the bolt being drawn across.

Alicia strained to listen. She was in no condition to move fast, but she pressed her ear against the door, hoping to catch something useful.

'Yes?' Hector answered.

'Mother?' came a voice, but Alicia couldn't make out the words.

'Yes, I know. I heard it on the radio. Rubin's been shot and killed by the police in Portsmouth. It's all over the news,' Hector's voice sounded distant. 'What do you want me to do with the girl?'

Alicia's heart skipped a beat. She had expected this moment, feared it even, but hearing the confirmation still felt like a punch to the gut.

'Alright, leave it to me. I'll take care of her,' said Hector before hanging up.

Alicia staggered back from the door, her legs buckling as she fell back onto the bed. The news hit her like a freight train. Rubin was dead. Charles Stanley was dead. And now, her fate seemed sealed. They had no reason to keep her alive anymore.

She glanced down at her battered body. Her eyes were swollen, the psychotropic drugs still warping her perception, making it impossible to think clearly. Downes sat and pondered her fate. How were they going to kill her? She thought of her family, would they ever know what had happened to her? Suppose they never found her body? She suddenly felt immensely vulnerable, as the seeming inevitability of her death drew nearer. She knew she couldn't afford to wallow in despair or self-pity. She was in a small room, physically incapacitated, and with no one coming to her rescue, but if they wanted her dead, she was determined to make them pay a heavy price for it.

The door opened again, and Hector stepped inside. This was her moment—perhaps her only chance. As he entered, Alicia grabbed the mug of hot tea and hurled it at his face. He flinched, his eyes squinting in pain, giving her the split second she needed. She grabbed the metal tray from his hands and smashed it against his head with every ounce of strength she had left. Over and over, the tray clattered against his skull until he staggered, his knees buckling beneath him.

She stomped down on his hand, then kicked out at his body, before scrambling her way toward the door. She fumbled with the handle, her swollen fingers unable to grasp it properly. Finally, the door creaked open, and Alicia ran as fast as she was able, stumbling through into the open air, disoriented, and blind to everything around her.

Travers, stationed at a nearby vantage point, had been monitoring the building through his binoculars. He saw her—the figure of Alicia running away from the cottage, unsteady and in a daze, heading toward the cliffs. Then, Hector's large form appeared in pursuit.

'She's moving toward the arch,' Travers radioed to DI Roberts, a sense of urgency in his voice. 'There's someone after her, I think it's Hector Devereux.'

Without waiting for a response, Travers leapt to his feet. He sprinted toward the cottage, eyes fixed on Alicia and her pursuer. As he ran, he spotted an old hand axe embedded in a block of wood just outside the cottage. Instinctively he grabbed it, the rusted blade feeling solid in his grip.

Ahead, Alicia was stumbling, barely aware of the danger closing in on her. Her movements were erratic, and she was heading straight for the cliff edge. Travers' heart raced. He couldn't shout out to her—if he did, her pursuer would catch her before he could reach them.

Alicia reached the rocky outcrop, stopping abruptly, as though realizing there was nowhere left to run. She turned to face her would-be executioner.

Travers was closing the distance, his eyes locked on the figure ahead—Hector Devereux, brandishing a large knife. Alicia Downes had collapsed to her knees, exhausted. Her energy, fuelled by adrenaline moments before, had now been entirely spent. She could barely see Hector, who stood only twenty yards away. Travers knew time was running out. He had only seconds to make a difference.

Scrambling quickly across the narrow ridge of the iconic arch, Travers moved with precision, knowing that one misstep could send him plummeting to his death. As he neared, he screamed Hector's name, his voice cutting through the tension. Hector stopped, turning slowly to face his pursuer. Behind him, Alicia, battered and bruised, lifted her head weakly, her vacant eyes locking onto Travers.

Hector, holding the knife with menacing intent, advanced toward Travers. His face was a mask of cold resolve, ready to kill. There was no time to wait for Roberts. Travers had to make a choice: stand and fight, or leave Alicia to face her fate alone, and leave his conscience forever burdened by the weight of inaction.

He hesitated for a moment, a lifetime of insecurity and calculated thought flashing before him. He had never been a man of aggression or action. But this was different. In front of him stood a killer, a man prepared to take a life—Alicia's or his.

The two men faced each other, as if in some twisted gunfight from the old West, each waiting for the other to make the first move. Then Hector lunged, his long knife aimed for Travers' chest. Instinctively, Travers parried the blow with his left arm, the knife slicing through the air, just missing. Without thinking, he swung the axe in his right hand, the blade cleaving toward Hector's side. Hector caught his wrist mid-swing, and the two men grappled, their bodies entwining as they fell to the ground, struggling for control.

Though weak, Downes rallied. She crawled toward the men, determined to help despite the overwhelming fatigue and pain in her limbs. The two men rolled over the narrow promontory, each vying for dominance. Hector managed to pin Travers by the throat, his knife just inches from Travers' chest.

Travers could feel the weight of Hector's body bearing down on him, the blade inching closer. His eyes were now wide with uncontrolled anger. Sweat dripped from Hector's forehead, landing on Travers' face. He couldn't hold on much longer. Desperation surged within him. He lurched his body to the side, letting Hector's full weight bring the knife down, crashing against the jagged stone where Travers had been seconds before.

With a forceful strike, Travers hit Hector on the back of his head with the axe shaft, stunning him and leaving him motionless. Travers reached for Alicia, her limp body now close by. He cradled her in his arms and looked into her almost lifeless eyes, once bright with life and passion, but now dimmed and barely flickering.

For a brief moment, Alicia's eyes widened. But before Travers could react, Hector's arm coiled around his neck, yanking him away from Alicia. He was thrown toward the cliff's edge.

Air squeezed out of Travers' lungs as Hector tightened his grip, choking him. Gasping for breath, Travers fought against the crushing hold, his vision growing hazy. But Downes, despite her exhaustion, wasn't done. She grabbed Hector's leg, sinking her teeth into the fleshy part of his calf. Blood poured from the wound. Hector screamed, releasing Travers as his focus shifted towards the young woman. He struck Downs across her face sending her sprawling across the rocks.

Travers rolled away, scrambling to his feet. Hector, too, was getting back up. Travers closed the distance and, with a mighty kick, sent Hector stumbling toward the edge of the arch. Hector grasped at the rocky outcrop, trying desperately to keep from falling.

Travers moved toward him, blood pouring from Hector's nose and mouth. He looked at Alicia—her body, broken and lifeless, splayed across the limestone rocks like a discarded rag doll.

Hector lunged forward, grabbing Travers' left ankle with a vice-like grip, attempting to drag him over the side. Travers kicked and punched, but Hector's hold was unrelenting. Every movement brought him closer to the drop.

In a final desperate bid, Travers spotted the hand axe he had dropped during the struggle. It was almost within reach. His fingers brushed the base of the handle, but it was agonizingly out of his grasp.

With one final push, Travers strained every muscle, extending his arm and lunging for the weapon. His fingertips grazed the axe handle, and with a final, concerted effort, he grabbed it.

The deliverance was in his hands. With a single, powerful strike, Travers brought the axe down on Hector's wrist. The blade cleaved through muscle and bone, severing Hector's hand entirely.

Hector let out a grisly scream of anguish as he clutched his severed wrist with his left hand, desperately trying to stem the blood gushing from the stump. His body swayed for a moment before Travers delivered a powerful kick to Hector's chest. The impact sent the man reeling backwards, and with one last, panicked grasp at the cliff's edge, he fell. Two hundred feet down to the rough waters below, his screams fading into nothingness.

Travers collapsed onto the rocky cliff top, his chest heaving as he drew in ragged breaths, his whole body trembling with the aftershocks of adrenaline. He lay there for a moment, allowing the reality of what had just transpired to sink in.

He turned toward Alicia, still lying motionless on the rocks. His legs felt like rubber as he struggled to his feet. His mind raced—was she alive? Could he save her in time? He hurried over to her, kneeling down. Her body was bloodied and bruised, but there was a weak pulse, her breathing shallow but present. He clasped her, heart pounding in his chest, but relief began to seep through him as he realised she was still with him.

As he looked down at her bloodied face, Alicia's eyelids fluttered. Her eyes barely opened, and yet, in them, he thought he saw the faintest hint of a smile. Her fingers tightened around his arm.

'It's all over, Alicia,' he whispered softly. 'You're going to be okay. We'll get you out of here.'

Downes gave a weak smile, but her strength gave out and she fell back into his arms, unconscious once again. Travers' heart ached, but he didn't have time to linger. He heard the sound of footsteps behind him. Looking around, he saw DI Roberts and one of his officers approaching, scrambling across the rocky outcrop.

'Where's the other guy?' Roberts called out, scanning the scene.

'Mostly down there,' Travers replied, nodding toward the churning sea below.

'The air ambulance is on its way from Bournemouth,' Roberts said, his voice calm and reassuring. 'Won't be long now.'

Travers watched as the air ambulance arrived, the helicopter's whirring blades creating a violent wind that tousled his hair. The paramedics swiftly assessed Downes, stabilizing her before loading her onto the helicopter. As they took off, Travers looked around at the crime scene—at the blood-soaked knife, at the remnants of Hector, now little more than a gruesome memory.

He turned back to Roberts. 'Do you have a couple of evidence bags on you?'

Roberts handed over two bags, then gestured toward the scene with a nod. 'I've got a recovery team on the way to pick up Devereux. How're you feeling?'

'I'm okay, thanks,' Travers replied. His voice was steady, but his eyes were far away. 'What happens now?'

Roberts looked at him. 'Now? We'll take your friend Olga in for questioning. After we talk to Miss Downes, I'm sure we'll have more than enough to press charges against her.'

Travers' frowned. 'Olga Devereux is the rotten, diseased heart of all this mess. She has the blood of your people and mine on her hands, and many others'

'She'll get what's coming to her, don't worry,' Roberts insisted, his tone firm. 'We'll bring her in, on suspicion of murder. Then, she'll answer for everything.'

Travers was quiet for a moment, his mind racing. Finally, he spoke again. 'I'd like to see her first, Inspector, before you arrest her. I have a score to settle with that woman.'

Roberts raised an eyebrow but gave a wry smile. 'Yes, I've heard about your little 'undercover operation' with her. I'd offer you a pair of handcuffs, but I gather she's got plenty of her own you could use!'

Travers snorted, though his face remained unforgiving. 'All right, I'll wait outside while you two get reacquainted, and don't do anything stupid. I don't want you both sharing a paddy wagon, understand?' Roberts continued.

'Really, Inspector, as if I would,' Travers replied with a sly grin, though there was an edge to his voice.

With the air ambulance now a speck in the sky, Travers followed DI Roberts back across the cliff, his eyes scanning the landscape, now eerily quiet. As they reached the police car, the other members of Roberts's team were already combing through the stone cottage, looking for evidence. Travers paused for a moment, his thoughts heavy, then reached for his phone, flicking through contacts until he landed on 'O.' He pressed the call button, holding the phone to his ear as the familiar ring echoed.

The line clicked, and the familiar, soft, seductive voice answered. 'Olga Devereux.'

'Olga, it's Greg Travers. I need to see you. I'm heading back to London tomorrow for a very important meeting, and it's urgent. I've got something you'll want to hear.'

'A meeting? I'm afraid not. I'm leaving tomorrow. I'm busy packing,' Olga's voice appeared indifferent to Travers entreaties.

'Two hundred million,' Travers said, cutting her off, his voice confident and persuasive. 'A major contract is coming up for renewal. I have the particulars with me, I think you should see it Olga.'

There was a brief silence on the other end, the faint sound of rustling papers. Then, Olga's voice returned, shaded with curiosity. 'Two hundred million?' She paused again. 'Alright, Greg. I'm at home. Come over to Parkson. We'll discuss it, but you'll have to be quick.'

Travers smiled, looking up at Roberts. 'Avarice, I love it. She just couldn't resist it. Come on, Inspector. She's on her island, getting ready to run.'

Roberts shot him a look of intrigue, but said nothing as he turned the car towards the quay. 'The Dorset Marine Police have a boat in the harbour. They'll lay off the island unless they're needed. I'll stay with the boat and wait for you to bring your 'girlfriend' out.'

Travers chuckled sardonically, the tension lifting slightly. 'That's the kind of remark Stanley would have made,' he muttered, reflecting for a brief moment. While Roberts was momentarily distracted, he reached over and grabbed one of the evidence bags from the back seat, slipping it into his jacket pocket.

They arrived at the quay, where a motorboat was ready to take them to Parkson Island. Roberts gave him one last look as Travers climbed into the boat.

'Don't do anything reckless, Greg. This isn't over yet.'

'Don't worry, Inspector. This is payback time, by the book, my book.'

Roberts and Travers clambered aboard the enclosed motorboat, and the boat's master fired up the engine. The vessel glided out of the bustling harbour, cutting a path through the water toward the island. About twenty minutes later, they arrived at the southern jetty, where Travers stepped off the boat and made his way toward the boathouse. A staff member, impassive and efficient, greeted him and escorted him through the electronically controlled entrance. They walked down the narrow corridor, finally reaching the large open atrium of Olga Devereux's home.

The assistant knocked several times on a wooden door before it opened. Olga appeared, her smile as warm as ever, but there was a flicker of something—perhaps curiosity or even anxiety—as she greeted him. She took his hand and led him into the large living room. The fresh sea air swept through the open French doors, carrying the scent of salt and damp wood.

'Would you like a drink, Greg?' Olga asked, her voice dripping with polished hospitality.

'No, thank you,' Travers replied, his eyes scanning the room. 'So, you're leaving tomorrow?'

Olga smiled slightly, her eyes gleaming with the allure of her extravagant lifestyle. 'Well, you know how it is—it's a global business. I'm combining business with pleasure. How is the world of Government Procurement? What's the deal with the contract?'

Travers noted the large array of suitcases and boxes scattered around the otherwise well-ordered room. He raised an eyebrow.

'That's a lot of bags,' Travers observed. 'It looks like you are planning on being away for a while, are you? It's just as well I'm here, I can give you a hand.'

Travers walked around to the back of Olga's ornate wooden writing desk. Then he reached into his coat pocket. 'Here,' he said, tossing the contents onto the table.

Olga froze, her expression flickering between confusion and fear as she glanced down. Her gaze locked onto the severed, blood-soaked hand resting in front of her.

'Do you recognize it?' Travers' voice was like cold steel. 'That ring—do you recognize it? It belongs to that bastard son of yours.'

Devereux staggered back, her face drained of colour as she gasped in horror. Her hands shook as she reached forward, grabbing the dismembered hand and clutching it to her chest, her expression twisting from grief to rage.

'Where is he? Where is Hector?' she hissed, her voice now venomous.

'Where he belongs,' Travers replied coldly. 'On a mortuary table, about to be dissected. The game's up, Olga. You don't just have blood on your hands—you're drowning in it. Alicia Downes is in the hospital, drugged and beaten half to death by you and Hector. If I had my way, you wouldn't walk out of this room alive. You're depraved, rotten to the core.'

Travers reached into his pocket, producing his identification. 'MI5,' he said flatly.

Olga's eyes narrowed, her lips curling into a dismissive sneer. 'MI5, I see. Well, well, so Procurement didn't work out then, did it?'

She laughed lightly, but there was no humour in it. 'You don't seriously think I'm going to spend the rest of my life in jail, do you? You really have no idea what real power and influence are, do you, Greg?'

Travers stepped forward, his presence now dark and commanding. 'Time to go, Olga. The police are waiting outside. You've kept them waiting long enough. Oh, and by the way, I hope you enjoyed your last fuck, because the only 'screws' you'll be having from now on are the kind that hammer on your prison cell door at 6:30 in the morning to wake you up.'

Travers turned and walked toward the door, with Olga Devereux on his arm. As they approached the boat, DI Roberts stepped out to meet them.

'Detective Inspector Roberts,' Travers said with a satisfied smile. 'May I present Mrs. Olga Devereux: billionaire philanthropist, multinational corporate chief executive, fraudster, kidnapper, and multiple murderer.'

Olga's face twisted in fury, but Roberts remained unfazed, calmly handcuffing her hands behind her back. 'Mrs. Devereux,' he said dryly, 'From what I hear, you're used to these.'

After reading her rights, he guided her into the boat, and the trio sailed back towards the quay. Roberts had already arranged for a squad car to meet them on arrival, and as the boat docked, Roberts helped Devereux onto dry land.

Before entering the police car, Devereux turned to Travers with a malicious glint in her eye. 'Greg,' she whispered, her voice low and dangerous, 'if I were you, I'd ask for a posting overseas. Somewhere quiet, far, far away. Because I have a very long reach. You've murdered my son. One day, one day soon, you will look over your shoulder, and I'll be there—waiting for you.'

Travers' expression hardened. 'Don't threaten me, Olga. You're a bitch—a depraved one at that. You're going to rot in prison, and what's left of you will rot in hell.'

He watched as she was ushered into the back seat of the police car, the door slamming shut with a finality that seemed to echo in the air. The car sped off, leaving Travers standing there, the weight of the moment settling in. Finally, his job was done and justice served.

Roberts turned to him, a small smirk playing at his lips. 'Well, Greg, I think that about wraps it up. We've got a search warrant for Devereux's office and her pad in Albatross House. Some of my colleagues are already on the job, and we'll be all over her island within the hour. Are you coming back to the station with us?'

Travers shook his head; his thoughts were elsewhere. 'No thanks, I'll let you clear up here, Detective Inspector. I'm going to the hospital to see how Alicia is.'

THE END

Author Biography

After nearly 38 years working for Barclays Bank International Ltd, subsequently Barclays Bank Plc, one of the largest banks in the world, Martin Fraser took his chance and the opportunity to follow his dream.

Born in 1961, his mother taught music, while his father worked for the Signals Research and Development Establishment, the Military Research Centre in Christchurch, developing Military communications satellites.

From a young age, he developed a lifelong passion for history, reading, films, music, photography and sport, which helped to fuel Martin's imagination and fill his inquiring mind with possibilities. With both parents, older brother Grenville and uncle, all writers or musicians, it was inevitable that Martin should harbour an artistic seed waiting to germinate and burst onto the world.

On countless occasions, Martin would sit at his desk and dream of leaving the bank and unleashing his creative talents, but personal circumstances wouldn't allow it. Eventually, though, when the chance came, Martin didn't hesitate.

In 2022, that dream was realised with the completion of his first novel, The Shadow of the Albatross, a fast-moving international thriller set in the millionaire's playground of nearby Sandbanks in Dorset, Central London, and Wimbledon Village, featuring nefarious billionaire Olga Devereux. In 2023, Martin finished the first follow-up novel entitled The Cerberus File, set in London, Poole, and Jersey. Plans are already well advanced for the as-yet-untitled third novel to feature MI5 Intelligence Officer Greg Travers.

Martin lives in Poole with his beloved Rescue dog Oscar. Martin eschews the current TV trend for grim, dour, confusing thrillers that leave one feeling distinctly un-thrilled and more often than not end with an unsatisfyingly damp squib. As Martin says, "A thriller should thrill, if it doesn't, what's the point?"